Divided Loyalties

DENNIS HAMLEY

WALKER BOOKS
AND SUBSIDIARIES
LONDON • BOSTON • SYDNEY • AUCKLAND

This is a work of fiction. Names, characters, places and incidents are
either the product of the author's imagination or, if real,
are used fictitiously.

First published 2008 by Walker Books Ltd
87 Vauxhall Walk, London SE11 5HJ

2 4 6 8 10 9 7 5 3 1

Text © 2008 Dennis Hamley

Cover design © 2008 Walker Books Ltd
Girl image © iStockphoto/German patrol image © Bettman/Corbis

The right of Dennis Hamley to be identified as author of this work
has been asserted by him in accordance with the Copyright,
Designs and Patents Act 1988

This book has been typeset in M Baskerville
Printed and bound in Great Britain by Cox and Wyman Ltd, Reading, Berkshire

British Library Cataloguing in Publication Data:
a catalogue record for this book
is available from the British Library

ISBN 978-1-4063-0407-7

www.walkerbooks.co.uk

Books by the same author

Pageants of Despair
Hare's Choice
The War and Freddy
Death Penalty
Spirit of the Place
Out of the Mouths of Babes
Ellen's People

Dennis Hamley was born in 1935 in Kent and grew up in Winslow, Buckinghamshire. After "two disastrous but funny years in the RAF" he studied English at Cambridge. He went on to gain a PhD and worked as a teacher and lecturer before becoming a full-time writer. His first novel, *Pageants of Despair*, was published in 1974. S hen he has written numerous historical stories for chil , including *Very Far From Here* (1976), *Landings* (1979) and *The War and Freddy* (1991), which was shortlisted for the Smarties Book Prize. He is also the author of the Joslin de Lay Mysteries series. The events of World War I and II have inspired much of his work including *Ellen's People* and its sequel, *Divided Loyalties*:

"I was only three when World War II started; my childhood was spent in its shadow and it has always been a strong influence on me. I remember lying in bed and hearing the drone of German bombers overhead, on their way to London. I thought it all rather exciting."

Dennis lives in Oxford. He has two children and four grandchildren.

*In memory of Agnes,
my beloved wife.*

ACKNOWLEDGEMENTS

My thanks are due once again to the staff of the Imperial War Museum Reading Room for letting me see many documents, especially the remarkable testimony of Hermann Wallach, a German Jewish refugee who fled to Britain before the war and was interned as an enemy alien for his pains. His experiences were fascinating and disturbing and tell a virtually unknown story. I have drawn from his descriptions considerably in Part 6 of this book and followed his locations and chronology.

Of the many books I have read, two stand out as being both useful and remarkable. The first is *Tail-End Charlies* by John Nichol and Tony Rennell (Penguin), the most vivid account that I have yet read, full of personal experiences, of the last battles of the Bomber War; the second is *Witnessess of War: Children's Lives Under the Nazis* by Nicholas Stargardt (Cape), a stark, moving, horrifying story.

I have received much help and gained many insights from my good friend Leslie Wilson, a fine novelist who has covered some of the same ground in her books and has direct and personal knowledge of German attitudes and understandings, as well as information about aspects of ordinary German life, between, during and after the two World Wars that I was not aware of and for which I am very, very grateful.

I also am indebted to several websites that have provided me with much essential information on the organization of emergency hospitals, life at Bomber Command Operational Training Units, the Hitler Youth, the rebuilding of Volkswagen and the Battle of Kursk, the greatest tank battle in history – a distinction it will, with luck, keep for ever. But the most useful website of all was www.battle-of-britain.com, which has an hour-by-hour account of the whole battle and told me a lot about the air raid on RAF Biggin Hill on 30 August 1940. However, even this was not as important to me as my father's own experiences during that raid: for this reason he appears fleetingly as a character in the story.

CONTENTS

Summer
1935

WALTER AND PAUL

1.1

Most evenings Walter goes clay pigeon shooting with his best mate, Harry Brindley. He loves the feel of the shotgun's stock pressed into his shoulder, the loud report, the recoil and sharp smell of cordite when he fires. And, best of all, the clay pigeon in bits when he hits it square on.

"How do you want 'em, Wally?" a voice calls from the traps.

"Any way you like," Walter answers. "High and slow, low and fast, it's all the same to me."

The first clay disc whizzes out almost parallel with the ground. Walter fires and smashes it. The second climbs high, a lazy parabola until he shivers it to pieces at its highest point.

"Not bad," says Harry.

"You do better," Walter grunts as he reloads the shotgun.

"You're on." Harry also destroys two clay discs, so honours are even.

The shooting, on this glorious summer day, continues until it's too dark to see. Walter destroys disc after disc, impatient when it's someone else's turn. He is fifteen – Harry is a year older. Walter doesn't know what Harry thinks of when he pulls the trigger, probably just his aim. But Walter thinks of something specific, terrible and always there.

He thinks of what it would be like if the target wasn't a clay pigeon but his father.

As they leave the range, Walter regretfully hands the shotgun to Harry. It belongs to Harry's farm-labourer father, who shoots crows and pigeons and also bags a few rabbits for Sunday dinner. It's as much as his job's worth to shoot pheasants or partridges. But Harry has, often.

"Pity you haven't got your own gun," says Harry as they walk home. "I get fed up with lugging two out every night."

"You know why I haven't," Walter replies. "*He* won't let me and he won't have one himself either. Says he doesn't hold with them. That's bloody silly; he fired enough in the war. There aren't many men in Peterspury without a shot-gun."

"Cheer up, Wally," says Harry. "You'll soon afford your own."

"On the wages he pays?" Walter scoffs. "Not a chance."

Harry shrugs. "I've hid some beer and packets of Woodbines in the shed at home. Fancy some?"

"Not half," says Walter. They traipse back to Harry's house knowing that by now Harry's dad will be safely in the Crooked Billet.

If Harry had pushed Walter a bit more about his father, he wouldn't have known what to say. Walter's hatred goes far back, to days he hardly remembers, days of torment, tears and impotent rage. He can never, ever forgive his father and, even worse, never change it.

It is nearly midnight when Walter finally reaches home. Paul and Anna have been asleep for hours. "Little creeps," he mutters.

His mum and dad are still up and waiting. "What time do you call this?" Mum demands as soon as he opens the door.

"Don't ask me, look at the clock," he grunts, swaying a little.

At once he's sorry. In any other house a father would really tear into him, but all his dad says is, "Well, you're home now, so least said, soonest mended. I'll lock up."

Mum sighs and goes upstairs to bed. Dad says to Walter, "You'd better get to bed yourself. We've got a big job on tomorrow. The vicar's Austin has completely seized up."

Walter stamps upstairs to his room. Why is his father always so *reasonable*? Sometimes Walter wishes he would rant, scream and take his belt to him. But he never will. And it makes his son hate him even more.

"There'll be a hell of a row one day," Walter mutters to himself as he slumps down on his bed. "It can't come soon enough."

1.2

My name is Paul and I'll be eleven in November. It's the summer holidays now and we're going to visit Granny and Grandad, my father's parents, soon. It will be the first time I've seen them, because they live such a long way away.

I live with Mum and Dad, my little sister Anna – she's only eight – and Walter, my big brother, in a village called Peterspury, which is near Northampton. My dad owns a garage.

Back in April, I took the scholarship exam to get into Wicester Grammar School. There were only four of us taking it, Jimmy Warner's daughter Mavis, Jean Dickens, Freddy Wilshaw and me. We were the only ones to get through the preliminary exam. I didn't enjoy it very much. There was this horrible intelligence test with lots of hard questions and they made my head ache. So I was really fed up because I was sure I'd failed.

Wicester is a town three miles up the A5 from Peterspury. The ancient Romans built the road and Roman soldiers used to march past where Dad's garage is now. Of course, they didn't know it was the A5 then. They called it Watling Street. A lot of people don't know how to pronounce "Wicester". You have to say it "Wister". Sometimes at school the girls play a skipping game in the playground. It's a bit rude and it goes like this:

My sicester's micester
Took my sicester
Out to Wicester
For some tea.

Then this micester
Left my sicester
While he picester
'Gainst a tree.

Another micester
Saw my sicester
And he kicester
Cheekily.

Now this micester
Has my sicester.
What a twicester,
OUT GOES HE!

The weekend after I took the scholarship exam, a man from Morris Motors came over from the car factory in Oxford to see if our garage was good enough to sell new ones. I was serving petrol, like on most Saturdays, thankful to be out of the house. Mum and Dad have given Anna a violin. It used to be Great-Uncle Fred's. When she tries to play it's like cats fighting and I can't stand it. So there we were, Dad, Walter, Jimmy Warner and me.

Walter works in the garage. Dad says he'll be a really good mechanic one day. But he likes clay pigeon shooting best. He once asked if he could have his own shotgun and then there was a row. Dad said no and Walter shouted, "When I'm old enough, you can't stop me!"

"No, I suppose I can't," said Dad. "But that's a long way off. Right now you can shoot all the clay pigeons you want with somebody else's gun but I won't have you shooting anything that's alive."

"Pity you didn't think like that in the war," Walter replied and stalked out of the room, slamming the door behind him.

Dad looked really upset. "I am right, aren't I?" he said to Mum.

"Of course you are, my love," said Mum.

Walter is often very bad-tempered when Dad's around and it makes me wonder how they get on at work. Walter doesn't like being called Walter. "It's horrible," he said to me once. "It doesn't sound a proper English name."

"I think it's nice," I replied. "They named you after Dad's father."

"Well, tell 'em thanks for nothing," he said.

His mates all call him "Wally". But I call him "Walter"

18

and I don't care how cross he gets.

We haven't always lived here. We came here when I was five. We used to live in Sussex, in a village called Lambsfield, where I was born. Dad repaired cars there as well, with Uncle Jack. Uncle Jack has only got one leg. He lost the other in the war. When he came home he started a bike repair shop. After Mum and Dad got married, Dad worked with him. When the war was over there were a lot more cars and vans on the road and soon they were mending more cars than bikes.

Then Dad's Uncle Fred died and left everything to Dad: his house, garden and smallholding where he grew fruit and vegetables. Dad said he didn't know much about growing vegetables and that he'd build a garage on it instead. We'd been living in Nanny and Nandad's house and there wasn't really room for all of us. Dad was very depressed about it. "I hate being beholden to them," he said, but when I asked what "beholden" meant, Mum told me to run off and play. So we moved, though Mum was sad about leaving Nanny and Nandad, and so was I.

The first thing Dad did was ask Jimmy Warner, who used to work for Uncle Fred, if he'd like to be a mechanic. Jimmy had been in the war and couldn't breathe properly because he'd been in a poison gas attack. Dad always put old soldiers first. He fought in the war too and was badly wounded. That's where he met Mum, when she was a nurse in an army hospital. Dad once told me that Mum saved his life, though he didn't say how.

Dad gets very cross about what happened to a lot of soldiers after the war. "I've seen them begging and selling matches in the streets," he told us. "And it's not just here

19

in England, it's all over Europe. People have very short memories. We fought for our countries with good hearts, we watched our friends die and this is all the thanks we get." When Uncle Jack and Auntie Enid come to stay, Dad and Jack go on like this for hours until Mum says, "Oh, for heaven's sake, get off down to the Crooked Billet and moan to someone else."

Sometimes Dad has nightmares. I can hear him through the wall, screaming out in his sleep. Then I hear Mum's voice, very soft, calming him down. When Uncle Jack comes here, he sometimes does the same. They can't help it. It's the war, it's stuck inside their heads for ever.

That's why Dad and Uncle Jack are such good friends. Not just because they're brothers-in-law but because they both went through so much. The funny thing is, they fought on different sides.

Anyway, I was telling you about when the man from Oxford came to see the garage. I was waiting by the petrol pumps, watching cars go by and hoping one would stop so I could serve them and take some money.

At ten o'clock a big, black car drove in and a man in a smart, grey suit got out and asked to see the garage owner. He and Dad shook hands and talked for a long time, though I couldn't hear what they said. Then Dad showed him round. The man looked at all the tools and climbed down into the motor pit. When Dad took him into the office, I tiptoed up to the window and looked through. Dad had opened all his account books and the man was sitting at the desk looking through them. Then he got up, so I scooted away and stood by the pumps as though I hadn't moved. They came out and shook hands again and the man said, "You'll hear from us soon, Mr Vögler." Before he left he came to me and said, "I'll have a top-up of petrol after all, sonny."

Dad shouted, "Have it on the house, Mr Winter."

"I wouldn't dream of it, Mr Vögler, I'll pay like everybody else," replied Mr Winter. He gave me a pound note and when I gave him the change he slipped half a crown into my hand and said, "That's for being such a good pump attendant." Then he drove off.

That night over supper, Mum looked at Dad and said, "Well?"

"I don't know," said Dad. "We'll have to wait and see."

"The suspense will kill me," said Walter.

Then Mum said, "Whether we get what we want or not, we'll go on a holiday in August."

"To Brighton?" Anna asked excitedly.

"I'd rather go to Blackpool," I said.

"Neither," said Mum. "Your father and I have decided it's time we went to Germany to see his parents."

"Well, you can count me out," said Walter at once.

Walter, Anna and I have never been to Germany, though Dad is teaching Anna and me to speak German. Mostly Dad goes on his own and Mum stays behind with us. I sometimes wonder if there's something going on that they won't tell us. He never seems very happy before he goes and hardly says a word when he comes back.

But now Mum was smiling, as if she was looking forward to it. "They live in a lovely place and there's a cousin just your age there, Paul. His name is Helmut and I'm sure you'll get on well."

We'll see about that, I thought to myself.

"What about Adolf Hitler?" asked Walter.

"He's just a daft little man with a funny moustache, like Charlie Chaplin," I said. I thought it was a silly question.

"You're a right twerp, aren't you, Paul?"

"Don't talk to your brother like that," said Mum. But Walter had already walked out of the room.

"Well, I don't care, he is a daft little man even if he *is* leader of Germany," I said. "Terry Burton called his new puppy Hitler." Mum laughed but Dad looked grave. "Mr Proffitt says he can't do any harm," I went on. "I mean Mr Hitler, not Terry's puppy."

"Paul," said Dad. "Mr Proffitt is a good teacher but this time I think he may be wrong. I fear that one day something bad will happen."

I thought Mum would say, "Don't be so silly, Matthias," because she often did, but instead she reached out and took Dad's hand. Dad sighed, "I hoped we'd left all that behind us," and Mum answered, "I know, my love. But it won't spoil our visit to Regelstein because I'm sure they all feel the same as us about Mr Hitler."

"Perhaps so," said Dad.

Anyway, next week we broke up for the Easter holidays. Uncle Jack and Auntie Enid came to stay, bringing Nanny and Nandad Wilkins with them and we all had a good time.

A fortnight later the postman brought a letter addressed to Dad. He read it and said, "Mr Winter was impressed. We've got it."

"Got what, Dad?" I asked.

22

"Your father is an authorized car dealer now and can sell new cars," said Mum. "Isn't that wonderful?" She kissed him and said, "You deserve it, my love."

"So does Jimmy," said Dad. "He's worked just as hard. And Walter here, of course."

"Thanks," said Walter, sounding sarcastic.

Mum smiled at Anna. "We can pay for violin lessons now," she said. *Good*, I thought. *Perhaps she'll get better.*

A few days later, a special carrier arrived with a big package which Dad unwrapped. Inside was a big white metal plate with a bull's head in red and MORRIS CARS, AUTHORIZED DEALER in blue. "I'll put it up this morning," said Dad, sounding very satisfied. "I'm sure people will want to buy the new Morris Eight, even if it costs two hundred pounds. One day everybody will have a car and then we can be really big," he said.

"Don't be silly, Matthias," said Mum. "People won't be that rich."

"You wait and see," said Dad.

"But who can afford them, what about all the poverty and unemployment and strikes and marches down from the north?"

"It'll pass," said Dad. "Anyway, we don't get that sort of trouble out here in the country."

"That's not a very nice attitude," said Mum.

Dad looked quite fierce. "What goes on in Britain now is nothing, *nothing*, to how it was in my Germany," he said. "How would you like it if a loaf cost fifty pounds and money was so worthless you wheeled your wages home in a barrow? That's if you'd got any." It wasn't often that Dad sounded angry but he did whenever he

23

talked about Germany.

Two weeks later, the first three new cars arrived. Dad stuck the prices on the windscreens and displayed them on the forecourt. He sold a Morris 8 two days later and Mum cooked a chicken for dinner to celebrate.

A month after that, Mr Proffitt read the scholarship results out at assembly. My heart was thumping. "It gives me great pleasure to tell you that two of our number have passed the scholarship," he said. "They are –" he paused a moment and peered at the letter – "Jean Dickens and –" another pause and I nearly passed out – "Paul Vögler."

I let out a big sigh of relief, and then heard subdued crying next to me. Mavis Warner, Jimmy's daughter. "I'm sorry, Mavis," I whispered. I shot a glance towards Freddy Wilshaw. He had a face like thunder. "I'll get my own back on you for this, Jerry boy," he whispered.

Everybody said "well done" to Jean. Tony Straighton added, "It's nice to see it go to someone who deserves it." Nobody came up to me and by the end of the day I felt really miserable.

Years ago, when I was still in Standard 1, Mum and Dad asked me if I ever had any teasing or bullying because I was half German, but I hadn't. "Don't be afraid to tell us," said Dad.

"Honestly, I haven't," I said and it was true, today was the very first time. Tony Straighton was supposed to be my best friend, but some friend he turned out to be.

I only had June and the first part of July to get through before I left. Those last six weeks weren't very nice, though a few people, like Mavis and Billy French, whose father kept the Crooked Billet, said they were pleased and not to worry about what the others said. I didn't tell Mum and Dad because I knew it would only upset them.

Still, the term ended at last and there was a prizegiving. I won some books for passing the scholarship and coming top in our class. Mr Proffitt called Jean Dickens and me into his office and told us that he knew we'd do well and be a credit to Peterspury and that we must never forget the school that gave us our big start in life.

Well I won't, but I wanted to say that it wasn't *just* the school that given me the start, it was Mum and Dad as well.

Then it was the summer holidays and we were off to Germany, to see Granny and Grandad and the mysterious Helmut in Regelstein. Early one morning, when it was still dark and the fields were covered in low-lying mist, Jimmy Warner drove us to Northampton railway station and our journey began.

1.3

After the rest of the family have left, Walter stays in bed for six hours, sometimes dozing, sometimes gazing at the ceiling. The unfamiliar silence begins to get him down. When the church clock strikes nine he reluctantly pushes off the bedclothes. He's already an hour late for work. "Doesn't matter," he yawns. "Jimmy daren't say a word: I'm the boss's son." He pulls his clothes on and slouches downstairs.

In the kitchen he makes tea, puts a lump of lard in the frying pan, and watches it sizzle. Then he cracks open an egg, cuts a doorstep slice of bread, shoves it in the pan as well, finds some rashers and adds them to the frying heap.

He switches the wireless on, turns it up loud and swallows a mouthful of bacon and yolk-soaked, fried bread. The wireless, after a few crackles and whistles, warms up and the prim, precise voice of the BBC newsreader fills the kitchen. "Stuck-up sod," Walter mutters, and switches it off.

He takes a long swallow of tea, finishes his breakfast and tips mug, plate, knife and fork into the sink, where they'll probably stay until the family comes home.

The church clock strikes the half hour. The sink is full and there's a mess of crumbs, congealing fat and puddles of cold tea on the table. "I don't give a toss," he says to himself and wanders over to the garage. Jimmy is there, his head under the bonnet of Dr Rudd's Rover. He straightens up. "What time do you call this?" he demands.

"Overslept," Walter says sullenly.

"Look at you," says Jimmy. "Death warmed up. I'm three times your age, only got one lung, and here I am, bright as a button, up at three this morning, drove to the station and two hours work done already."

"More fool you," mutters Walter.

"I heard that," says Jimmy. "Just because your dad's not here doesn't mean you can say what you like."

"What do you want me to do?" Walter asks.

"The spark plugs on the vet's Lanchester need changing," Jimmy replies. "Get on with it."

When Jimmy finishes on the doctor's Rover he turns his attention to the vicar's Austin 7. At ten o'clock, he emerges from underneath it and says, "Shape yourself, Walter, the delivery lorry's here soon." Even as he speaks, the lorry arrives with a load of new cars.

"That's three Morris Eights and two Twelves," says Jimmy as he signs for them. "Pity your dad's not here. He'd have liked this."

"That's his fault," says Walter as they push them to the forecourt.

At one o'clock they take half an hour off for lunch. Jimmy opens his packet of sandwiches and vacuum flask of tea while Walter trails back to the house. He opens the door and sniffs. A pungent, dangerous smell. Gas. He must have left the oven on. He turns it off and rushes round the house opening all the windows. When the smell has gone he tries to light a gas ring to boil the kettle, but nothing happens. The gas has run out: the meter needs money. He finds a shilling piece, shoves it in the slot and breathes a sigh of relief. He boils the kettle, cuts bread and a lump of cheese, makes a mug of tea and chews contentedly until it's time to go back.

So the day passes until at half past five Walter stops working on Mr Craddock's Standard 10 and tells Jimmy, "I'm off home now."

"You should be here till six," says Jimmy. "I'll tell your father."

"See if I care," shrugs Walter. He doesn't go back to the house. Instead he walks to Harry Brindley's dad's cottage.

Harry is waiting. "We'll go shooting up at Colby's Wood," he says. "Bag a few squirrels."

"Shotguns?" asks Walter hopefully.

"The old bugger's locked them up. It's airguns tonight."

As they cross the fields, they take a few potshots at rabbits but they're too fast for them. When dusk begins to fall they've shot nothing.

"Proper poachers bring torches," Harry tells Walter.

"We're not poachers," Walter says.

"We could be," Harry replies. "We could make a fortune."

"I'd need a proper gun," says Walter. "But he'll never let me."

"You want to stand up for your rights," says Harry.

"Easier said than done in our house."

"I've got some bottles of beer in my haversack," says Harry.

"Good," replies Walter. "I've got a real thirst on me."

Not only does Harry produce four bottles out of the haversack, but also a packet of Woodbines and a box of Swan Vestas matches. They sit down on the grass and light up their cigarettes.

"I bet they don't know you smoke," says Harry.

"I couldn't give a monkey's," Walter replies.

Harry opens the bottles and they swig and smoke reflectively until it gets cold and Harry says, "Time to get back."

The next day is much like the one before. Spark plugs, gaskets, fan belts, carburettors, punctures, collapsed shock absorbers, cracked radiators and cylinder blocks, stripped gearboxes. Once Walter becomes fully engrossed in the work he is almost as happy as when he's clay pigeon shooting. He and Jimmy don't talk much but Walter knows the old soldier can't say he isn't good at his job.

Sometimes, when Jimmy isn't looking, he goes to the showroom and sits in a new car, smelling the leather, holding the steering wheel, fondling the gear stick and wishing, wishing it was his. Other times he wanders round the used car lot, calculating when he can afford one and whether, since he's taught himself to drive, they'd make him take a test. None of the old blokes bringing cars to the garage has passed a test, they've picked it up for themselves. Why should it be different for him?

Every evening he goes off with Harry, sometimes shooting in Colby's Wood or at the clay pigeon range. Or they catch the green United Counties bus to Northampton, hoping to meet a couple of girls and take them to the pictures. They always fail, which means they never go to the pictures themselves, for what's the point if there's no girl to take into the back row where the usherettes' torches can't reach? Instead they wander the streets, buy fish and chips, eat them on a bench in the park and then catch the last bus home.

Sometimes Walter thinks about the family, miles away in Germany. Mum will hate it, he decides. Paul will love it, but then, he'll like anything, the soft little sod. Anna's so dopey she won't know what's going on. Anyway, that lot over there, they are nothing to do with him. They're his dad's people and he doesn't have to know them.

Walter's family will be home tonight. "Let's get this place tidied up," says Jimmy. "I want it all shipshape and Bristol fashion, as they say."

It's one thing getting the garage looking decent but quite another cleaning the house. Walter stares at the pile of dirty plates in the sink and the filthy sheets, pillowcases and blankets on his bed and feels helpless. He wonders whether, after a fortnight, he should take off his vest and underpants and rinse them out and then decides it isn't worth it. Mum does all the washing. *Sod the lot of it,* he thinks.

Before leaving the bedroom he finds another shirt, takes a jacket off its hanger in the wardrobe and puts them both on. He can't remember wearing a jacket since he left school, but this one isn't too small and, amazingly, it looks quite good. Surely it will bring the Northampton girls running. Then he recalls he's got no money, so he can't go to

Northampton.

He is just about to close the wardrobe door when he sees a large metal object, once silver, now sadly tarnished, on the floor. He picks it up and looks at it, mystified, wondering what it is and how it got there. Then he remembers. Of course. It's a musical instrument Mum and Dad call the oom-pah. Great-Uncle Fred left it to him after he died. "Fred be blowed," he mutters. "His real name was bloody Friedrich."

The instrument has been there for years, shoved to the back and forgotten. The valves are stuck, but nevertheless he puts the mouthpiece to his lips and blows. Nothing. He blows harder until his face turns red. Not a sound. He throws it to the floor. "Bloody useless. What else can you expect from a Jerry?"

Downstairs in the kitchen, Walter chews stale bread and mouldy cheese and then leaves for Harry's place. He's hardly gone a couple of steps before he thinks, *No, I'll sort that useless object out once and for all.* He goes to his room, picks the instrument up and heads back to the kitchen. Here he's struck by a niggle of conscience, so he writes

GONE OUT. DON'T WAIT UP.

on a piece of paper and leaves it on the table.

The weather has held for the last fortnight, but now the clouds have gathered. As Walter walks towards Harry's place, the first drops of rain spit onto his face. When he gets there, Harry sees the instrument and asks, "Wally, what the bloody hell have you got there?"

"Some rubbish my Kraut uncle left me," says Walter.

31

"Old Fred Vögler? My dad thought he was all right."

"Well, he wasn't, and I don't want his rotten old oom-pah. I want to get rid of it so I don't have to see it again."

The rain is harder now and they're in for a good soaking. "Sod this for a lark," says Harry. "I'm not going shooting in this."

"I haven't got any money," says Walter. "So I can't go to Northampton."

"That's all right," Harry tells him. "You come with me." He leads him up the straggly garden to the shed at the far end. They go inside, Harry closes the door and drags a wooden box from under a shelf. He lifts the lid, takes out a pair of old overalls and says, "Look in there."

"Crikey," Walter exclaims. "There must be twenty bottles."

"You name it, I've got it," says Harry proudly. "Mild, bitter, brown, light, stout, a bottle of sherry the old devil bought in for Christmas and didn't like. And look at this." He picks out three bottles underneath the rest. "Johnny Walker."

Walter examines the bottles of whisky. "Someone's drunk out of them," he points out.

"I know," says Harry. "I pinch it off the old man when he gets sozzled every night. He's forgotten about them next morning. I tell him he's drunk the lot and the empties are in the dustbin. The daft old git buys himself some more. Never fails. I've got forty fags here as well. Woodbines."

He opens two bottles of beer and hands one to Walter. They light up and for a while drag on the Woodbines and swig from the bottles contentedly. The rain rattles on the window and thrums on the felt roof. Harry takes a Johnny

Walker, unscrews the top and says, "Whisky chaser." He takes a gulp, wipes the top of the bottle on his sleeve and passes it over.

The unaccustomed fiery liquid burns Walter's throat and ends up warm in his stomach. He splutters, feels light-headed and takes another swallow. "One swig each," says Harry. "We have to pace ourselves." But Walter's tongue is beginning to loosen. Sooner or later he will say things pent up, unspoken, even unthought, since before he can remember and with every word, part of him will feel he's soaring to undreamt of heights, another part that he's falling into pits of disloyalty and guilt.

He drinks more beer, takes a gulp of whisky, then a swallow from the sherry bottle. It's brown and unexpectedly sweet: he nearly retches and suddenly feels quite ill. "What's up, Wally?" says Harry. "You look like you lost a quid and found threepence."

"It's all right for you," Walter mutters. "You've got a proper father."

"What, *that* drunken old git?" says Harry.

"At least he's an English old git," says Walter.

"What's that got to do with it? He's all right, your dad, even if he is a bit of a prick about shotguns."

"You wouldn't want a Fritz for a father."

"Ho, wouldn't I? If he had his own garage selling new cars, he could be a bloody Martian for all I care."

"You don't understand," says Walter angrily.

"What's there to understand?"

"Shut up, I'm not talking about it," says Walter and opens yet another bottle of beer. They continue to drink the beer and whisky. Once Walter takes another gulp from

33

the sherry bottle. It doesn't seem so sweet now and the ground he is straying on no longer feels quite so forbidden. "They must think I'm a fool," he says.

"Who?" asks Harry.

"Him and my mother. I can count and I know what's what."

"What are you talking about?" says Harry.

"They got married in November and I was born in March, that's what."

"What's so bad about that? There's lots in Peterspury like it. The vicar's always marrying couples with the bride four months gone."

"Their husbands aren't Huns."

"Oh, that's it, is it? Well, you never know, maybe he isn't your real father. Perhaps he only married your mum because he was sorry for her because someone had put a bun in her oven. What's certain is that your mum opened her legs to someone she shouldn't have, whether it was him or some other bloke."

"I'll punch your bloody nose if you say that again," says Walter.

"It takes two," says Harry. "If it wasn't your dad, stands to reason it must have been someone else."

Walter picks up the whisky bottle and takes a longer drink as he considers this. "Careful," says Harry. "I want some of that as well."

Walter hands the bottle back and wipes his mouth with the back of his hand. "He'd no right to come over here after killing all our lads. That could have been your father he killed and then what would you say?" His voice is getting very slurred.

34

Harry shakes his head. "No fear of that. My old bugger stayed safe on the farm. God alone knows how he dodged being conscripted. He says he hid in a barn."

"Of course," says Walter, "if it was someone else, then I wouldn't be half and half like I am, I'd be all English."

"No you wouldn't," says Harry. "You wouldn't be here. You'd be a different person. You wouldn't even *exist*."

By now Walter's brain is completely befuddled. He knows there is something wrong either with what he just said or with what Harry just told him, but what is it? "I don't care what you say," he says. "He should have buggered off back home."

"What stopped him?"

Walter can't think of an answer to that. In fact, he is almost beyond thinking of anything at all. He takes a last swig of whisky, finishes off the sherry and the beer and then says, "I hate the bastard."

"Well, tell him then," says Harry.

"I can't," says Walter.

"Why not? Are you frit?"

"Course I'm bloody not. I don't want to upset me mum."

"I know you, Wally, there's more to it than that."

Walter knows there is, much more, but his befuddled mind can't tease it out. He dimly sees the silver instrument still on the floor. "I'll sort that sodding thing out," he says. He tries to jump on it but falls against a shelf. Empty paint pots drop on his head. He gets up again and stamps hard on it. Harry joins in and they stamp and stamp until the once shiny instrument, which blasted out many a German march and Austrian waltz, is a twisted mass of metal.

Harry takes a spade, they go outside and, shrieking with laughter, Harry digs a hole, Walter drops the instrument into it and together they heap wet earth over the top until it is no more. "Best place for it," says Walter. "Bloody shame the ones who gave it to me aren't down there with it."

"One of them is," says Harry.

The next thing Walter remembers is lying in bed at home with a headache such as he's never had before and in his ears the sounds of his returned family bustling around downstairs.

1938

MEETING HELMUT

2.1

I'm thirteen now. I remember coming home from Germany the first time we went and finding Walter wasn't in. We were woken up at two in the morning by a loud knocking on the door. It was PC Coppard propping up Walter, who was dead drunk. "I found him staggering along the road," he said. "I knew you were back tonight so I frogmarched him here. It was that or put him in the cells." Mum and Dad had to get him into bed. When they asked him about it next day he told them to mind their own business.

A lot has happened since then. Nobody thinks Mr Hitler is a funny little man any more. People used to say there'd never be another army in Germany, but Hitler's built up a big one. Tony Straighton asked, "Is your dad going to join?"

"Of course he isn't," I replied.

Dad's upset as well, because some of his friends are saying the same. Yesterday Mr Ingram, who was a sergeant major in the war, shouted at him in the High Street, "Once a Jerry, always a Jerry, eh, Matt?"

Dad was very angry. "What can I do about it, Ellen?" I heard him say to Mum. "Must I just put up with it?"

"Take no notice," Mum answered. "You've worked hard. People respect you. You can't help what Hitler does."

Dad replied, "I told Jimmy that Britain ought to start building their armed forces up again and he said, 'Don't you worry about Hitler, he'll fade away like the rest of them.' I told him he didn't know how angry the German people were after the last war, and I was as angry as any even though I came to live over here." He paused, and then said, "Sometimes deep down I'm rather pleased to see my country making itself strong again. I just wish it wasn't because of that man."

The funny thing is that some people here think Hitler is right. The other day at supper, Dad said, "Mr Wigley the undertaker brought his hearse in this morning. He stood in my office and said, 'I reckon your Herr Hitler has got the right idea. He's a man after my own heart. Kicks out the undesirables and defectives.' 'Do you include Jews?' I asked him. 'Why not?' he said. 'Hitler does, and communists too. The mess this country's in, we need someone like him in charge. I can't understand you, Matt. If I'm a loyal Englishman, you should be a loyal German. Why don't you support your own?' 'I *am* a loyal German,' I said. 'But not to Hitler because I don't agree with him.'"

"Daddy," said Anna. "Does that mean you don't like Uncle Hermann and Auntie Anneliese any more?"

"Of course not," said Dad. "How could I not like my own family?"

I often think back to our first visit to Germany, especially now we're going again this summer. I really liked Uncle Hermann and Auntie Anneliese but best of all were Granny and Grandad Vögler, who really spoilt Anna and me with chocolates and told us all sorts of things about Dad when he was a boy. Then there was Helmut. Yes, I suppose I did like Helmut, but something happened there that I can't forget and keep on worrying over. And I can't forget the conversation Anna had on the journey about the Lorelei song either.

We were on the train from Cologne to Frankfurt. After the train left Bonn, Dad said, "Now you'll see how beautiful the River Rhine is."

He was right. It was wide with wooded hills on both sides and rugged dark rocks jutting out at bends. The water shone blue almost like the sea. When the train stopped at a station called Koblenz, a man and his wife got on and sat opposite us. They smiled and said, "*Guten Morgen*," which is German for "Good morning". Dad answered and the lady turned to us and said something that sounded nice but came out so fast that I couldn't understand it, in spite of my time learning German with Dad.

"I beg your pardon," I said, and Dad told me, "The lady is asking you how old you are."

I couldn't remember the German for eleven, so I said it in English instead. The man smiled, "So you are an English boy. How do you like our lovely country?"

"I don't know. I haven't seen it yet," I answered in German, just to show that I could.

Anna was peering through the window. "Look at that

big rock jutting out into the river."

"Ah yes," said the lady. "We're near St Goarshausen and that is the rock of the Lorelei. There's an old story about it."

"Ooh, lovely," said Anna. "Would you tell it to us, please?"

"Of course I will," the lady said. "Once upon a time there was a young woman with lovely, long, blonde hair. Her name was Lorelei. But her lover sailed away and ever since she has waited on her rock, singing her song to bring him back, all in vain. But when sailors on the Rhine hear her sing they come too close. Her song is so beautiful and they so much want to hear the words in case she is singing to them. And what happens then, do you think?"

"The ships run onto the rocks and sink and all the sailors drown?"

"Clever English girl," said the lady. "That's exactly right. Her voice has lured many good mariners to their deaths. It's a good story, isn't it?"

"Yes," I answered, and Anna asked, "What was the song she sang?"

"Nobody knows," said the lady. "But it was very beautiful."

"I wish I knew what it sounded like," said Anna. "I'll find out one day."

"If ever you do, I hope you'll tell me," said the lady. "We get off at the next station and I don't suppose you'll have found out by then."

I sometimes think Anna's a bit cracked in the head. She can't seem to think of anything else but music. She's always singing to herself and I have to admit that she's not bad on her violin now she's having lessons. Anyway, that Lorelei business has really got stuck in my brain and I don't quite know why. I sometimes ask Anna if she knows what the song sounds like but she always says, "Not yet," as if one day she will.

The other thing I can't get out of my head is Helmut and the tree. That really made me angry – and it scared me a bit too. When the train arrived in the big station in Frankfurt, Uncle Hermann, Auntie Anneliese, Granny and Grandad and Helmut were all waiting. Helmut had fair hair and was a bit taller than me. He gave me a funny look, as if to say, "I'm the boss here and don't forget it."

When we got to Regelstein, Auntie Anneliese showed Anna and me to our rooms. Mine looked out over the back garden. At the end was a tall sycamore tree. After we had eaten a huge evening meal, Helmut said, "Paul, come outside with me." I followed him into the back garden and Anna tagged along behind. Helmut led us to the tree. "I can climb it," he said. "Watch me."

A rope dangled from the lowest branch. He swung himself up with it and then climbed the tree as easily as climbing a ladder. When he got to the top, he called down, "I dare you to come up here with me."

Well, I'd climbed trees at home, especially horse chestnuts because it was easier to pick conkers rather than throwing stones to get at them. But this tree looked very high and seemed to sway in the wind.

"Don't do it," said Anna. "You'll break your neck."

Deep down, I thought she might be right, but Helmut had dared me and if I didn't do it he'd think English boys were all cowards. So I shouted, "I'm coming," and started

45

to climb.

He'd made it look easy, so swinging myself up onto the lowest branch didn't worry me at all. But then it got difficult. "Ooh, be careful, Paul," I heard Anna call. On I went, feeling my way so cautiously that I hardly seemed to move. Helmut kept calling, "Hurry up, I haven't got all day," and each time his voice seemed further away. I was hot and sweaty and scared in case I lost my footing or a branch broke. I didn't dare look up or down so all I saw was tree bark in front of my eyes. Finally I heard Helmut say, "I was getting tired of waiting." He was sitting on a branch just above me. He smiled and said, "Come and sit next to me. You did well, Paul. But you were very slow."

"Of course I was," I panted. "It was my first time. I bet by the time we leave I'll be able to climb it as fast as you can."

"No, Paul, you won't," he said as if there was no argument.

"Yes I will," I replied. "And to prove it we'll have a race on our last day."

"If you wish," he said, as if he didn't really care. But *I* cared. I decided to practise until I could climb the tree in my sleep.

So early every morning, I practised climbing the tree. I couldn't remember which branches Helmut used, so I tried my own way and found it easier to climb up the other side. By the end of the week I could reach the top really fast and my hands had toughened up. Well, I'd give Helmut a good race, anyway.

The day came for us to leave. Everything was packed and the train from Regelstein to Frankfurt left in two hours. "There's just time for our race," I said to Helmut.

"Oh, be careful, Paul," begged Anna.

Helmut looked at the tree. "We can't climb it at the same time," he said. "We'd get in each other's way. We must climb separately and have someone time us."

"Why shouldn't we climb together?" I replied. "I'll go up my new way. We won't even touch each other. Then it's a proper race."

"My idea is best," argued Helmut. "Anna can time us," but Anna didn't know how to.

"All right then," said Helmut. "My father will."

"Not on his own," I said. "He might cheat."

"My father would not cheat," said Helmut indignantly. "He has a good watch which always tells the right time."

"So does mine," I replied. "I don't mind them both timing us. That shouldn't stop us having a proper race."

"Well, if you want to get beaten then that's all right with me."

"You won't beat me," I replied. "My way's best."

Helmut told Dad and Uncle Hermann what we were going to do and they seemed to think it was a good idea. In fact, they got so excited you'd have thought they were having the race, not us.

"We'll synchronize our watches," promised Dad. Uncle Hermann said, "Say when you're ready and I'll start you."

So we took hold of our ropes, and waited. "Five seconds to go," said Uncle Hermann. "Five, four, three, two, one, GO!"

This was a lot different from a practice. Helmut was climbing faster than the first time. I was soon out of breath, sweat dripped into my eyes and I was scared of losing my grip. I could see his feet level with my chin. I nearly gave up and gasped, "All right, you win," but as I grasped the branch above me his foot came down and would have landed right on my knuckles if I hadn't snatched my hand away at the last minute. That did it. If he was going to cheat, I wouldn't give up. I was so angry I shinned up the last branches like a monkey. I was going faster than Helmut, overtaking him, reaching the topmost branch first and making sure he couldn't get to it, though not by stepping on him. He looked flabbergasted when I drew level. He stopped for a second and I seized my chance. I heard a crack as if a branch was snapping. One last heave and I was at the top.

"Beat you," I shouted. Then I looked down. The branch Helmut was on was breaking under his weight and he was hanging by his hands from one above.

"You did that on purpose!" he screamed.

"Did what?"

"Pulled on the branch. You could have killed me."

"I never touched it," I said.

"Yes you did. I can't hold on, I'm going to fall!"

"No you're not. Here, I'll save you."

I bent down carefully, holding onto my branch with one hand and grasping his wrist with the other. I could see his frightened face, about as frightened as mine, a crisscross of branches and leaves below us and, far down like little puppets, Dad and Uncle Hermann. I could hear Anna screaming, "Mummy, Mummy, come quick."

Suddenly things got even worse. I wasn't just nearly overbalancing, Helmut seemed to be pulling me. "What are you doing?" I yelled, but he didn't answer. Then his grip loosened. For an awful moment I thought he'd fallen, but then I saw he'd pulled my arm down to reach a lower branch and hold it there so he could stand safely. Trembling, I dragged myself back to the top branch.

"Are you all right?" said Helmut.

"Yes. What about you?"

"Fine," said Helmut. He paused and then said, "Thanks."

"I won," I said. I wasn't going to let him forget it.

"You wouldn't have if that branch hadn't snapped," said Helmut.

"Why did you try to tread on my hand?" I said.

"What do you mean? I didn't tread on your hand," he replied.

"Yes, you did."

"No I didn't. I'm not a cheat."

"Yes you are!"

"Then so are you. Why did you try to make the branch break?"

"I didn't!"

"Yes you did. I'll fight you and make you sorry."

"I don't care, I'll win that as well."

We argued all the way down the tree and when we reached the ground, he squared up to me and I did the same to him, like Joe Louis and Max Schmeling fighting for the world heavyweight championship.

"Mummy, they're going to hit each other," Anna screamed.

"Do something, Hermann," Auntie Anneliese shouted and Uncle Hermann and Dad jumped in and pulled us apart.

49

"What do you think you're doing?" Uncle Hermann roared. "You nearly killed yourselves up there and all you can do is fight."

"He tried to tread on my fingers!" I cried.

"He broke the branch and he called me a cheat!" shouted Helmut.

"Well, you are!"

"That's enough!" said Dad.

"Anyway, I won," I said.

"Only because you made the branch crack," said Helmut.

"Stop it, the two of you!" Auntie Anneliese cried.

We stood getting our breaths back and glaring at each other. Then Helmut said, "Honestly, I didn't try to step on your fingers and if you thought I did, I'm sorry."

"All right, then. I'm sorry I called you a cheat and I didn't make the branch crack. You were just too heavy for it."

"That's more like it," said Dad and Anna stopped crying and dried her eyes.

"But I still won," I said.

We left after that. There were lots of kisses and "Don't make it so long before the next time." Helmut and I shook hands and looked warily at each other. When we were in the train Mum said, "That wasn't as bad as I thought it was going to be," and Dad said, "Our wonderful son nearly ruined it for us."

"It wasn't me, it was Helmut," I said and Mum answered, "Don't start again, Paul."

Dad smiled and said, "Well, he didn't let us down in the end."

We changed trains at Cologne. The train to Ostend ran through the night and the boat to Dover left next morning. As we watched Calais disappear behind us, Dad suddenly said, "I'm not very happy."

"Why not, Daddy?" asked Anna.

"Take no notice of me," he said. "I'm being silly. But I wish…"

"What do you wish?" asked Anna.

"My family must never follow Herr Hitler. He's not good for Germany," Dad answered.

"That's not a wish," said Anna.

"Yes it is," said Dad. "In a way." And he didn't say another word until we were on the train to London. Neither did I. I was thinking about Helmut and the tree. He did try to step on my fingers and I didn't try to break the branch. But I bet he was sitting in his room thinking exactly the opposite. Well, he was wrong.

Three years have passed. I'll soon be seeing him again and I haven't changed my mind.

2.2

Over these last three years, Peterspury has changed. People are afraid there'll be another war and I sometimes think they blame us for it. Nobody's nasty, nobody says anything straight out, at least, not to me, but Dad's sometimes very quiet and I notice he doesn't pop in to the Crooked Billet for a drink as often as he used to. When I told them at school that we were going to Germany for our summer holiday, I got some very funny looks.

Walter hasn't been drinking or, if he has, he's hidden it very well. In fact we haven't seen a lot of him because he spends more time than ever clay pigeon shooting. He was out all last Saturday and when he came home in the evening he brought a couple of rabbits. "Here's tomorrow's dinner," he said. "Rabbit pie. Lovely."

"I hope you didn't shoot those," said Dad accusingly.

"No," said Walter. "Harry did. He shot four and gave two to me."

"I thought you were shooting clay pigeons," said Mum.

"We were," Walter replied. "Harry shot the rabbits this morning."

"I don't believe you," said Dad. "You know what I said about having a shotgun."

"Of course I know," replied Walter. "But I'm eighteen now and you can't stop me."

"Maybe I can't, but I can stop your wages. Just remember that." He looked at the rabbits. "Get rid of them."

Walter shrugged his shoulders. "Suit yourself," he said.

But Mum said, "Matthias, don't be silly! I won't waste good food. I don't care where it's from as long as they haven't been poaching."

"Harry shot them at Buckland's Farm," said Walter. "The farmer was there, he knows all about it."

"I'll ask him when I see him," said Dad.

Whether he did or he didn't, Mum gave us stewed rabbit for Sunday dinner and it was lovely.

I'm in Form 3 at the grammar school. We do French and this year we've started German and Latin. I'm quite good at French, though I'm best at German, because Dad and I speak it together. I can't make head or tail of Latin and I hate Latin homework, it makes my head ache. But I like everything else, Maths, History, Geography and Science, where we do experiments which make some great bangs and stinks. I have to play rugby and they made me fullback because I'm good at catching the ball. But I still play football in the evenings and at weekends with all my old friends and nobody's said I shouldn't be going to the grammar school again, not even Tony Straighton.

Anna didn't pass the scholarship, so she'll have to stay at the village school. She's very upset. I'm sorry too because I hoped Jean Dickens and I wouldn't be the only ones in

Peterspury who went there except for the few at the posh end of the village whose parents can pay. Still, everyone says it's better for boys to go anyway because girls who get to be nurses or teachers will have to stop when they get married and have children to look after. That doesn't seem fair to me, but it's how it is.

Yesterday Walter brought three more rabbits home. Dad said nothing but Mum said, "I'll make us a pie this week. I hope we won't be eating rabbit for the rest of our lives."

We had the pie for Sunday dinner and there was enough over to last two more days. "Never tell me I don't do my share in this family," said Walter and Mum said, "When did I say you didn't?"

The garage is doing really well now. It's the only Morris dealership for miles and Dad's made enough money to have new tools in the garage and new petrol pumps which work automatically so you don't have to pump the petrol up yourself. What's more, we've had a proper new bathroom built with a hot water system. It's better than filling a bath in the kitchen with water boiled in the kettle.

One night, I heard Mum and Dad talking. They didn't know I was listening and soon I knew a secret that I wasn't supposed to.

"Well, I say she deserves it," Mum was saying. "It's not as though we can't afford it now."

"Is it worth the expense?" Dad said. "She'll probably be married when she's twenty. We're already paying for violin lessons."

"Matthias Vögler, I'm shocked at you," said Mum. "Of

course she should have her chance. It's only fair. And she loves her music so much. Her violin teacher says she could be really good."

"What will Walter think?" said Dad.

"When Walter was eleven we'd hardly two pennies to rub together. I expect he'll resent it, but what can we do?"

I knew at once what they were talking about. They were going to pay for Anna to go to the grammar school. I was pleased. But Walter would feel more out of things than ever.

Last Saturday Dad asked me to help him plant some late runner beans in the garden. He sent me into the shed to get some long bamboo canes. They lay on the floor under the window. I picked up a pile and saw something hidden underneath them, long, hard and wrapped in oily cloth. I picked it up and unwrapped it. A double-barrelled shotgun. It wasn't new but the action was well oiled and the barrels glinted a sinister dark grey, like a battleship. Suddenly I was scared. It must be Walter's, but what a silly place to hide a gun. What if Dad had got the canes out himself?

Next day Walter had his breakfast, then said, "I'm off out with Harry." He left by the front door, which surprised me, but when I looked out of the kitchen window I thought I saw something moving in the shed. He must have gone round the back, climbed over the fence, slipped into the shed and taken the gun.

He came back in the evening, this time with a brace of pheasants. Dad was furious. "The only way you could have got these was by trespassing and poaching. If you go to court, don't expect me to help you."

"Of course we didn't go poaching," said Walter indignantly. "They escaped out of the woods and Harry shot them as they ran across the road. He got four and gave two to me."

Dad gave him a long, searching look and then said, "I hope you're telling me the truth."

I knew he wasn't. Those pheasants didn't cross the A5, they were in Colby's Wood and Walter shot them with that gun.

"We can't eat them tomorrow," said Walter. "You have to hang them for a week and get them nice and ripe."

"I know all about pheasants," said Mum. "When I was in service at Hartcross Park, they were always eating them. The cellar stank with the things hanging up. Not that Lady Launton gave us any." She paused, then said, "I always wondered what they were like. I'll do them for next week." So it looked as though Mum believed Walter, which meant Dad would go along with her for the sake of a quiet life. But I was worried. What if Dad found out? I'd have to let Walter know I'd found the shotgun.

Next day when I came home from school I went straight to the shed. The shotgun was still there. Walter came home about six o'clock, ready for his tea. After we'd eaten, I had to get on with my homework.

"Tell Mum I'm off out with Harry," said Walter.

As he was opening the door, I said, "I found the gun in the shed."

He turned back to me. "You what?"

"It was under the bamboo canes."

"And are you going to tell your beloved father?"

"Of course I'm not. I just thought I'd warn you. It's not a very good place to hide things."

Walter sat down. "And what if I don't care? What if I *want* him to find it? You didn't think of that, did you?"

"Why not just tell him then?"

He gave me a long look and then said, "So I can have a proper row with the bastard. If I confess first he'll be all reasonable and forgiving like he always is."

"You can't call him that name you just said," I managed in a weak, little voice.

"Oh, can't I? Well, I bloody well did."

"Walter, what's he done to you to deserve this?"

"Don't call me Walter. I'm Wally and don't you forget it."

"All right, but what's he done to you?"

"Done? If you used that so-called brain of yours you might find out. I reckon all the algebra you do at that school has made you forget how to count."

"What do you mean?" I asked.

"If you've not got wit enough to work it out, then I'm not working it out for you. Tell Mum not to wait up." Just before he stormed out he turned and said, "And you breathe just one word of what I've just told you and I'll kill you."

"But you haven't told me anything," I called after him. He slammed the door so hard that Mum came rushing downstairs. "What's happened?" she gasped.

"Walter's gone out," I replied. "He says not to wait up for him."

Mum looked sad. "I'm afraid that's the way with Walter all the time now." She looked at me closely. "Did you two have an argument?"

"No, Mum. Honestly."

"Something was said, wasn't it?"

"No." She must have known I was lying.

"Well, I can't force you to tell me. Now you can help me peel the potatoes."

I nearly said, "I haven't done my homework yet," but didn't.

Saturday. Dad was at the garage, Mum and Anna had gone shopping. This time Walter left through the back door. I followed him to the shed and, as he picked up the gun and replaced the canes, I said, "Walter, what did you mean about working it out? Work what out?"

"Shut up, I'm in a hurry," he replied.

"But I want to know."

He fixed me with an angry glare. "I'll tell you what it is," he said. "Our father's a bloody Jerry and he did something he shouldn't and if he hadn't I wouldn't be in the mess I am now."

"He can't help being German, it's how he was born. We're not German, we're English."

"You're not, you're half Jerry and so's Anna. But Mum's not and I'm sure as hell that I'm not."

"That's silly," I said. "You're the same as me."

"Am I?" he said, with a sort of leer.

"What do you mean?"

"What I say. Now shut up about it."

That made me angry. "No, I won't! Tell me what you mean."

"Look," he said. "You're either English or you're

German. If there's a war and you don't know which side you're on, they'll shoot you. I won't believe I'm half German, so I must be all English. Now do you understand?"

No, I didn't. "Everyone says there isn't going to be a war," I said.

"Well, I hope there is, a bloody, great, big one and I'll be first in the queue to join up. Now, get out of my way. I'm off to smash a few clay pigeons and knock over some pheasants and wish that every one of them was a Jerry soldier and the biggest pheasant of all was that evil sod Hitler. Tell that to your father when he comes home."

"No, I won't," I replied. "You'll have to." Then I added daringly, "If you're not too scared."

He glared at me again. "I'll wring your neck, you little bugger," he said. And then he was gone. I suppose this means he won't be coming to Germany this time either.

On the first Monday of the holidays, Walter didn't turn up for work. He wasn't home until nearly eleven. He marched straight to his bedroom and went out early next day, long before anyone else got up. When Dad went to the garage Walter wasn't there and a secondhand Ford 8 had disappeared.

"Jimmy said I should call the police," said Dad when he came home. "But I won't because I know very well who's got it."

"Not Walter?" Mum cried. "You can't be sure."

"Who else? I won't set the police on my own son."

Walter didn't come home that night, or the night after, or the night after that. Eventually Mum said, "If you don't call the police, I will."

"Walter will be fine," Dad told her. "He can look after himself, he drives a car as well as I can. He'll have the time of his life in that Ford."

"He's just a boy," said Mum. "Please call the police."

"I'll do no such thing," Dad said. "But I'll go round to the Brindleys. Perhaps Harry knows what's happened to him."

When he came back he said, "Jacob Brindley says they've gone off together for a few days. They'll be fine. They're old enough to look after themselves."

"If we don't hear from him I won't go to Germany," said Mum.

Two days later a postcard arrived, one of those rude ones you get at the seaside. On it was scribbled: *Don't worry about me, I'm all right.* The postmark was blurred, so we still didn't know where he was.

"What did I tell you?" said Dad. "He's a big lad, he needs his freedom."

"It's not good enough," Mum replied. "I won't rest easy until he's home."

Three days later another rude postcard arrived. Mum read it and then threw it on the table. Dad picked it up.

"What does it say?" asked Anna.

"See for yourself," said Dad and passed it to us. This time Walter had scrawled: *Wish you were here. Only joking.* This time I could read the postmark. "He's gone to Skegness," I said.

"Ooh, he is lucky," said Anna. "I wish we were going to the seaside."

"Instead of Germany?" Mum asked her.

"Oh no, of course I want to go to Germany," said Anna, but I could see where she'd rather be and deep down inside I couldn't help agreeing with her.

2.3

So we're off to Germany again. Walter still wasn't back when we left, Mum said she thought the second postcard was so horrible that she felt resigned to it. Jimmy drove us to the station again. "Don't worry about young Walter," he said as he dropped us off. "He'll be back and I'll keep an eye on him when he is."

It was windy in the Channel and the clouds were grey with flecks of rain in the air. I felt queasy on the ship and Anna was sick over the side. The train journey seemed very long and by the time Granny and Grandad Vögler met us at Frankfurt I felt tired and washed out.

Helmut was with them again – but what a different Helmut. His face looked hard, not in a cruel way but strong. He was wearing a light khaki shirt with badges on it, black shorts and a dagger on his belt. He stood up very straight and clicked his heels, just like the film star Erich von Stroheim who we sometimes saw in films in Northampton. He held out his hand rather stiffly and said, "*Guten Morgen.*"

Anna stared at him. "Why are you wearing a uniform?"

Mum frowned at her. "Don't be so rude, Anna."

As the train for Regelstein steamed out, Grandad and Granny Vögler chatted in German to Dad, about Uncle Hermann making a lot of money building a barracks at an army camp. Then Anna said to Helmut, "You haven't told us about your uniform yet."

"I do not think you will like what I shall say," said Helmut.

"Yes we will. I think it's a nice uniform," said Anna.

"Why shouldn't we like it?" I asked.

"Because the British do not like our Führer," said Helmut. "But the Führer does not care what people in other countries think."

"What's that got to do with your uniform?" I asked.

"I am a member of the Hitler Youth Organization," Helmut replied.

"Is that like the Boy Scouts?" I asked.

"Do the Boy Scouts make you love your fatherland?" said Helmut. "Do they teach you that you must defend it against all its enemies? Do they make you feel that loyalty to your Führer is the most important thing in your life?"

"I don't know, I'm not one of them," I replied.

"If you don't feel it is your duty to join the Scouts, then Britain must be a poorer place than Germany," Helmut said.

"Well, it's not," I snapped.

"That will do, Helmut," said Grandad. "You must not say things to make your cousin angry."

He was right – I was angry. Things had changed since last time. I had a different room too, so I couldn't look out of the window at the sycamore tree.

* * *

A week has gone by and we're going home early and I'm not a bit sorry. Germany is different. There are big red banners with swastikas on them wherever you look. The streets are full of men in uniforms with swastika armbands. There are shops with broken windows and

JUDEN RAUS

painted on the wall. I asked Helmut why the Germans wanted the Jews out.

"Because they are decadent and will bring down the German people," he explained. "They are not true Germans."

"But they must be," I said. "They've got German names. Didn't they fight in the war?"

"They have stolen their names and should not have been allowed to fight. Because of them our country was betrayed."

I didn't know what to say to that, so I shut up. But that evening Dad asked Grandad Vögler the same question and he answered, "You must understand, Matthias, that the Jews have taken over the whole of the furniture industry and are trying to run the banks to suit their own ends. If they are not stopped, Germany will be bankrupt again and all the advantages we have won under the Führer will be lost. The Führer saved us from ruin and we are all grateful to him."

It was a better reason than the one Helmut gave me,

though it still didn't seem good enough. I couldn't see how the man who ran the baker's shop at the end of the street and had a sign painted on his window was anything to do with the furniture industry or running a bank.

I wondered if Helmut would challenge me to a race up the tree again: after two days he hadn't and I wondered if I should do the challenging. But he was so much bigger now. Anyway, he had other things to think about. Auntie Anneliese and Uncle Hermann were very proud because he was marching with the Hitler Youth in a big rally in Nuremburg in three days' time. "Baldur von Schirach will be there," said Uncle Hermann. "Perhaps he will pick Helmut out and set him on the path of great things."

"Who's Baldur whatever-it-is?" I asked.

"The man who started the Hitler Youth," Uncle Hermann replied.

All the top members of the Nazi Party would be there: Goebbels, Goering, Ribbentrop, Adolf Hitler himself. I hardly saw Helmut because he was always out practising for the rally. "I expect you're dying to see us rehearsing," he said to me. "But strangers are forbidden to watch."

"Of course, we shall all go to the rally," said Uncle Hermann. "You will find it very instructive and inspiring, Paul." He seemed to expect an answer, so I muttered, "I'm sure I will, Uncle Hermann."

Without Helmut, I spent most of my time with Anna. Not that I minded, but she was quiet and not much fun really and besides, I hadn't come all this way to play with my little sister. Uncle Hermann worked all day and half the night, so we either went for walks round Regelstein or into Frankfurt with Granny and Grandad. Grandad tried starting conversations but Mum and Dad weren't very talkative. I tried talking to Granny but nothing I said seemed to come out right.

On the evening before the rally, Helmut came home very excited. Because he was a model member of the Hitler Youth, an example to all German boys, he was to be presented to Hitler personally. Auntie Anneliese cried, "Oh, Helmut, I'm so proud of you."

Next day we set off for Nuremburg in Uncle Hermann's big Mercedes. Helmut had gone early in the morning on a special coach.

"We have seats reserved for us because Helmut is in the parade," said Uncle Hermann proudly. "Just think how wonderful it will be when we see the Führer actually talking to him."

It was over a hundred miles to Nuremburg, but the new Autobahn made the journey seem quite short. "It's thanks to the Führer that we have such wonderful roads," said Uncle Hermann. "And wait until you see the Zeppelinfeld. It is a perfect stadium for our great rallies."

When we arrived in Nuremburg and I saw the Zeppelinfeld, its huge stands full of people, the vast arena and the hundreds of big red banners with swastikas on them, I gasped with amazement. Our reserved places must have had one of the best views in the place. There was a big dais at one end and men in uniforms sat there. Uncle Hermann was looking at the dais through a pair of binoculars. "There's Goering," he said. "I can see Albert Speer and Rudolf Hess. And see that thin man with them? Dr Goebbels. Very clever fellow. Heinrich Himmler's there too. And Baldur von Schirach. Matthias, have a look." He passed the binoculars to Dad, who shook his head and said, "Not now, Hermann."

"I'm sure Paul would like to see such great men close up," said Uncle Hermann and gave me the binoculars. At first it was a blur. "I'll adjust them for you," said Uncle Hermann. This time I saw everything in sharp detail. Goering, big, smiling, a fat, smooth face. Goebbels, with a scrawny neck and huge Adam's apple. Rudolf Hess, tall, thin, almost like a skeleton. In the middle of them was a vacant place.

There was an expectant hum round the crowd: then a band appeared, playing a stirring march, trumpets and drums and cymbals crashing. After the band came rank on rank of marching boys, drilled so that they moved like a well oiled machine. "There they are, the Hitler Youth," Auntie Anneliese squealed. "Can you see Helmut?" I stared through the binoculars but couldn't find him. "Give them to me," said Uncle Hermann. "I know where he'll be." He almost snatched them, put them to his eyes and said, "There he is, in the little group at the front. They're the ones who will meet the Führer." I followed Uncle Hermann's pointing finger but I was blowed if I could see him.

"Oh, Hermann, don't you feel proud?" Auntie Anneliese cried, and clutched his arm. Uncle kept the binoculars to his eyes. "Of course I do," he said gruffly.

After the Hitler Youth came the soldiers, marching stiffly like robots, lifting their legs high in the air with every step as if they were kicking a football. "Why do they march like that?" I whispered to Dad and he murmured, "It's called goose-stepping."

"It must make them very tired," I said.

Uncle Hermann heard me and said, "Oh no, soldiers of the Third Reich will not be tired."

Then there was a huge roar of diesel engines and a squadron of tanks squealed into the stadium. There was another expectant hush, though this time full of a tension which I felt clearly. Then came a piercing fanfare of trumpets: everybody looked to a spot far away to the left of the square – and suddenly the tension snapped.

A chant began: "*Sieg Heil! Sieg Heil! Sieg Heil!*" again and again, a rhythm you could drown in. The noise swirled round me and made me feel faint. Every right arm was lifted up – the Nazi salute. I knew because we often played games at school making fun of it. I wondered if I would ever make fun of it again.

Then I saw a small figure in a brown uniform making his way along the front of the dais. My heart beat very fast. I was watching Adolf Hitler himself, not a hundred yards away from me. From where I was he looked tiny, dwarfed by the huge men round him, yet every eye was drawn to him. He acknowledged the salutes with an almost casual movement of his right hand and took the empty place at the front of the dais as a hush came over the packed stadium.

Someone barked out an order. The little group in which Helmut stood marched up the steps to the dais and stood facing Hitler. Baldur von Schirach stood next to him. The boys slowly filed past them and stopped in turn before Hitler for the briefest of moments. Von Schirach spoke to him about each one: he nodded and sometimes laughed. Then he bent down and spoke to the boy. Sometimes he touched the boy's shoulder, sometimes his head. When Helmut stood before him I snatched a glance at Uncle Hermann and Auntie Anneliese. They were holding hands as if they were in a trance.

At last Hitler had seen every boy and they filed down the steps and back to their places in the arena. Then Hitler started his speech.

I expect that, if it hadn't been distorted by the loud-speakers, I would have understood more of it. I know he was saying things about Germans being the master race, that they must keep their purity and that lesser people, *Untermenschen*, he called them, must be got rid of and that there should be more room in the world, *Lebensraum*, for real Germans to flourish. The rest went over my head as a wordless noise, a piercing, raucous, sometimes high, some-times low, always menacing voice. The crowd seemed hypnotized. I looked towards Mum and Dad. Mum had grasped Dad's hand and was squeezing it.

Sometimes as he spoke there was a huge roar from the crowd and more chants of "*Sieg Heil*". I knew everybody in the square was getting worked up. Except Mum and Dad, who still held hands, with Dad pale and Mum looking at him anxiously.

That evening, back in Regelstein and eating supper, Uncle Hermann asked, "Well, Paul, what did you think of our great day out?"

"It was very loud," I said.

He chuckled. "It was indeed, Paul, it was indeed. And so it should be, so the whole world can hear. Don't you agree, Matthias?"

69

Dad didn't answer but carefully cut a slice of salami.

"Paul, you have been given a great privilege today," Uncle Hermann continued. "Very few German boys have been in the presence of the Führer himself so an English boy must feel very proud."

"But part of you is German, isn't it, Paul?" said Auntie Anneliese.

"Half, I suppose," I muttered.

"I hope it will be the better half," said Uncle Hermann, laughing.

"Where's Helmut?" Anna asked.

"He has stayed behind with the Hitler Youth," said Auntie Anneliese. "Tonight they go to camp. Oh, he's been given such an honour. He will have a lot to tell us when he gets home."

It took me a long time to get to sleep that night because the day's events went round and round in my head. When I finally did, strange, nasty dreams came but I couldn't remember them next morning. Mum woke me up very early. "Put your clothes on and pack your case, Paul," she said. "We're going home."

"But I thought we'd come for a fortnight," I said.

"We're going home," Mum repeated. "Now."

I washed and dressed quickly. Packing my case didn't take long and I lugged it downstairs. Dad sat at the table, eating rye bread and plum jam, drinking coffee and not speaking. Anna ate a bowl of cereal.

"Where's Auntie Anneliese?" I said.

No answer. I asked again.

"Hurry up with breakfast," said Mum. "We must be out of here."

Dad still said nothing. I didn't feel like eating.

A door opened above us. Auntie Anneliese ran downstairs, Uncle Hermann following her. "What are you doing?" she cried.

"I'm afraid we're going home," Dad said grimly.

"It's because Walter hasn't returned home and I'm worried," said Mum.

"I don't believe you," Uncle Hermann said. "You were not so worried about him when you came. There's something more, I see it in your faces."

Dad looked up and spoke at last. "I cannot stay here."

"What are you talking about? You're my brother."

"I know I'm your brother. But after yesterday I cannot stay here."

Uncle Hermann narrowed his eyes and spoke stiffly. "If what you saw yesterday offends you then you are no brother of mine. You are disloyal to your family, your people, your country. If you feel you must go, then please do. You are not welcome here."

Dad looked as though he had been hit. "Come on, children," said Mum. "We're going now."

Then I heard Granny's voice. "What's going on?" I looked up and there they both were, Granny and Grandad Vögler, still in their nightgowns, at the top of the stairs.

"I'm sorry, Mother," said Dad. "And you, my father. But we cannot stay here."

We left without another word, no goodbyes, and I felt awful about Granny and Grandad because it wasn't their fault, it was Hitler's.

2.4

It was a long, sad journey home. Dad's face was still pale. There were lines on it I hadn't seen before and his eyes had dark shadows round them. Mum gripped his arm and kept looking at him, as if searching for something in his face. They hardly spoke, to each other or to us.

As the train left Koblenz and was running beside the Rhine, Anna suddenly said, "Daddy, do you remember when we came here last time and the lady told us about the Lorelei story?"

"I'm surprised you can remember that, Anna," Dad replied.

"Oh yes, I can," she said. "The lady told us about Lorelei singing such a beautiful song that all the sailors were enchanted and wanted to hear it so much that their ships hit the rocks and they were drowned."

"Yes," said Dad. "It's an old story and a very sad one."

"I've wondered what that song sounded like ever since," Anna continued. "Sometimes I almost thought I could hear it. But yesterday I knew I'd got the song wrong. It wasn't a lovely tune, it was like Mr Hitler speaking. It's as if what he said was enchanting the people there, like Lorelei did to the sailors."

"You mean so they'll hit the rocks and drown?" I said.

Dad looked at Anna for a moment without speaking. Then he said, "You're very clever, my girl." He turned his face away and stared out of the window. Then he turned back and said, "I'm sorry, Anna. That sounded patronizing. It's not what I meant. I didn't mean clever. I meant wise. You speak the truth, more than you know."

It was late when we reached Calais, so we found a guesthouse to stay the night in. We woke to another grey, squally day and the crossing back to Dover was as bad as the crossing out. When we were off the ship Dad found a telephone box and rang Jimmy to tell him we'd be at Northampton in the afternoon. He was there to meet us and when we'd loaded our cases and set off, Mum said, "Has Walter come back?"

"No," Jimmy replied. "But the Ford has. It was on the forecourt yesterday morning. They must have brought it back in the night."

"Was it damaged?" asked Dad.

"No, it was fine," said Jimmy. "Only needed a wash. But they'd put a thousand miles on the clock."

"Never mind the car, what about Walter?" said Mum.

"Ah," said Jimmy. "I was coming to that. I went round to ask Jacob Brindley if he knew. You'll never guess what he said."

"No guessing, just tell us," said Dad.

"Walter and Harry, they've only gone and joined the RAF."

***

I was sure we'd find a note from Walter in the house. So was Mum, because the first thing she did was to look on every table and shelf. But there was nothing. She sat down on a kitchen chair as if all the stuffing had been knocked out of her.

"Paul and Anna, bring the luggage in, please," said Dad. "Jimmy will help you. I need to stay with your mother."

Jimmy helped us take the cases out of the car to the hall. "Should we unpack them?" Anna whispered.

"Yes," I replied and we set to work. We weren't sure where Mum's and Dad's stuff went so we left it all on their bed, but we put everything of ours back where it ought to be. We heard Mum sobbing in the kitchen. "Do you think we ought to go downstairs?" Anna was sounding very worried now.

I nearly said, "No," but changed my mind. "Yes. It's as much to do with us as it is with them."

Mum still sat in the chair and Dad knelt beside her, his arm round her shoulders, talking softly. She stopped crying and wiped her eyes. "Our eldest, our firstborn child," she said. "And he goes away without a word to his own family. I can't stand it, Matthias."

"He's dealt us a cruel blow," said Dad. "I feel it's my fault. I don't know what I've done to make him dislike me so much. I've tried to be a good father." Then he said something which made me catch my breath. "As long as you never regret marrying me and making things so difficult for yourself."

Mum grasped his hands and smiled. "Never, my love,"

74

she said. "Not for a single second. Never blame yourself for what Walter does."

Next week we tried to carry on as though nothing had happened. Surely Walter would write. But nothing came…

Then, a week later, the postman brought a small suitcase. We knew it was Walter's. There was a label tied to the handle with our address on one side and on the other was written:

314607 AC2 VÖGLER, W

Inside were a pair of trousers, shirt, jersey, vest and three pairs of underpants, all fairly dirty. There was no letter.

Mum gasped. "It's like the war, when they sent home the belongings of soldiers who were killed."

Anna cried, "Walter hasn't been killed, has he?"

"Of course not," said Dad. "He wears a uniform now. He has no use for those clothes any more."

"Well," I said. "Now we know where he is, we can visit him."

"He's at the reception base," said Dad. "We can't go there. Walter belongs to the Air Force now, not to us. We won't see him for months, and then only if he's thought better of how he behaved."

"What made him do it?" said Mum. "He didn't have to. There isn't a war on."

"No," said Dad. "Not yet." And I have never seen him look so troubled, not even on the train home when Anna talked about the Lorelei story.

1939–1940

ELLEN

3.1

We heard nothing from Walter for six weeks. I was so worried that I rang the RAF station that had sent his suitcase back. They told me he was on basic training, "square-bashing" the man called it, in the north of England. But one Friday evening Walter turned up without warning, in blue uniform and shiny boots. "Got a forty-eight-hour pass," he muttered. "I hitch-hiked down. Getting lifts is easy when you're in uniform."

We were so pleased to see him. After supper Matthias asked him to go for a drink in the Crooked Billet. Walter refused. "I'm only here the night," he said. "I'm off to London in the morning to meet up with some mates." Next morning Matthias drove him to the station. When Matthias returned, I said, "I bet he didn't thank you."

We both know that Matthias has lost Walter for good now. Four months have passed since that weekend and we haven't seen him since, though he did send two postcards, the first to say that he was training on aircraft engines, the second that he was at Biggin Hill working on Hawker Hurricanes.

I can't help thinking that some of the great turning points of our lives have occurred within these months. Sometimes, when Matthias was working in the garage and the children were at school I felt almost drowned under waves of despair. My husband was estranged from his family and our son was estranged from us. There would be war: we knew it and so did our family in Germany, though it had remained unspoken. Brother would take arms against brother while son wished he could take arms against father.

When I felt this desperation taking me I thought over the past: how, while it delighted me and I would not have it any other way, it had brought us to this. I rejoiced at its blessings at the same time as tracing its inevitable progress.

I love all my children equally but sometimes I feel closer to Anna. When I look at her, I see myself. She's quiet and lets the boys get away with too much, but she'll surprise them one day. She has talent.

About the boys – any mother would be proud of a son like Paul. He's clever, works hard at school and, underneath it all, I think he's tough. But what can I say about Walter? We never told him he was the reason we married. He probably knows, though he doesn't realize we would have married anyway.

A lot of people didn't like it when they knew Matthias and I were getting married. Lambsfield was split in two. Some, the Straker family and their friends the Langleys and Pinkneys in the forefront, did their best to shake Matthias and make us leave the village. The other half couldn't have been more supportive. At first Ma didn't like the idea of our marriage and was outraged when I became pregnant, but, as always, she came round in the end.

When Walter was born our happiness seemed complete. But when he went to the village school, he suffered a lot from other children because his father was German. Paul was born four years later and Anna two years after that and I prayed they would never go through what Walter did.

When Matthias's Uncle Friedrich died he left Matthias his smallholding and market garden. "I don't know much about market gardening but I do know about cars," said Matthias. "We'll build our own garage there." So we left Lambsfield and came to Peterspury.

Uncle Friedrich, I remember, was a lovely man: fat, jolly and generous. He told us he came to England with a German band playing on the seafront in Brighton, Blackpool and Eastbourne in the summer and in park bandstands in London in the winter. But he met a girl and bought the smallholding so he could get married and support her. When she let him down he didn't go back to Germany. He stayed in England and did pretty well as a market gardener.

But music was his first love. He had two instruments, a big euphonium, the "oom-pah" he called it, for the band, and a violin for himself. He often played them to us when we visited. And he played beautifully. He left the euphonium to Walter and the violin to Anna in his will. I've no idea where Walter's euphonium is, but the violin has come to be the centre of Anna's life. As well as the violin, Friedrich bequeathed his love of music to Anna.

3.2

So 1938 is here and how have things turned out? The world is a troubling, dangerous place. I'm told there are people in high places in Britain who support Hitler. I fear for my children. "I'm used to not sleeping," Ma once said to me. "All mothers are." Now I know what she meant.

In September, Mr Chamberlain, the Prime Minister, came back from seeing Hitler, waving a piece of paper which he said was the Munich Agreement and meant peace in our time. He'd let Hitler occupy part of Czechoslovakia as long as he did nothing against Britain and France. Matthias actually shouted at the wireless set. "He won't stop there! Austria, Czechoslovakia, what will he want next?" But most people are thankful. No war. I slept easy that night. I never thought of people in Czechoslovakia. Out of sight, out of mind, I suppose.

Poor Matthias. His loyalties are stretched to breaking point. I see it in his face as he listens to the news or reads the paper. He hears about *Kristallnacht*, when all over Germany the windows of Jewish-owned shops were smashed by Nazi mobs. Last night, he said, "If I'd gone home after the last war, would I have smashed Jewish shop windows as well?"

"Not you, Matthias," I replied. "Never you."

"And Helmut and Paul were friends. Now Helmut's a Nazi in the Hitler Youth. Might Paul have been a Nazi if we lived there?"

"Never," I cried.

"And what about Anna?" he went on.

"Matthias, why are you saying such things?"

"You misunderstand me," he said. "I was thinking of what she said about the Lorelei's song and Hitler." He stared gloomily into the fire. "She was right. A girl of eleven can see it when millions of my countrymen can't. I live here now and I see how despicable it all is. Would I if I were still there?"

"It depends where your loyalties lie," I said.

Paul and Matthias do lots of things together, even going to Northampton to watch football in the winter and cricket in summer. He's close to Anna as well. Two out of three children isn't so bad.

Two months after the Munich Agreement, Hermann wrote to say their father was ill but there was no need for Matthias to go. "It can't be serious," said Matthias. Another letter came a week after. Mathias's father was dead. "Why didn't they send a telegram?" he cried. "I never said goodbye." He left for Regelstein next morning and was gone for a week. When he returned he looked really ill.

"How was the funeral?" I asked.

"How do you think?" he replied. Then he took my hand

and said, "I'm sorry. I didn't mean to snap. It was awful. My old home is now a terrible place. I could not stay there. I know there will be another war."

Paul is doing well at Wicester Grammar School. The teachers tell us he is very strong in languages, French and, not surprisingly, German. Sending Anna was worth every penny. She loves it there and is especially good at music. She plays Friedrich's old violin beautifully. "I wonder where she gets it from." Matthias once said.

"Your uncle of course," I replied. "Friedrich should have left his euphonium to her as well, not Walter. I wonder where that euphonium went. I'm sure it used to be in Walter's wardrobe."

I once asked Walter and he said burglars must have taken it. "Don't be silly," I answered. "Where have you put it?"

"Nowhere!" he shouted. "You're always on at me. You never believe a word I say."

I'm sure Paul and Anna will turn out well. I just pray that what happens in the next years will allow them to.

This year, 1939, has been the worst year yet. Hitler has got Czechoslovakia and now wants Poland. Britain says that if he invades Poland, we'll declare war.

"That means he will," said Matthias. "He wants to pick a fight."

A few in the village, such as Mr Ingram, are saying nasty things about Matthias. Someone shouted "Nazi spy" the other day.

"Why don't you stop them?" I said.

"How can I?" he replied. "They can't forget I'm German."

"Well, they should have by now. You should fight back."

"Should I?" he said. "Do you want our windows broken?"

Then government circulars came through the post about what to do in an air raid. I nearly tore them up. Who'd bomb Peterspury? For Matthias, the one bright spot was winning the football club draw for the two Cup Final tickets. "I'll take Paul to Wembley," he said delightedly. "For one day I can stop worrying."

The twenty-ninth of April dawned and they left early to catch the train for London. They were back late at night. Paul was full of talk about the match, the crowds, Wembley Stadium itself. But when he'd gone to bed, Matthias said, "So much for thinking I could forget about everything for a day." He opened the programme in the middle, where they showed the teams. There was a notice at the foot of the page:

NATIONAL SERVICE

A MESSAGE TO ALL

YOU SHOULD UNDERSTAND THAT THE HORROR AND DANGER OF MODERN WAR MAY BE BROUGHT TO YOUR OWN DOOR

It said that everybody should volunteer for some form of national service, air raid wardens, rescue workers. "*It is your duty to do so. It is absolutely necessary to your future.*"

"Even at the Cup Final," Matthias said. "What chance have we got?"

85

* * *

In August the papers were full of the news that Germany and Russia had signed a non-aggression pact saying that neither would ever attack the other. "Hitler hates communists," Matthias exclaimed. "I know why he's done it. He doesn't want to fight in the east and the west at the same time. Now he only need fight us. Nothing can stop war now."

I think it was the Nazi-Soviet pact that plunged Matthias into complete depression. One night as we lay in bed he said, "Ellen, do you realize that if war comes they'll take me away, like they took Friedrich?"

"Why should they? You're not a spy. Everybody knows you. The village can't do without you. Who'd mend their cars for a start?"

"There are some in Peterspury who would gladly see me go," said Matthias. "What will happen will happen. We can't stop it."

September came and with it the news we all dreaded. Hitler had invaded Poland. Though he said it was the other way round and Germany was only defending itself, nobody was fooled. Mr Chamberlain demanded that he withdraw. On the morning of 3 September, Mr Chamberlain spoke on the wireless. "I have to tell you now that no such undertaking has been received and –" his voice sounded old and tired – "consequently this country is at war with Germany."

I was on my own when I heard. I sat down numb and drained and thought: *Does Matthias know? Shall I tell him? I'll go anyway. I can't sit here on my own all day.* Then the front

86

door opened and Matthias blundered in. I put my arms around him and hugged him. "It's all right, my love, we'll come through this."

His face was deathly pale. "It's finished," he said, almost in a whisper. "It's all finished. Everything I ever wanted. Finished."

3.3

It's 1940 and war was declared six months ago. We know terrible things are happening in Poland, and in Finland too, where Russian troops have invaded. But here it's quiet. Some London evacuees came in October. Most families took two or more but we weren't asked. I mentioned it to Mrs Carter in the grocer's shop and she said, "Well, it's because of your husband, isn't it."

I felt as if she'd slapped me across the face. We were enemies in our own village. But worse was to come. Paul and Anna were at school and Matthias was eating breakfast. I answered a knock at the door. Three policemen stood there. I didn't know two of them, an inspector and a sergeant. The other was George, PC Coppard.

"Has Matt gone to the garage yet, Ellen?" he asked.

"No," I replied. "Why?"

"We have to talk to him for a minute."

Matt came to the door. "What's going on?" he asked.

The inspector stepped forward. "Matthias Vögler, we are required by law to detain you in custody as an enemy alien."

Matthias turned to George. "But I've lived here in Peterspury for twelve years. I'm secretary of the football club. I'm almost a native." As an afterthought he added, "My son's in the RAF."

"I know that and you know that," said George awkwardly. "But we're at war and the law is the law. The government wants to round up all the spies and rascals and if they take in a few they shouldn't, that's the luck of the draw."

"Mr Vögler," said the sergeant. "We'd be obliged if you would pack a suitcase with enough clothes for a week. You'll be properly equipped at the detention centre. You have half an hour to get ready."

"Where are you taking me?" Matthias asked.

"To Wicester Racecourse. Everyone for internment in Northants and North Bucks goes there to start with."

"I want some time alone with my wife before I go," said Matthias.

George looked at the inspector. "I reckon we can hold on for an hour," the inspector said.

When they were gone we packed the case and put it in the hall. Matthias looked so desperate that I almost doubted that he would survive internment. In the last war he'd escaped death by a hair's breadth and I had saved him. Now I thought: *I don't think I can save you this time.*

Looking back on that precious hour, I've often wondered how we might have used it if we'd had more warning. Made great declarations of love? Sworn undying hatred towards Adolf Hitler and all his works? Snatched a last few minutes of lovemaking? We did none of these things. We could only clasp hands and look at each other as if fixing each other's faces in our minds for ever. It seemed only a few minutes before there was a quiet tap on the door and George Coppard's voice sounded through the letterbox. "Time's up, I'm afraid, Matt."

Matthias picked up his case. "Goodbye, my love," he said. "I shall write." Then he walked out of the house to the car. George opened the rear door. Matthias got in and sat next to the sergeant. The inspector climbed into the front passenger seat and the car moved off.

I watched it disappear up the A5, with Matthias looking back through the rear window. I waved, saw his hand lift in return and kept waving until the car was too far away to see him any more.

"Will you be all right, Ellen?" George asked. "Shall I send someone round to stay with you?"

"I'll be fine," I replied. "But thank you."

"Well, if you're sure," he said. "I'd better be about my duties."

I turned back into the house. I have never felt so empty, so drained. The clock's ticking sounded like hammer blows in the silence. At midday I put the wireless on. The latest about the navy chasing the battleship *Graf Spee* to the River Plate, news about Poland and Finland, the RAF in France, naval patrols in the North Sea, anti-aircraft guns round London. Then came a programme of dance music, Jack Payne and his band. I loved it once: I had no wish to hear it now. I switched the wireless off, sat in a kitchen chair and stared blindly out of the window, too depressed even to cry.

Paul and Anna sensed something was wrong the moment they came in the house. "What's happened,

90

Mummy?" said Anna as Paul asked, "Where's Dad?" I made them sit down and told them. Paul sat very still while Anna snuggled up to me and put her arms round my neck. "Things might be hard for you at school now," I said. "Please don't get angry or lose your tempers."

"Don't worry, Mum, we won't," said Anna.

"I know," I replied. Then we sat silent for a long time, wondering what the next months might bring.

August 1938–
September 1940

WALTER'S CAREER

4.1

Walter knows he wants to join the RAF long before the war starts. When he sees his family preparing to go to Germany again he is outraged. The time has come to show them he'll have no part in this. A plan is forming in his mind – but he doesn't want to carry it out alone. So he takes Monday off work and goes round to see Harry.

He comes back late that night with everything sorted out, packs a case and at first light gets up and steals out of the house. Nobody wakes up. He goes to the garage, unlocks the office door and opens the cupboard where customers' car keys are kept. For some time now he's had his eye on the second-hand Ford 8 brought in for part-exchange. He'd have it if he'd got the money, but he hasn't. He'll take it anyway, he thinks, because he's perfectly entitled to. He's the eldest son of the boss and the garage will be his one day.

He unlocks the driver's door, then cranks the car up. The engine starts with a loud cough. He sits in the driving seat, pulls out the choke and listens to the engine idling as it warms up.

There's no sign of life: nobody has heard. He slips the car into first gear, drives down the village street and then up the potholed track leading to Harry's dad's cottage.

Harry is waiting. He opens the passenger door, throws his bag on the back seat and says, "Where to?"

"It's about time I had a holiday by the sea," Walter replies and heads out to the main road.

Five hours later and they are in Skegness. Walter parks the car on the seafront, gets out, stretches, looks at the water sparkling in bright sunshine, takes a deep breath and exclaims, "Just smell that air. We're going to have the time of our lives."

Sadly, he's wrong. Next day the clouds rush in and a cold wind blows off the grey, heaving North Sea; their bed and breakfast is horrible and the girls who flock in from Lincoln and Nottingham are even less forthcoming than those in Northampton. He sends two postcards home, not because he feels guilty but to make sure they don't get the police to look for him. But as the days pass he grows more and more disillusioned. "I'm pissed off with this," he tells Harry after a week. "We're going."

"Where to?" asks Harry.

"Back home."

"But you said…"

"I know what I said. But I have to get this car back. I've got other fish to fry."

He doesn't speak for nearly an hour as he drives. Harry watches him, unsure of what's happening. This is a new Walter: Harry is certain he's preparing a surprise and the feeling is deeply unsettling.

Harry doesn't drive yet and doesn't see much chance of

doing it. He envies Walter. The man with the car keys has power over the passenger. Suddenly, as Walter pulls out to overtake a lorry, he realizes, with a lurching heart, what that might mean.

The lorry is doing a steady thirty miles an hour. Even with his foot on the floorboards Walter finds it hard to get more than forty-five out of the Ford, so they pass it with agonizing slowness. Harry closes his eyes: he knows a car will come straight at them and they'll be killed. Half his life seems to pass before they are level with the lorry's cab. The driver looks down and mouths something. "And you!" roars Walter. Harry opens his eyes to see him give a two-fingered sign and the lorry driver shaking his fist.

Walter is smiling. "That shut him up," he says. He's happy now. "As soon as I've dumped this pile of scrap back in the garage, I'll join the RAF," he shouted. "There's a recruiting office in Northampton. I've got my bag so I don't even need to go in the house. And I'm never coming back to Peterspury again. Are you with me?"

Harry thinks for a moment. "Yes," he says at last. "I bloody well am. Anything to get out of that dump. Better let them know at home though, or they'll have the police after us."

When they reach Peterspury they call first at Harry's house. Harry's father isn't there so Harry leaves a note:

GONE TO JOIN RAF. DON'T WORRY.

"I won't leave a note at our place," says Walter. "Let my father find out from yours, before he tries to make me join the bloody Luftwaffe."

97

"Now what?" says Harry when they've left the car at the garage.

"Last bus to Northampton," Walter replies.

They are just in time to catch it. "Cheerio, Peterspury. Cheerio, Kraut father. And good riddance," says Walter as he gets on.

The recruiting office in Northampton is closed. "Now what?" Harry asks.

"How much money have you got?"

Harry turns out his pockets. "Three shillings and six-pence. That won't get us far."

"I've got half-a-crown," says Walter.

So they spend the night on a park bench. Next morning, shivering with cold and bones aching, they find a public convenience where they have a quick swill and smooth their hair down with water. At nine o'clock they are at the recruiting office. The sergeant behind the desk says there are a few, little aptitude tests they must do before signing on. "Nobody said anything about tests," says Walter.

"This isn't the army," the sergeant replied. "We pick and choose in His Majesty's Royal Air Force. You can do them now if you like."

When they finish, the sergeant collects their papers and looks at their names. "Which one of you is Vögler?"

"Me," says Walter reluctantly.

"You're sure you're not a spy?"

"Never," said Walter indignantly. "I'm as English as you are. My father has a car dealership near Wicester."

"All right laddie, keep your hair on," said the sergeant.

"You'll hear from us in two weeks. Have I got your addresses?"

Before Harry can say his in Peterspury, Walter cuts in with, "We're working in Northampton. We're just moving to a new place but I can't quite remember the address. I'll be round to tell you a bit later."

When they are outside, Harry says, "What are you talking about? We haven't got jobs and nowhere to live either."

"Before this morning's out we'll have both," Walter replies. "We'll find lodgings first. How does a B&B sound?"

"Not if it's like Skegness," says Harry.

"If it's cheap enough it's good enough," says Walter.

They find one in a small terraced house. Shared room, shared bed, breakfast between 7 and 7.30 a.m., five shillings a night. "Take it or leave it," says the landlady.

"It's horrible," Harry mutters.

"It'll do well, Missus," says Walter. "We'll leave our stuff here and be back this evening."

"Mrs Jenkins is my name and I'll thank you to use it," says the landlady, shutting the door on them.

"This is no good," says Harry. "I'm going home."

"Suit yourself," shrugs Walter.

When Harry doesn't answer, Walter says, "Work next."

Harry shakes his head, "You can't get a job just like that."

"Easy," Walter replies. "We'll find a building site. Casual labour and no questions asked."

They find three houses being built on a plot along the Stony Stratford road. Apart from a few bricklayers there is no sign of life. Walter approaches the nearest. "Where's the foreman?" he asks.

The bricklayer points towards a small wooden shack. The foreman sits inside drinking a mug of tea and reading the racing page in the *Daily Mirror*. "Do you want labourers?" asks Walter.

The foreman looks them up and down. "Done it before, have you?" he says.

"Lots of times," Walter fibs, at the same moment as Harry says, "No. Why are you kicking my ankle, Wally?"

"What's the wages?" Walter asks.

"I'll see how you get on this afternoon," says the foreman. "After that I either sack you or keep you on. Three quid a week."

"Sounds OK," says Walter.

"Right," says the foreman. "Go and get something to eat. Be back here at one sharp. And I'm Mr Hicks to you."

"See?" says Walter as they left. "Nothing to it. Three quid a week's a quid more than I expected. That's thirty-five bob on the B&B and twenty-five bob for us. Not bad."

"He's got to take us on first," says Harry.

They find a café up the road, buy egg and chips with the last of their money and are back at the site dead on the appointed time. The day is warm now and the next six hours are spent shovelling sand, cement and shingle into the concrete mixer, pouring out the mixed concrete, loading it into wheelbarrows and tipping the loads in newly dug footings. Late in the afternoon a lorry from the London Brick Company arrives and they unload and stack the bricks. By half-past six they are worn out and their hands are bleeding.

Mr Hicks watches every move they make. "Not bad, lads," he says when knocking-off time comes. "You'll get better at it."

"Can we have a sub on our wages?" says Walter.

"You've got a nerve," says Mr Hicks. "All right, will two quid each till pay day suit you?"

"Done," says Walter, grinning.

Mr Hicks unlocks a cashbox and takes out four one-pound notes. "Eight sharp tomorrow," he says. "And if I have to sack you I'll be taking that four quid back."

For the next fortnight Walter and Harry work hard, whatever the weather. They are too tired to go into town in the evening, so they either have something at the café or buy fish and chips from a van and eat them in their dismal shared room. After two weeks they are tanned and fit and their hands well toughened up. Walter is enjoying every moment but Harry's face is growing longer and longer. At last the RAF get in touch. They are in and must report to the reception unit in a week's time.

"Where is it?" says Harry.

"Just up the road near Bedford," says Walter. "We can get there on the bus. Piece of cake."

"Piece of what?" says Harry.

"It's something they say in the Air Force," Walter replies. "You'd better learn it."

Harry begins to wonder whether he really wants to.

Though RAF life might not appeal to some, Walter loves it from the moment they give him a pair of black boots made with dimpled leather which must be smooth and shiny and the toecaps like mirrors in three days' time. Harry looks at his despairingly and says, "This is impossible. Do they make them like this on purpose?"

"Of course they do," says Walter, starting the long process with boot polish, soft cloth and bags of spit. "It's so they know who's going to be any good."

Harry's stricken look suggests he knows already.

The first few days are hectic. They are issued with two uniforms, best blue and working blue, blue shirts, black ties, vests and underpants, then lectured on how privileged they are to be part of the World's Finest Fighting Force.

Harry grows more morose by the day as he toils away at his boots. By now, Walter's toecaps are beautifully smooth and he can see his face in them. Harry's have more or less the same dimples as when they were first issued. Suddenly he throws them on the floor. "I can't do it," he cries. "I hate the bloody RAF. What possessed me to listen to you?"

"It's too late now," says Walter. "You've signed on."

"Perhaps I've got flat feet. They discharge you for that."

The medical tests start next day. Harry does not have flat feet.

"Perhaps I'm short-sighted and never knew," says Harry hopefully.

They are given the eyesight test. Harry has 20/20 vision. That night Walter hears him talking in his sleep.

The hearing test is next day. They are led to a brick wall and told to march, one by one in reverse alphabetical order, towards it and halt one foot away. A sergeant stands forty feet away and says something very softly. The recruit has to repeat it. All do. Now it's Harry's turn. He faces the wall. The sergeant murmurs, "Sausage and bacon." Harry says nothing.

The sergeant moves nearer. "Sausage and bacon," he repeats, slightly louder this time. Again Harry doesn't move. The sergeant comes nearer and shouts. Harry doesn't move a muscle.

"I'll make you hear me if it's the last thing I do," the sergeant roars. Still Harry doesn't answer. The sergeant stands about ten feet away and says "One." No response. A step closer, voice louder. "Two." Not a flicker. Nearer still, louder still. Not a thing. At last he is hardly six inches from Harry's left ear. He takes a deep breath and bellows, "SEVEN!"

Harry turns and smiles. "Eggs?"

"You'll never get away with this," Walter mutters. But he is wrong. Before the day's end Harry has handed back his shirts, shoes and nightmare boots. Then he comes to fetch his suitcase. "I'm off now, Wally. Dad'll be really proud of me. Beats hiding in a barn any day."

"They'll have you back in before your feet touch the ground when the war starts," says Walter.

"Come off it," Harry replies. "What do they want with someone who's stone deaf? Shall I tell your mum and dad how you're doing?"

"No! Don't say a word."

"Well, so long, pal. See you around some time."

"Not if I can help it," says Walter. After Harry leaves, he suddenly feels very lonely. The man from Liverpool in the bed opposite says, "I didn't know your mate was deaf."

"He isn't," replies Walter grimly.

The scouser whistles. "Cheeky sod," he says admiringly.

* * *

103

Harry, however, is soon forgotten. The thirty-nine recruits from all over the country, Cornwall to Inverness, begin to mix and make friends. For Walter, the first is Mikey Kennedy, the scouser opposite.

Within days the hut becomes home. It is long, built of dark creosoted wood with floors of brown lino which must be kept as highly polished as their boots, washbasins outside an end door and a coke stove in the middle which roasts those near it and leaves the rest freezing. On each of the hut's narrow iron bedsteads is a bedding pack – consisting of a pillow, three sheets, three blankets, all neatly folded – and a hard, lumpy horsehair mattress.

The final day on the reception base arrives. The men feel they've picked up all there is to know about the RAF. Their cases, full of belongings from their former lives, are labelled and sent back to their homes. Now they are aircraftsmen 2nd class, mere sprogs, sticking out like sore thumbs in their brand-new, unmarked uniforms and dragging their stark white kitbags.

At nine o'clock they muster on the parade ground to be given their postings. A flight sergeant stands in front of them. "Look at you," he says. "God help our country, that's all I can say; you'll give Hitler a right good laugh. You're off to West Kirby now for two month's square-bashing. And the best of luck: you aren't half going to need it."

West Kirby looms large in RAF lore, a hard, hard place. But Mikey Kennedy whispers, "It's only five minutes from home, Wally. I'll show you the sights of Liverpool."

They are driven north in coaches and reach West Kirby in the late afternoon. They stop at the guardroom, are

104

checked by RAF police and waved forward to the huge arid desert of a parade ground. They pick up their kit bags, shamble off the coach and wonder what has hit them.

Raucous shouting and demented screeching assaults their ears. Corporals and sergeants, all impossibly smart with blindingly white webbing belts swarm round them, bully them into three ranks, terrorize them into clumsy, shuffling marching, herd them into their huts, make them dump their kit and form up again for the march to the cookhouse and shout at them to take their irons. "Knives and forks to human beings," mutters Mikey.

Even in the cookhouse they aren't left alone but driven out almost before they have time to swallow, let alone digest, the tough meat and half raw potatoes. They are hustled off to the stores to get their bedding and then back to the hut to make their beds.

Their corporal, a small, red-faced, aggressive Welshman, bawls at them all the time and when they have finished, walks round the hut looking at each bed, kicking the sheets and blankets off and shouting, "Horrible. Do it again." After they've remade their beds at least three times, he finally disappears into his little cubicle at one end of the hut. Walter lies exhausted beneath the scratchy grey blankets and thinks, *is this how it's going to be? I thought I knew it all but I know nothing. Have I made a big mistake?*

4.2

Square-bashing is hard. Endless drill on the parade ground. Heavy boots thudding down on gravel. Orders are screamed at them. Quick march! Slow march! At the double! Arms drill: slope arms, present arms, order arms. Doing everything with a rifle, except fire it.

Walter loves some moments – naming the parts on a rifle or stripping down a bren gun. But he'll never need these skills: he'd have to be aircrew and he hasn't even applied. Machine guns fascinate him, but so do aero engines. He'll work on them instead.

Every night he staggers back to the hut muttering, "I'm knackered." He thinks wistfully of Harry at home, probably preparing for an evening's gentle clay pigeon shooting. But things will get better. After a month they'll get a 48-hour pass – a whole weekend away! "Can't wait to get back home," sighs Fred Scrimshaw, working out train times to Norwich. "Save your money," says Charlie Briggs. "Hitch-hike. It's easy for airmen."

Walter sits on his bed and wonders if he'll bother going back to Peterspury.

As he is thinking, Mikey turns to him. "Wally me old mucker, don't sit dreaming of beer and women you can't have. I'll show you a good time in the 'Pool. Any time you like. How about this week?"

"There'll be a hell of a row if we're caught," says Walter.

"Not a chance. A kid of three could get out of this place."

"How?" Walter asks.

"I've got a mate in the RAF who knows these things. If you walk around with paper and pencil looking busy, nobody stops you. That's what we'll do and get out dead easy any night we like."

"We'll end up in the glasshouse."

"No we won't," Mikey replies. "How about tomorrow?"

"Suits me," says Walter. "I won't get much fun at home."

They slip out after cookhouse parade. Mikey dodges behind the big coal bunker, three huts from theirs, and Walter follows. Mikey lifts up a flat stone. Underneath are two clipboards, each with a pencil attached by a string and a bulldog clip clamping on sheets of paper.

"What are these for?" Walter asks.

"You've got to look as though you're taking notes," says Mikey. "Do it with bags of swank as though you mean it."

So Walter tries and Mikey watches him approvingly. At last they come, unchallenged, to the fence, concrete posts and steel netting. Mikey pulls at the netting and it comes up to show a gap easy to slip through. "Shocking," he says. "Someone should be told. The men could get out."

107

"How did you know it was here?" Walter asks.

"I live here, don't I? I didn't waste my time before I joined up."

They slip through the gap. Another flat stone lies outside. Mikey picks it up and put the clipboards carefully in a little hollow scraped out of the earth. "There's a bus stop down the road," he says.

"Won't we look obvious in our uniforms?" says Walter.

"There's army, RAF, Navy all round Liverpool," Mikey replies. "The place is full of uniforms. All the girls love a uniform."

"Mikey," says Walter. "You're wasted in the Air Force."

"That's why I joined," he replies. "There's more fiddles in the services than you'll find in civvy street."

They catch a bus to Birkenhead and a ferry across the Mersey to Liverpool, sample more pubs and clubs than Walter can count and pick up a couple of girls who seem willing. "Those girls were great," says Walter as they catch the bus back.

"I told them we'll be back in a week," Mikey replies. "They think we're going on a secret mission in the morning. Next time we'll have finished it and be waiting for our medals. We've got a date outside Yates's Wine Lodge and then we're going to stay out all night."

"Did they believe that rubbish about medals?" asks Walter.

"I told you, Wally. Uniforms turn women crazy. I reckon you're well in with that Doreen."

The man's a genius, Walter thinks. They get off the bus and slip through the fence. "Take notes like before," Mikey whispers.

They move unhurried towards the huts, examining stones, lamp posts, dustbins, anything above ground. Suddenly a torch shines in their faces and a voice shouts, "What time do you call this? Why aren't you in your billets?" Walter's heart nearly stops.

"Special late-night audit for Wing Commander Fortescue, Sergeant," says Mikey calmly.

"Oh," says the sergeant. "Well in that case, carry on, airmen."

"Who's Wing Commander Fortescue?" Walter whispers.

"Christ knows," Mikey replies. "I saw his name on a noticeboard. That sergeant wouldn't dare ask questions about an officer. That's how the Air Force works, young Wally, and if you remember it you can't go wrong."

"Mikey, you're a real piss artist and no mistake," says Walter.

They creep into the hut. Fred Scrimshaw is awake. "Lucky for you there wasn't a snap kit inspection," he says.

"Fortune favours the brave," Mikey replied.

Walter likes that. *I'm one of the brave.* His head is spinning as he relives the evening. Especially Doreen. His fingers itch and tingle with her, memories to carry him through till the next time, when he won't be back at eleven. This is how to treat the Air Force. Keep your nose clean, appear to play by its rules. That way you'll know how to break them. The only way to survive.

Walter wonders what to do about the weekend pass. Mikey hadn't asked him to stay with him. The London lads have arranged to meet up in Piccadilly on Saturday and have a night on the town. He'd love to join them. But what about

Friday? There's only one answer. Go home, not for his father, not for his brother or sister, but for his mother. He owes her that.

They pick up their passes at midday on Friday. Most make for Lime Street station. Walter sets off looking for lifts. He is picked up by a lorry bound for Stockport, a builder's van, a young man in a little red MG, a vicar in his Austin 7, three miles on the back of a tractor, last of all a coal lorry which brings him down the final miles of the A5 to Peterspury and home for the first time in three months.

It doesn't go well. His father asks him to go to the pub. Walter takes great pleasure in refusing. What upsets him, though, is being somehow unable to talk to his mother. He goes to bed almost feeling as if he's in an anonymous bed and breakfast. When he catches the train to London next morning he wonders if he will ever see his home again.

He has a terrific time in London with the lads and when they split up at three in the morning, he is glad of a warm waiting room to sleep off his roaring headache in time for the Liverpool train. When he returns he finds Mikey back already. "Mikey," Walter asks. "What trade will you go for when we're out of here?"

"Driver in the motor pool or i/c stores," Mikey replies and winked slyly. "Good skives. A man like me could do well in either."

Before square-bashing ends they make two more trips to the city. Same routine, except for not returning until the tannoy was blasting out, "Wakey, wakey, rise and shine, it's half-past six, you've had your time."

Walter is still in a dream about being up a dark alleyway with Doreen. "How far have you got with her?" asks Fred and Walter replies triumphantly, "All the way, mate, all the way."

"You bloody liar," says Fred.

"I mean it," says Walter, and he did, well, nearly. He just needs a little more time. He doesn't go home after the passing-out parade but spends his week's leave going out with Doreen and sleeping on the floor at Mikey's place until he has to report for trade training.

"Where do you go now?" Doreen asks the day before he leaves. "Another secret mission?"

"Yeah, top secret," Walter replies. "But I'll be back in a few weeks."

"You can stuff that," says Doreen. "I want a good time, not moping after the likes of you."

So that's the end of Doreen. "She can sod off. Saved me the trouble of dumping her," Walter says and almost means it. But when the week's leave is up, he is sad because he and Mikey have come to the parting of the ways.

4.3

Walter enjoys trade training at his new base in Gloucestershire, where he learns to how to be an aero-engine fitter. He strips down old engines which may be clapped out but work the same as the Merlins in the Spitfires and Hurricanes. He longs to get his hands on a Rolls-Royce Merlin engine. It's in a different class, more powerful than anything else flying. It can throw the Hurricane, a sleek contraption of aluminium and canvas, around the sky and let it streak along straight and level at 340 miles an hour. Passing trade training, being promoted to Leading Aircraftsman and then posted to Biggin Hill in Kent to work on Hurricanes is like winning the football pools. He soon forgets about Doreen. He's pleased when war is declared. Now he'll show the Jerries, his father and the rest of the world just who is best.

Although air raid warnings sounded the moment Mr Chamberlain switched off his microphone, after declaring war on Germany, for the first month not a single Luftwaffe bomber is to be seen. It seems to Walter that the war is showing a distressing tendency not to start.

Walter's squadron is sent to France a month later. The locals' welcome of the intrepid British airmen come to save them from the Boche almost makes up for leaving the pubs and girls of Biggin Hill. But as the months go by and still no Germans appear, the novelty begins to wear off.

November 1939, Lille-Sedan, near the Belgian border. Walter is perched on the starboard wing of a Hurricane working on its engine and thinking that without him the public school twerp who flies it couldn't even get off the ground.

Squadron Leader Stewartby, the public school twerp himself, strolls out of the officers' mess and says, "All ship-shape, LAC Vögler?"

"Yes sir," he answers.

"I'll take her up for a couple of circuits," says Stewartby. "Must be ready for when Jerry comes."

Walter closes the engine cowling and jumps lightly off the wing. "She's as good as I can make her, sir," he says.

"Good man," Stewartby replies as he straps himself in. Walter pulls the chocks away, the plane taxis forward, gathers speed and rises smoothly away over the grass air-field. Its wheels retract and soon it's high above him.

"Don't you dare mess my Hurricane up, you clumsy idiot," he mutters and wanders to the squalid hut called the airmen's mess.

Squadron Leader Stewartby climbs to twenty thousand feet and indulges in a few minutes of aerobatics. "Bloody show-off. Waste of fuel and risking the plane," Walter mutters. Now the Hurricane is coming in low, not fifty feet up, at three hundred miles an hour, straight for him, engine

113

screaming, and he ducks involuntarily. The noise brings other pilots out of their huts: they cheer wildly and wave their arms. Walter is furious. They seem to think Hurricanes are big, though dangerous, toys. At last Squadron Leader Stewartby has had enough. He lands, unbuckles his harness, jumps down from the cockpit and says, "First-rate, Vögler. You're jolly good at looking after these engine thingies. She's smooth as a sewing machine. Jolly fast one too." He laughs at his own joke, if joke it is. "Just bed her down for the night." As he walks away, Walter says savagely, "I'll give her a bag of oats if you like."

Six months pass and at last the war is here. The Germans are coming. The Hurricanes take off every day, climbing rapidly in the morning air. Most come back, some whole, some shot up, some crash-landing. The survivors have hair-raising tales to tell. Ground crews hardly sleep getting planes airworthy for next day: patching up, repairing engines, servicing Browning machine guns, often still hot, loading ammunition. Sometimes there's blood to scrub out of the cockpit.

Pilots no longer stroll out to the planes as if going for a spin in their sports cars. They run to the Hurricanes; when they land, they stumble out, pale, sometimes shaking. No "piece of cake" now; there's damage to report. "Glycol leaking everywhere," or "Fuel tank hit," or "Starboard Browning's jammed again," they cry. The ground crew know what to do, while the pilots get drunk and sleep fitfully until tomorrow's sorties. There's little joy of battle or glory, only anger that there are so few Hurricanes to fight

114

so many Messerschmitts.

"What are we doing out here?" says Walter's corporal. "Jerry will go through France like a dose of salts. We can't stand up against them on our own. We should be at home looking after our own."

"We'll just have to try, Corp," says Walter. "I reckon something big's coming up before we see England again."

Events will prove Walter is right.

Another day dawns. "Scramble, scramble," comes the cry and pilots sprint to their planes. Walter jumps down as Stewartby climbs in. "Good man, Vögler," he says, as always. The engine barks into life, the propellor turns once, twice, then is a blur. Walter pulls the chocks away. The Hurricane taxis across the field and then, leading its group of three, climbs steadily into the air. More follow until the squadron is a pattern of dots in the sky. The ground crews drink tea, play cards and wait.

Time hangs slowly. An hour, two hours. Then there is a roaring in the sky and the Hurricanes appear. Twenty-one left Lille-Sedan in the morning. Walter counts them as they land. Fourteen, fifteen, sixteen, seventeen. They touch the ground, some smoothly, others roughly, while two, their undercarriages jammed, skid wildly on their bellies, fetch up far across the airfield, tip over onto one wing and their pilots scramble out and run like hell in case their planes blow up. Neither do and they will be worked on all night in order to fight another day.

Now the sky is empty and ominously silent. Four gone. A heavy toll. Pilots slouch back to the mess, trailing kit behind them. One shakes his head as he passes Walter.

"Bad day, bad day," he says. There will be empty beds tonight, a pall of sadness over RAF Lille-Sedan.

Squadron Leader Stewartby is among the missing four. For all that Walter called him a twerp, he feels a pang of real sadness. He wonders if, in spite of the rank-conscious officer-erk relationship, the off-handed drawl of "Good man, Vögler," there was a real, unspoken friendship between them.

He stays out on the airfield. He won't move while his Hurricane is missing. At last, faint at first, he hears the unmistakeable sound of a Rolls-Royce Merlin. But it is laboured, sick, something bad has happened. Now it appears, losing height fast. It is his: he knows by the recognition letters on the fuselage. But it loses height too quickly: it won't clear the perimeter fence. The undercarriage is down, but one wheel has not dropped properly and the other will collapse when it hits the ground. Somehow the Hurricane clears the perimeter fence. Part of the rudder is shot away, smoke pours out of the engine. Walter shouts, "Sod the plane – save yourself!"

But Stewartby cannot. The Hurricane ploughs into the ground, its nose burrows into the earth and the propellor blades crumple. Walter runs towards it. He hears a faint shout from the huts: "It's going to blow up!"

But he won't stop. He sees a figure struggling to slide the cockpit canopy back. "It's all right, sir," he shouts. "I'm coming."

Then there is the crump of a muffled explosion and the stricken Hurricane is enveloped by a ball of flame. Walter throws himself to the ground. Dimly he hears the fire wagon approaching: foam and water are pumped into the wreck until the flames are out and it stands there, a charred metal skeleton. But he stays on the ground, not watching.

When the fire crew has gone he gets up, looks at the twisted heap and knows that in it are the remains of Squadron Leader Stewartby, who loved the Hurricane as much as he did, who fought to bring it in safely and was burned alive for his pains. He sinks to his knees and tears stream down his face. Now he knows what manner of war he is part of and he beats his fists on the grass in frustration at the powerlessness he feels.

4.4

More planes and pilots arrive. The Germans have indeed gone through France like a dose of salts. The British Expeditionary Force is being pushed back into the sea. The soldiers must be taken off the beaches and brought home, which means air cover twenty-four hours a day while Messerschmitts and Stukas cause havoc as the troops wait.

Nobody sleeps. The squadron takes off, stays in the air for two hours, comes back further depleted. A brief rest, then off again and even fewer return. The RAF is taking a terrible toll.

But don't worry, the pilots say, the Luftwaffe is taking a greater. They speak of amazing scenes below: men in their thousands waiting on the wide beaches where children once dug sandcastles. Flotillas of fishing boats, pleasure steamers, river launches come close inshore: lines of men wade out to them and are pulled aboard. Further out, Navy destroyers keep watch. Messerschmitts and shrieking Stukas spread slaughter on the beach while the Hurricanes try to beat them off. Returning pilots are weary, their eyes bloodshot. "It's a miracle," they say. "The army is getting away. France is lost but we'll soon be home to defend our own."

In August 1940, they are. Walter is back at Biggin Hill, among the familiar billets, cookhouse, Naafi, hangars, and blast pens. Now they have France, the Germans are starting on Britain. The squadrons are always in the sky as Luftwaffe bombers make sporadic raids. Life is as hectic as it was at Lille-Sedan. He receives a letter from his mother: he reads it quickly, then again slowly, to absorb its momentous news. His father has been taken away and interned as an enemy alien. He laughs. Then he says, "Poor Mum."

"Poor Mum." For the first time he has acknowledged that his English mother may actually love his German father. At last he understands her sorrow, and yes, feels differently about Peterspury, his brother and sister. He almost wishes for his time again so he can start afresh. But he cannot, will not, feel differently about his father. It's *his* people who conquered France, who wrecked his Hurricane and killed Squadron Leader Stewartby. *I will not believe his blood is in my veins*, he fiercely thinks. *Internment? Let them throw away the key. Let him die in it.*

He is due a forty-eight hour pass and gets it on Friday 9 August. Some of his mates will catch trains to destinations all over the country, others will stay in London to have a good time. After arriving in a blacked-out Charing Cross station they'll find rooms in the Union Jack Club and then hit the town.

Walter sets off with this group. Then he has a sudden

119

impulse. "See you Sunday," he says abruptly and, while they are asking, "Where are you off to, Wally?" dives into the Underground, surfaces again at Euston and catches a train to Northampton. As it puffs northwards he wonders what on earth has possessed him. He catches the bus home, along roads with every signpost removed. Even the garage nameboard has disappeared: no "Vögler's", no "Tel: Peterspury 37".

Good, he thinks. *When the Germans invade they won't know where they are and my father's not here to tell them.*

His heart beats fast as he rings the doorbell. Anna opens the door. She isn't the little girl he remembers: she's thirteen and wears the red and green blazer of Wicester Grammar School. "Walter!" she gasps and runs to the kitchen shouting, "Mum, Mum! Walter's here!"

His mother appears. "Walter!" she cries and throws her arms round him. "Walter, my dear, dear son. I thought I'd never see you again."

He extricates himself from her embrace and says, "I'm only here because…" He sees her face and stops.

"Because what?"

"Because…" But he can't continue.

"Don't say it. I know," says Mum. "It's because your father isn't here. It's all right, Walter. I know how you feel. The pity is he doesn't feel the same about you."

"I can't help that," Walter replies.

"I'm glad you've come," says Mum quickly. "Matthias was all right the last time we heard. Perhaps he'll be home sooner than we think. If only you could find it in your heart to welcome him."

"Perhaps," says Walter. "We'll see." He knows he won't.

"Have you eaten?" asks Mum. "I can give you a good dinner. Jimmy Warner brought some broad beans and new potatoes from his allotment. Your friend Harry gave us a rabbit and I've stewed it."

"How is Harry?" Walter asks.

His mother gives him an odd look. "He's doing very well," she says.

"What at?"

"You'd better go round and see for yourself," says Mum.

They sit down to rabbit stew, broad beans and potatoes. "Jimmy gives us lots of vegetables," says Mum. "People are very good to us—"

"Now you've lost the two men of the house," Walter finishes the sentence for her.

"What about me?" says Paul. "Don't I count?"

"You?" says Walter. "You stick to your algebra and Latin." Paul grins weakly, unsure if that's a joke or an insult. Walter regrets his remark and says, "Anyway, Paul, how are you getting on?"

"I did well in the School Certs," Paul replies. "I'll be in the sixth form in September. I'd like to go to university."

"Lucky for some," says Walter. He turns to Anna, "I expect you're the same."

"I'm going to be a musician," Anna answers. "I've got grade seven in violin and grade six in piano already and my teacher thinks I'll be good enough to go to music college when I'm eighteen."

"If Hitler lets you," says Walter.

There's another awkward silence.

"What's it like in the RAF?" Paul asks.

"Where do I start?" Walter replies.

"Is it dangerous?" asks Anna.

"Too bloody right it's dangerous," says Walter.

"Language," Mum says warningly.

"Sorry, you'll have to put up with it." Walter snaps. "I won't say it's *jolly* dangerous because it's sodding well not jolly. On duty twenty-four hours a day, snatch sleep when we can, always planes to get fit to fly again, watch men we know take off and not come back. Jerry bombers make low level bombing runs and all I can do is watch. Sometimes they crash on the airfield and so do ours and we have to drag the bodies out. In France there was this squadron leader, I looked after his Hurricane, I pampered that plane, we got on all right, him and me, but he got shot up and crashed and the Hurricane caught fire and exploded. I watched him burn alive and couldn't help him. How do you think that made me feel?"

All this comes out in one breath and they look at him as if hypnotized. "Sure beats School Certificate and grade seven violin," he says.

Paul looks down at the tablecloth. Anna's face crumples as if she's going to cry. Mum bites her lip and looks fixedly out of the window. Walter is sorry for them. He decides to say something conciliatory.

"Anyway, how is my father finding internment?"

"He's safe and looked after quite well," says Mum. "The last we heard he was on the Isle of Man."

"He's staying at the Hotel Metropole in Douglas," adds Paul.

"He's *what?*" cries Walter incredulously.

"The Hotel Metropole," Paul repeats.

"I don't believe this!" says Walter. "You mean *I'm* dodging bombs and bullets and dying on my feet through lack of sleep, and scraping blood and guts out of wrecked planes for this bloody country, while a Jerry's pigging it in a seaside hotel? I'm going to complain to somebody about this, it's not right."

"I don't think it's quite the way it sounds," says Mum.

"What *is* it then? Here am I defending you and if I don't manage it, Hitler will turn up here and I don't give much for your chances. And when he's sorted you out he'll go to the Isle of Man, find my Jerry father in this Hotel Metropole and give him a glass of champagne and the Iron Cross. I tell you, Mum, your precious husband has been laughing at us all these years."

"I think," says Mum frostily, "that you'd better not say any more."

Walter knows he has gone too far. To break the silence, Mum says, "I've got suet pudding if anybody wants it."

Nobody does. Walter stands up. "I think I'd better go," he says.

"Please, Walter, no," says Mum. "I know that you can't help how you feel. You're wrong but I won't be angry with you. I'll make up a bed in your room. Anyway, the last bus has gone."

"All right," he says. "Thanks."

"Why don't you go to the pub?" says Mum. "I'm sure there'll be people there who'd be really glad to see you."

"Yes," says Walter. "Yes, I will."

"I'll give you a key. Don't make too much noise when you come in."

Suddenly he reaches out and hugs her and says,

"Thanks, Mum. I try to be a good son, I really do. But sometimes I can't quite manage it."

"I know, my love," says Mum. "Now, off you go and have a good time."

The Crooked Billet is enveloped in its usual homely fug of tobacco smoke. Men drink pints of beer and line up more on the counter. In one corner they're playing darts: in another, old men shuffle dominoes. Slowly, they become aware of him: talk dies, heads turn and someone exclaims, "Bloody hell! Look what the cat brought in."

Walter is tempted to say, "Sod you then," and stalk out, but someone laughs and first one person, then another comes over and says, "Welcome home," and "Really pleased to see you," and "What'll you have, Wally?" They are all there, the old regulars, Harry Brindley's father, half sozzled as always, Jimmy Warner nursing his half-pint, Arthur Dickens, Bill Straighton, Reg Wilshaw, familiar faces and all happy to see him.

"Why aren't you lot in the army?" he asks.

"Have a heart, Wally," says Bill Straighton. "We're far too old."

Walter looks round again. It's true: there's no one under forty here. All the young ones have gone. Except one who's just entered the pub. He sees Walter. "Hello, mate," he says.

"Harry!" Walter exclaims. "Where did you get that smart clobber?"

Harry is wearing a sharp, pin-striped suit, white, silk shirt and blue tie. His black shoes shine. He taps the side of his nose with his forefinger and says, "I've got contacts. I do all right."

"Why weren't you called up when the war started?" Walter asks.

"I'm not fit. I've got discharge papers saying I'm stone deaf."

"But you aren't," says Walter.

"I know that and you know that," Harry replies. "Mind you, I nearly got found out when the Military Police came round for me."

"Surely they'd notice you could hear as well as they could?"

"Well, they didn't. Funny, wasn't it? Still, they were glad of their bottles of Scotch and I expect their wives were pleased with their new silk underwear. Let me show you something." He leads Walter outside, to where an Austin Ruby saloon car is parked. "Mine," he says proudly.

"What's it for?" Walter asks. "You can't get petrol now."

"Can't I?" says Harry. "There's a barn full of cans at home."

"How did it get there?"

For the second time, Harry taps his nose with his finger. "I know where the good stuff is. Can't let people starve on wartime rations, can we?" He looks at his gold wristwatch and says, "Time to start work." He opens the car door. Walter sees boxes and parcels on the front seat. "Let's see what I can tempt you with," says Harry and brings out a bottle. "Cop hold of that," he says. "Finest malt whisky. Here, have another. These'll put hairs on the chests of the boys in blue. Have you got a girlfriend?" Walter shakes his head. "Take these and you soon will." Three boxes of chocolates and six pairs of silk stockings. "I'm cutting my own throat but have them for free for old time's sake."

"Where did they come from?" Walter asks.

"That would be telling," Harry replies.

"You'll end up in prison."

"Not me. There are too many in Peterspury who like a pound of Stilton or a joint of beef to eke out their ration books."

"What if George Coppard finds out?"

Harry laughs derisively. "Our village bobby is quite partial to a glass of brandy at night, though his wife prefers gin. Besides, I gave him some good information."

"What about?" Walter asks.

"Nothing much," says Harry. "By the way, is it true that your dad and all the family went to a Nazi rally and heard Hitler give a speech? And didn't your cousin get presented to Hitler personally?"

"Have you been saying things about my family?"

"Not me, mate. I got it from Freddy Wilshaw. He got it from Jean Dickens at the grammar school. It seems your Paul had been telling everybody."

"Well, I can't help you there. It's the first I've heard of it."

"Pity. Ah well, that's me as a government agent finished. I'll have to stick to the black market."

Now Walter is full of real anger. "Bloody hell, Harry, here's me busting a gut to save your miserable skin and here's you twisting the public right, left and centre."

"How am I twisting the public? I'm giving them a taste of the good things in life when everything is miserable."

"And I bet you make them pay."

"Well, I don't do it for nothing."

"I'll shop you myself."

"Come on, Wally, calm down. Here's another bottle of Scotch. Shove 'em all in your kitbag so nobody notices. Your uniform looks scruffy. Do you want a new best blue, hardly worn?"

"Where did it come from?"

"It's mine. I didn't hand it in when I left. Five bob to you."

"Bugger off," says Walter. He picks up the box and slouches home, angry, not at what Harry does but that he's not doing it with him.

The house is in darkness. He unlocks the door, puts the hall light on and tiptoes upstairs. A voice calls from the kitchen. "Walter, is that you?"

"Yes, Mum," he says, going into the kitchen. It is in darkness, so he switches the light on. She is sitting at the kitchen table, elbows resting on it, hands cupping her face.

"You're in early," she remarks. "Did you see Harry?"

"Yes."

"I thought you might. He makes most of his money on Friday nights. Is that why you came away?"

"Yes. He made me angry. But he made me envious as well."

"Don't be. He'll get his comeuppance. The law doesn't take kindly to black marketeers. When he came home he got in with some shady characters. Now he's in on every fiddle going. I can't understand why he's not been called up."

"He's deaf."

"Pull the other one."

"That's why he's out of the RAF. He wangled it, the

crafty sod."

"That's Harry all over. Be glad you're who you are, Walter."

He thinks about this. Then he says, "Do you mean that?"

"Walter, how can you ask? You're my son. I love you."

"But I run off and don't come back, and you hate it when I say things about my father. I can't help it, Mum, it's the way things are."

"I know," she says. "Walter, do you realize that you and he are very much alike? You both come out with what you think and you're both as honest as the day is long. You're doing your bit for your country with a good heart and so did Matthias. You're brave like him, but I know that you're scared like him as well. And he loves you, Walter." She turns her face away: when she looks back again her brow is furrowed. Walter sees not only strain on her face but anger. "Why do you hate him so much?"

Walter makes no answer.

She goes on. "I listened to you trying to make Paul and Anna feel small because you're at the war and they're not. That's not fair on the children; they can't help being younger than you and if they were your age they'd be doing their bit as well."

"It'll do them good to know what I'm going through while they're just skiving around," he replies.

She's angry now. "Do you think you're the only one who knows what war is like? I saw as much horror and danger in that hospital in France as you do now – and more. And your father saw worse. What you've gone through so far is nothing compared to what he faced in the

128

trenches. *Nothing*."

"But it was for the other bloody side," says Walter.

"It doesn't matter which side it was, he faced it every day. And so did your Uncle Jack. That's why they get on so well. They went through the same thing. Now they respect each other."

Walter can't think of a reply to this.

"Cat got your tongue?" she asks.

"You married the enemy," he mutters.

She purses her lips as if she cannot bring herself to speak. There's a fury in her face that Walter has never seen before. Suddenly he is frightened.

"You've got a lot to learn," she says at last and falls silent again.

He feels she is willing him to speak. If he does, he must say things he's kept to himself for years. But he says it anyway. "If it wasn't for me, you wouldn't have married him."

"Walter, I'd have married Matthias whether you came or not."

"He shouldn't have done what he did. He was trying to kill us all a few months before. And he comes over here and does *that* to you."

Tears well up in her eyes. "Oh, Walter," she says. "Is that why you're so angry? Did you think he raped me?"

"He shouldn't have done it. Not to you. Even if I was the result, he still shouldn't have done it."

Now she's no longer crying and Walter flinches at the hard anger in her voice. "Walter, it's about time you heard a few home truths."

"What about?" he asks sullenly.

"I married your father because I loved him. You weren't

129

an accident. We knew we'd be married, whatever people around us thought. You weren't just conceived in our bodies, you were conceived first in our minds, our feelings. What we did was natural, inevitable even, and we knew, no matter what difficulties we'd have, especially with me being pregnant before we married and Matthias being German, how our lives would be."

"That doesn't help me," Walter mutters.

She shouts in exasperation. "Well, it damned well should."

Walter clamps his mouth tight shut and won't answer.

She calms down now. "It's true, I saved his life when he was brought in wounded. And I looked after him while he was in the hospital. I was afraid to go into the German ward at first, but then I looked out for him and we talked. When he'd been taken away I dreamed about him. I think I loved him even then, but I thought it was no use, I'd never see him again. Then he turned up in Lambsfield, a prisoner of war. And when I saw him, I knew. So did he." She pauses and then says, "Walter, excuse me asking, but have you ever been in love?"

Walter thinks of Doreen. "No."

"When you are," says Mum, "you'll know too."

Walter thinks of Harry, the nylons and the chocolates and says, "I doubt it."

"You will," Mum replies firmly.

Walter shrugs his shoulders.

"It was hard for us before we got married. I was pregnant when I shouldn't be and a lot of people didn't like me marrying a German. For a long time even my own mother wouldn't accept it. But she came round, we got married and we were so happy. But some people still didn't like it."

I'm not surprised, Walter thinks.

"And then you were born."

"I hope you were pleased."

"Pleased? We were ecstatic. Though you weren't a very good baby, you cried a lot and you never seemed satisfied when we fed you."

"Start as you mean to go on, that's my motto," he says. "Perhaps my precious father was horrible to me and that's why I can't stand him."

"No, that's not why, Walter." Her anger has gone: her voice is gentle now. "He was a wonderful father to you."

"Why is it then?"

"Don't you remember when you went to school in Lambsfield?"

Walter tries, but only a confused jumble of impressions come, all of which seem unhappy. "Not really," he says.

"You had a bad time. Lots of children teased you, taunted you, the big boys bullied you, made you cry, because Matthias was German. It was so soon after the last war and some children there had lost their fathers and brothers and couldn't forget. All their anger and the grown-ups' anger through the children came onto you."

"I don't remember," says Walter.

"I think you've blanked it out. We tried to get the head-master to stop it but he couldn't. Matthias and I had already split the town down the middle and you were getting the brunt of it. It wasn't fair and we knew it. One day you came home crying. I can see you now, punching Matthias with your little fists and screaming, 'I hate you, I

131

hate you.'"

"I don't remember," Walter repeats stubbornly.

"Well, it's all gone now. It's in the past, it should all be forgotten."

"I can't forget what I don't remember."

"But it's the reason why you say you hate your father. Yet *he* didn't do it to you. In fact I didn't know a man could love his son so much. Can't you forget it all and start again?"

"No," says Walter.

There's anger in her voice again. "The war didn't start for you last year," she says. "You've been fighting it since you were a little boy."

"Maybe I have," he replies. "And maybe it's not over yet. Perhaps it will never be. Not for me, anyway."

"You'll change your mind one day," she replies.

"No I won't," Walter says stubbornly.

His mother stands up. "In that case, there's nothing more to say."

"Yes there is. Harry asked me if it was true you all went to a Nazi rally and heard Hitler speak. Is it?"

"Yes," she replies. "And your cousin Helmut was presented personally to Hitler."

"How come I never knew?"

"You weren't here to tell."

He draws a deep breath. "Well, that's it then. My cousin's a proper Nazi. How can I have anything to do with that?" He knows it is finished. "I'll go in the morning. I won't trouble you for any breakfast."

"Put the light out as you go." Her voice is hard. He leaves her sitting in the dark and lugs Harry's box upstairs.

132

He changes into his RAF-issue pyjamas, climbs into bed and sleeps quickly and deeply.

He departs early in the morning, not even leaving a note to say goodbye. A refrain beats through his head. *I won't change how I feel, I'll never come back. I can't, I can't, I can't.*

When he reaches Euston he walks down Tottenham Court Road, Charing Cross Road, further, further, until he sees the Thames, grey, oily, flowing imperturbably to the sea. He walks east along the Embankment, hardly aware of the soldiers, sailors, airmen, many with girls on their arms, who throng past him. He carries on until St Paul's Cathedral looms over him. At last he stops and sits on a bench overlooking the river. He has no idea that this is the very seat on which his mother sat twenty-two years before, wondering what the future held for her, before she left for France and the first meeting with Matthias, her future husband.

As he sits, he thinks about the Nazi rally. He never expected Mum to say it was true. His own cousin, a close blood relation even though he'd never seen him, was presented to Hitler. It's his family, all of them, not just Helmut – and not just Germany either – that he's fighting, and they are fighting him. This war is personal. The sheer enormity of the thought crushes him. Helmut appears in his mind, a sinister figure, with a face a malevolent cross between his father and Paul. "They've betrayed me," he says aloud. He knows the last link with his family is broken.

4.5

After an hour by the river he walks back to Charing Cross station, imagining the Luftwaffe pounding everything to rubble. They will, he thinks, they will. He catches his train, returns to Biggin Hill and checks in at the guardroom by three o'clock. As he walks to the airmen's quarters he sees a Waaf striding briskly towards the ops block. She's small with blonde hair bunched under her peaked cap. He gives a loud wolf-whistle.

Usually when he whistles after girls he gets a withering glare in return. Not this time. She smiles and waves and he feels good. "I must find out who she is," he says to himself. When he reaches the airmen's quarters he feels almost happy. The place is full of airmen taking a much-needed break. The man sitting on the bed next to his says, "Blimey, Wally, you're back early. Wasn't it so good in London?"

"Who's the blonde Waaf in the ops block?" he asks.

"Do you mean Julie? Forget it, mate. Very choosy is our Julie."

"Didn't she choose you then?" he asks but gets no

answer. He unpacks his kitbag, puts Harry's box in his locker and locks the door. Then he lies on his bed thinking. He's finished with his family for ever. And that Julie – no chance, surely. But she did smile at him.

It's August and so far the Luftwaffe has left the big airfields more or less alone, except for a few sharp raids with one or two aircraft. The Germans are giving most grief to outlying airfields and radar stations. But whenever one of these RDF stations is hit, the radar is working again in twenty-four hours so Fighter Command is never taken by surprise.

The morning of Sunday 18 August is quiet but there's a strange foreboding in the air. Two squadrons are based here, one of Hurricanes, the other of Spitfires. At one o'clock, both are scrambled to intercept planes coming in over the Channel. The airfield is left undefended: Walter feels his chest tightening and his heart beating fast.

Incoming aircraft are identified. Nine Dorniers flying fast and low under the radar. But it seems that Biggin Hill is not today's target. RAF Kenley, just up the road, is to catch it today. They see the bombers, watch the battle overhead, the criss-crossing vapour trails, the occasional plane falling out of the sky. They hear the "Crump!" of explosions and watch black smoke climb into the air. Then comes the ominous drone of a large bomber force. The air raid sirens wail. Junker 88s, Heinkels, Dorniers, coming in low.

The Biggin Hill fighters are now miles away but squadrons from other airfields are overhead to defend them. Along with everyone else, Walter runs for the shelters. As he runs he keeps looking up. The air is full of bombers and Messerschmitt 109s. But the Spitfires and Hurricanes are among them. Time to take cover. He pushes into the crammed-tight airmen's shelter and waits in the dark until the all-clear sounds.

They emerge blinking into the sunlight, expecting to see desolation and ruin. But Biggin Hill is almost intact. There are no craters on the runways. Most bombs have landed harmlessly wide.

More people stream out of the shelters. Walter sees Julie among them. He runs towards her, as though by accident, and when he's close, he says, "We got out of that OK, then."

Julie turns to him with a radiant smile and says, "Yes, we live to fight another day. But they'll be back."

That smile lifts him for the rest of the day.

The weary days progress. The ground crews work tirelessly. The pilots take off and return minus one, two, three, sometimes more, rest until the next call to scramble, four separate sorties each day. New, untried pilots arrive and with them new planes, some fresh out of the factory, some repaired, a few cobbled together from the good bits of wrecks.

At night there may be a few hours' respite. The officers pile into red MGs to pubs in Westerham, Sevenoaks and old hostelries in tiny villages in the North Downs. The other ranks go to the Naafi, or crowd into the Coach and Horses in the village until kicked out at closing time to reel unsteadily back and finish off Walter's single malt.

Other airfields still suffer most. Goering and his

Luftwaffe are determined to destroy Fighter Command once and for all: Biggin Hill's turn will come.

Walter often looks for Julie but never sees her. Waafs in the ops block work all hours God sends.

Friday 30 August. It is another hectic day. The Hurricanes and Spitfires are in the air incessantly. There is no let-up. 6 p.m. Late for a daylight raid. Walter relaxes. His squadron is in the air and there is a little time to breathe easy.

A roar to the south. Planes coming fast and low. All eyes turn. A belated air raid siren wails. Then, breasting the rise at the southern end of the airfield, flying low to cheat the RDF, nine Junker 88s appear, fast, sleek and deadly.

Panic on the tarmac. People run as bombs fall round them. Some are hurled to the ground by the blast. Explosions tear great holes in earth, concrete, runways. Terrifying noise tears their eardrums: there's smoke, flame, flying lumps of concrete and stone, showers and clods of earth, shrapnel mixed with them. People are making for the shelters before the Junker 88s turn and make another run.

Walter runs with the rest. Out of the corner of his eye he sees Julie. In spite of the danger he pauses, changes course and runs towards her. He mustn't be killed before he has had a chance to speak to her.

"Julie, come with me," he shouts. "I'll look after you."

"I don't need looking after," she shouts back. "I know where I'm going." And then she is swallowed up in the fog of flame, smoke and ruin that the Junker 88s have spread.

Walter's diversion has cost vital seconds. The airmen's shelter is already shut. He doesn't panic. He just says,

"Well, Wally, it looks like this is it," and almost nonchalantly walks away as the Junkers scream over the airfield on their second run.

Planes parked on the airfield will be destroyed where they stand. They are his children and he cannot see them perish. Futilely he runs towards them as if he can ward off these murderous attacks. But the first receives a direct hit and he sees it disintegrate in a sheet of flame, the noise assaults his ears and the blast hurls him to the ground.

He picks himself up, dizzy. The ops block is badly damaged: other buildings are burning. He is looking at a vision of the apocalypse.

The Junkers come again. Walter is running blindly to nowhere, until a sudden impulse makes him stop. He is standing on the edge of a trench: instinct has stopped him falling straight into it. The Post Office people are laying telephone cables underground: slinging them from poles is the quickest way for the Luftwaffe to cut them.

A trench means protection. He jumps in and crouches below the parapet. A civilian is crouching there too. Walter is suspicious. "You're a civvy. What are you doing here?"

The man flashes a little red book at him. "My station pass," he says. "Telephone engineer."

"Sorry, mate," says Walter. "I thought you were a Jerry spy."

He doesn't hear the engineer's reply because there is a violent explosion not a hundred feet away. He just has time to think MISSED when the blast reaches them. It's as if a giant hand picks him up and deposits him eight feet from the trench. When he opens his eyes he finds he's sprawled on the ground. Beside him, the telephone engi-

138

neer picks himself up.

"You all right?" Walter gasps.

"I've felt better," is the reply.

The Junkers' farewell consists of machine gun strafing.

"Yeah," agrees Walter. "Back to the trench." But when he looks he sees it has collapsed into a small sea of clods of earth.

The engineer starts running towards the smoking buildings. Walter shouts, "Come back," then sets off after him. He seems outside himself looking on, leading a charmed, inviolable life amid the smoke, fire and chaos. He catches the man up and says, "Are you off your rocker? Where are we going?"

"Ops block," the engineer pants. "If my telephones still work, someone's got to operate them."

"You're a mad bugger," says Walter but follows just the same.

They run and run, their lungs bursting. Thankfully the Junker 88s are tired of strafing the airfield: they must save ammunition for the flight home. But the ops block is half destroyed and Walter doubts that any telephone will be intact.

He follows the engineer through the doorless entrance, picks his way over piles of bricks in what remains of a corridor and sees a large switchboard. Two Waafs sit at it, headsets on, calmly connecting calls – "Number please; trying to connect you; the number is ringing, caller." The engineer jumps into the nearest empty chair, puts a headset on and is soon going through the same routine. Walter looks on amazed. It's almost like a country exchange on a peaceful Sunday afternoon.

But then he hears the familiar ominous drone above: the Junker 88s were just the advance guard. Snarling whistles of bombs, deafening, reverberating explosions – and suddenly the engineer pulls his headset off and shouts, "Sod the bastards, they've cut the cables again. It's no use, girls."

The Waafs tear off their headsets as well and they all crouch under the switchboard. Then the tearing shriek of a bomb sounds too near: there is an ear-splitting explosion and an overpowering shock-wave. The far wall of the exchange collapses and the ceiling with it: they are smothered in powdered plaster, brick dust and wooden joists. The four fugitives cough and splutter. For the first time that day, Walter is afraid: that was nearly a direct hit. The cramped fearful wait under the ruins lasts for an eternity: the all-clear when it comes sounds unreal, impossible. They crawl out and look at each other, amazed they have survived. They are white as ghosts with plaster.

Suddenly, the engineer moans, "I feel terrible," and collapses. "Shell shock," says Walter. "Let's get him to the sickbay before we all flake out."

But there's no need: the fire crews and ambulances have come. Before he is helped into the ambulance Walter looks at the Waafs: it has just occurred to him that Julie may be one of them. But he's seen neither before. "Where did you come from?" he asks.

"We were here all the time," one says. "We never left our seats," says the other. He looks from them to the engineer on a stretcher and says, "You deserve medals, all three of you."

* * *

Walter spends three days in the sickbay. He too is shell-shocked, though mildly compared to the engineer. When he is let out he still feels weak and lightheaded. But he's been promised a week's leave, though not until things are quieter. *If I knew Julie well enough,* he thinks, *I could wangle it so I'm on leave when she is.*

While in the sickbay he hears terrible things. The airmen's shelter he was shut out of received a direct hit. All thirty-nine inside were killed. He feels a cold hand clutch at his heart. The Waafs' shelter was hit as well. Only one Waaf was killed but many were injured. Walter hopes and prays Julie wasn't one of them.

When he's discharged from the sickbay he sees devastation all round him. Yet the airfield is operational: the craters on the runways have been filled, temporary telephone lines put up and it's business as usual. Besides, the Luftwaffe seems to have tired of bombing airfields. They're bombing London instead.

He makes a resolution. "I'm sick of being bombed and shot at. I want do the shooting and bombing myself and I bloody well will."

A woman's voice calls his name. "Wally!" No, it can't be true – but it is, it is. Julie. She runs towards him, arms outstretched. "Wally!" she cries again. She reaches him and stops. She is not smiling. She reaches out a hand and touches his face shyly, almost fearfully. "Wally," she breathes. "You're not a ghost. It's really you."

"Of course it's me," says Walter.

Now she does smile, that wonderful, radiant smile she gave him before. "Oh, Wally, Wally, Wally, I thought you were dead. I thought you were in the airmen's shelter. Oh,

Wally." And she throws her arms round him and kisses him, long, passionately, and Walter responds and thinks that the terrible raid of 30 August may turn out to be one of the greatest events of his life. He looks at her small, beautiful face, sees the blonde hair under her cap, her happy, sparkling eyes. His heart beats fast and he tries to find something to say which will fit this momentous occasion. Finally he comes out with, "Would three boxes of chocolates and six pairs of silk stockings be any use to you?"

September 1940

HELMUT HAPPY

5.1

Helmut didn't mind being a postman. To get the job left by a man now fighting for Führer and Fatherland was an honour and being a leader in the Hitler Youth made him the envy of every boy in Regelstein. Besides, among his bundle of letters were draft orders for those too scared, weak or stupid to join up. He pushed them through letter boxes with venom. *That'll show you*, he thought. *Prison or worse if you won't go.*

It was a warm September morning. Mailbag on his back, he stopped outside Frau Schultz's house in Pixisstrasse with a letter from *Oberleutnant* Schultz. A Luftwaffe navigator bombing England every night. "May God punish England," Helmut said to himself. The Luftwaffe would destroy their Air Force just as the Wehrmacht destroyed their army.

It was a pity about Britain. They were brothers: they should be fighting with the Germans. But everyone knew that Britain was in the grip of the great Communist/Jewish conspiracy for world domination and had been tricked into the war. In Germany they saw this trick coming. The

Führer's timely actions saved the Fatherland.

Helmut smiled when he thought of the free gift the government had granted his father for his essential building work. A brand new Bedford army lorry, left behind by the British at Dunkirk. It had been quite useful, although it broke down often. He'd learned a lot about diesel engines by helping his father get it going again. Captured Bedford lorries were common sights now. Nothing could stop the march of the Fatherland.

Herr Winckelmann's house next. A postcard from his brother in Bavaria. Helmut liked old Herr Winckelmann. He had the Iron Cross from the last war, for bravery against the French at Verdun. Four long years in the last war and still the Kaiser couldn't get to Paris. This time? Three weeks. Revenge is sweet and *Blitzkrieg* is sure.

And what of himself? He was sixteen. But all the Hitler Youth leaders were at the war, so the promotion age had been lowered. Already he was *Scharführer*, leading three *Kameradschaften* totalling fifty boys. He was second only to Lothar, *Gefolgschaftsführer*, in charge of the whole company. The *Gefolgschaft* was Helmut's first loyalty, now even greater than to his parents. He had a wild hope that soon he might take Lothar's place. Lothar was waiting to be accepted into the SS. Helmut longed to join the SS. But the standard for getting in was so high. You must have pure Aryan blood, be a perfect physical specimen, the brave, brutal, young man that the Führer demanded. Helmut knew of someone rejected because of two fillings in his teeth.

Of course, he had a big advantage. He was special: he had been presented personally to the Führer. He often recalled that amazing day.

How could any other boy in the world begin to know what it was like to be so close to the Führer? Helmut sensed his hero's pulsating power. Its force field enveloped him. He even fancied he heard a strange humming from within the Führer's body, like a huge dynamo throbbing with energy. When the Führer reached out and touched his shoulder, it was as if electric shocks energized his muscles and made his nerves even more alert. And the Führer spoke, to him, Helmut Vögler, alone. "The future of the Fatherland rests on your shoulders, Helmut."

"Only because you touched them, my Führer," Helmut wanted to say, but of course he was struck dumb. Yet he had the courage to look up and into the Führer's face. The cold and unmoving features he knew from photographs and newsreels seemed relaxed, the eyes which never blinked were almost twinkling with pleasure. And Helmut was overcome by the feelings of joy, hope and invincibility which that face brought him. In that moment he knew: *Nothing will stop us from imposing our will.*

The long trudge up Lindenstrasse. Here was a letter for Herr and Frau Seydlitz. He frowned. He had his doubts about the Seydlitz family. Herr Seydlitz was definitely not Aryan. There was something about his sallow complexion and black hair. Could there be Jewish blood there? Herr Seydlitz should have an eye kept on him. "I must tell Lothar," Helmut said to himself as he continued delivering letters, knocking on front doors with parcels, a cheery cry of "*Guten Morgen. Heil Hitler,*" when it was opened and estimating the enthusiasm in the answering "*Heil*". Detecting hints of disloyalty was the duty of a member of the Hitler Youth.

Nearly lunchtime. Helmut returned to the Post Office, left his bag and cycled home for lunch. His father was at work, building another new army barrack block. His mother had prepared salami and sauerkraut and he wolfed it down. His mother was a good *Hausfrau*, an example to German womanhood. Yet he sometimes wondered if she was really dedicated heart and soul to the great German struggle. Of course, he would never denounce his own parents, though he'd heard of those who had.

He had little to say to his mother. His mind was on this afternoon's parade. They were to learn how to strip down machine guns and fire them. Afterwards they would go to an anti-aircraft battery site and learn how to be signallers, searchlight operators, maybe how to fire those wonderful quadruple 20mm anti-aircraft guns with their four barrels. It was good fun but Helmut couldn't see the point of being a *Flakhelfer*. No English bomber would ever appear over a German city. Some had got as far as Berlin and knocked off a few chimney pots but they were so slow and clumsy that the Luftwaffe blew them out of the skies. Still, the Führer never left anything to chance. Germany was safe in his hands.

Before he left, he made himself ready. His uniform was spotless: khaki shirt, black shorts, leather belt with the swastika buckle and cross-strap, short-bladed knife in one sheath on his belt and in another his proudest possession, the Hitler Youth dagger inscribed *Blut und Ehre* – Blood and Honour. His blood, ready to be shed for Germany; his honour, the code he would always live by. He looked in the mirror. Yes, he was every inch the good young Nazi.

The first person he met was Lothar. After their *Heil*

*Hitler*s, Lothar said, "I've news for you. I'm joining the SS. I leave next week. You are to be *Gefolgschaftsführer* in my place. It's all arranged."

"Thank you," said Helmut. "I shall be a good one. But I'd rather be going with you."

"Your turn will soon come," Lothar replied.

The ceremony confirming him as *Gefolgschaftsführer* was nearly as great as being presented to Hitler. The solemnity of the oath he swore, the heartiness of the patriotic songs, the fervour of the cries of "*Heil Hitler*" and the power of a hundred Nazi salutes as Herr *Obergebietsführer* Wilhelm Deisler, leader of all Hitler Youth in the Taunus, invested him with his new badges of rank – all these left him glowing with unalloyed pleasure and pride. He saw his mother and father smiling proudly as friends congratulated them on their remarkable son and wondered how he could ever have suspected that his mother was less than heart and soul for the Nazi cause. Yes, his life was set on an inevitable course and he would follow his star wherever it might take him.

March–October 1940

MATTHIAS IN EXILE

6.1

I sometimes wonder why I went so quietly when the police called. Shouldn't I have told them they had no right to invade my home? But it would have done no good. The Nazis had overrun Norway, Holland, Luxembourg, Denmark. France would be next and then even Britain herself. How could I be surprised that I, a German, was taken away?

There were nearly a hundred others already at Wicester Racecourse all sitting on the grass in the sunshine, like a gigantic picnic. The police handed me over to the army and I was searched for weapons. They confiscated the pocket knife I always carried for opening envelopes and peeling fruit. Did they think I'd stab them with it?

Then we were handed large sacks. A sergeant led us to the empty stables, and said, not unkindly, "I'm sorry, gentlemen, but I must ask you to fill the sacks with straw. These will be your mattresses."

"Do we sleep in here?" someone asked.

"No such luck," the sergeant replied.

He led us back into the sunshine and we sat on our new

mattresses to squash the lumps out. The man who had asked the question sat next to me so I introduced myself. "Matthias Vögler."

"Wolfgang Eberstark." He was a big man, burly and dark-haired. "Refugee. Been here two years. We had a bakery in Hamburg. After Kristallnacht I knew we had to go. How long have you been here?"

"Since 1919," I replied.

He looked at me narrowly. "So who did you escape from?"

"Nobody. I was over here and married an English girl."

"So soon after the armistice?"

"I was a prisoner of war."

"I see," he replied. "Who did you fight with?"

"The First Taunus regiment. Got wounded in the 1918 retreat and ended up in a British hospital."

"I was with the 2nd Hanseatics," he said. "Three years in the trenches and they gave me the Iron Cross. Then they broke my windows and scrawled insults on the walls. So you're not Jewish?"

"No," I replied.

"You've been here twenty years. You must be well settled. Why didn't you take British citizenship and save yourself all this?"

"I often thought about it," I replied. "But I'm not English, I'm German. I was born German and I'll die German."

"So if you hadn't met your English girl, would you have broken my windows too? I'm sorry to be brutal, but I have to ask."

"I hate what's happening in my country," I replied care-

156

fully. "It's a monstrous cancer and we must root it out before it destroys us. If I'd gone back in 1919, would I have held out against it? I hope I would. But who can tell?"

Wolfgang nodded. "We can never be sure what we would do if things were otherwise. Yours is as good an answer as I could expect."

Like all racecourses, Wicester had a tote where racegoers could place their bets. It was in a large hall and we were to sleep on the concrete floor. We put down our straw mattresses and made ourselves as comfortable as we could. I don't think many slept that night. I certainly didn't. The shock of being torn away from home and family and the fear of what might happen kept me awake. But next morning dawned sunny and warm again, we were given a good breakfast and felt much better. If this was internment then life might not be too bad.

I found out more about my companions. Many were German Jews; others were political refugees and persecuted priests. I was none of these and some were suspicious of me. They thought I might be a spy. I had to tell my story many times before everybody believed me.

Life was good for those first few days. We lazed in the sunshine, read newspapers and books, ate fairly good food, talked and played cards and football. The guards were friendly and helpful. We were allowed to write one letter home. Then someone spotted a newspaper report that long-stay internment camps were being prepared in the Isle of Man. That day the sun went in.

A week later we were put on coaches to Northampton station and herded onto a train with as many army guards as passengers. The train was hot, crowded and slow. We could only use the lavatories if a soldier stood outside with his rifle jammed in the doorway. Did they think we'd try to escape down the S-bend?

Six hours later the train stopped at a station with blacked-out nameboards. They put us in more coaches and drove us through darkening lanes to a place where soldiers were putting up rolls of barbed wire round a perimeter fence. The last time I'd seen such barbed wire was in the previous war, in the trenches, and fear struck my heart.

6.2

As far as we could see in the darkness, this was a deserted village of dilapidated houses. We stood bewildered and shivering while the guards kept getting the roll-call wrong and became angry and agitated. In the end an officer strode up and called it himself. It was still incorrect. These people were hopeless. After an hour they gave up the roll-call and tried, with similar incompetence, to divide us into equal groups.

It was very late when they finally marched us to the houses. Ours had two downstairs rooms, a kitchen, three bedrooms and a bathroom. But there was no furniture, gas or electricity. There were fifteen of us in the house. Wolfgang and I took an upstairs bedroom for ourselves and a Catholic priest who introduced himself as Father Zeigler joined us. He said he was hounded from his pulpit in Bavaria for preaching against the Nazis and fled to England to avoid the concentration camp. He was a small man with sandy hair, very mild and inoffensive, the last person you would expect to speak out. So here we were, three German prisoners in the land we had come to for better lives.

We were ordered outside again, formed up into a ragged troop and marched off to the stores. Here we were each given a flimsy camp bed, thin mattress, three blankets and a pillow. When we had made our beds by the light of Wolfgang's torch we looked at each other in despair.

"What have we come to?" said Father Zeigler.

"Matthias," said Wolfgang. "You should know England like the back of your hand. Where are we?"

"I've no idea," I replied. And after all this time I still have no idea, except that it was somewhere near Liverpool.

Next morning we were woken by a voice shouting, "Everyone out of bed, dressed and lined up outside in half an hour." Standing outside bleary-eyed and yawning, we saw what a bleak place this was. Some houses had boarded-up windows. There was barbed wire all round us and a watchtower, with armed soldiers surveying us.

We were marched to a hut lined with rough trestle tables, obviously our dining room. Here I had the worst breakfast of my life. A thin slice of bread, a piece of margarine the size of my fingernail, a bowl of porridge that looked and tasted like wallpaper paste and a mug of stewed tea with one tin of condensed milk between thirty of us.

"Perhaps they aren't organized properly yet," said Wolfgang.

For lunch we had half a partly rotten, nearly raw potato each, accompanied by six (I counted) butter beans. The evening meal was even worse. A bowl of soup like cabbage water, another thin slice of bread, a one-inch cube of hard cheese and a tiny lump of margarine.

"We can't survive on this," I said to Wolfgang. A restive, mutinous noise built up until the sergeant in charge shouted, "Shut up and be thankful for what you're given."

Next morning we marched to the meal hut in heavy, driving rain. Breakfast was the same as yesterday's. So was lunch except for a boiled cabbage stalk instead of butter beans. The evening meal was worse, with potato water instead of cabbage water as the soup.

The rain poured all day. That night I said, "At this rate we won't survive the winter. We'll get pneumonia."

"Our Lord will provide," said Father Zeigler.

"He'll have to do better than this," said Wolfgang.

"Wolfgang, we're both old soldiers," I said. "How did we get by when times were hard?"

"Foraging, wangling, bribery," Wolfgang replied. "Using our wits. Low cunning."

"Exactly," I replied. "So that's what we must do now."

Father Zeigler shook his head sadly.

"Have you noticed that people in charge can often be corrupted?" said Wolfgang. "What do we have to corrupt them with?"

We turned out our pockets. Altogether we had ten pounds between us that we had kept hidden when we handed our money in. Wolfgang produced a gold cigarette lighter, a silver cigarette case and a leather wallet. "Bargaining tools," he told me.

I had a gold signet ring and a fountain pen. We looked sadly at our little condemned pile. "When the money runs out we can sell these and go on buying," I said.

"Once we find a supplier he'll soon be so deep in it that he can't go back," said Wolfgang. "Once they're hooked, we can drive hard bargains. One word from us and they'll be court-martialled."

"Wonderful," I said. That was our plan and it sounded excellent.

Father Zeigler looked at us sorrowfully. "I take no part in this," he said. "You are committing sins. I shall pray for your souls. I'm sorry you aren't Catholics because I can't absolve you through confession."

"Father," said Wolfgang. "If we get you bread and wine, could you consecrate them? Then you could hold Masses for the Catholics."

Father Zeigler didn't answer.

"God moves in a mysterious way," I told him.

When I was a prisoner in 1918 I noticed that army prison guards were either annoyed at their menial duties or thankful they weren't at the front-line. Either way they could be tempted. The guard who woke us each morning was a Private Snaith. He was thin, pale, clumsy and spotty-faced and his uniform fitted where it touched. Wolfgang and I drew lots to see who would get at him first and Wolfgang won.

"Private Snaith," said Wolfgang next morning. "We're starving and sick. We need fresh fruit to give us vitamin C."

"Oh yeah?" Private Snaith replied. "If you don't like it you should have stayed in Jerryland. What can I do? There's a war on, you know."

"I've got a ten shilling note here that says you can do quite a lot. I was a soldier once. I know how little they pay you."

"I won't be locked up for a ten bob note," said Private Snaith.

"Of course not," Wolfgang replied. "However..." He

opened his wallet and flicked the edges of the notes inside like a card sharp. Private Snaith's eyes nearly popped out. "Oh, I don't just mean the money," Wolfgang continued. "You could sell the wallet for, let me see, at least three pounds. Here, feel the quality."

I swear Private Snaith's hands were shaking as he reached out for it. But Wolfgang drew it back and said, "No, I think we'll stick to cash."

Private Snaith swallowed and his Adam's apple seemed to somersault inside his neck. "What do you want me to get?" he said.

"Oh, let's say six packets of twenty cigarettes."

"I could try, I suppose."

"Some apples and plums. Corned beef. I've heard about this new American stuff called Spam. A few tins of Spam wouldn't come amiss."

"I'm told Spam contains ham," said Father Zeigler. "As a Jew you should not be eating it."

"I won't," Wolfgang replied. "I merely think of others."

"Give me the money," said Private Snaith.

"Oh no," said Wolfgang. "Strictly cash on delivery."

"Why should you trust me?" said Private Snaith.

"Because we could double your army pay," Wolfgang replied.

When Private Snaith had gone to the next house, Wolfgang laughed. "He'll do as he's told. He can't afford not to."

"This is sinful," said Father Zeigler.

"You said that before," said Wolfgang. "Father Zeigler, before the bad days started, I was an upright, respected Hamburg businessman, honest as the day is long. But I've had to live on my wits, think only of my family's survival and let the rest go hang. Now I'm here I don't care what I do to keep going and in a couple of weeks you'll be the same."

Private Snaith did not let us down. Next day he brought us six packets of cigarettes, five pounds of apples, five of plums and four tins of corned beef. Wolfgang handed over the ten shilling note and two half crowns as well. "Bonus for good work," he said.

Private Snaith strode to the next house with a spring in his step. "We have him now," said Wolfgang. "He'll get his friends in on the act and they'll spread it over the whole camp. They'll be the richest soldiers in the army. Ah, human nature."

All went well for three days. Then the toilet paper and soap ran out so a new supply was added to the list. Private Snaith never failed with our orders and whispered that he was making three pounds a week clear profit.

"Why not share your good fortune with your colleagues?" said Wolfgang. "We'll get you plenty of customers."

Private Snaith nodded. "Sounds good," he said. "Don't you want to know where I get all this stuff?"

"No," said Wolfgang firmly. "Never share secrets."

Soon, nearly everyone was in on the act. Those too honest or too simple had pale faces, blotchy skins, were losing weight fast and crowding into the squalid "hospital" with colds and 'flu. Even Father Zeigler bit down his objections ("For a greater good," he said) and held regular Masses with his consecrated bread and wine.

Even so, things got worse by the day. When we arrived,

there were about three hundred in the camp. But new groups kept arriving. Soon nearly a thousand were fighting for space. Our house had thirty in it. In our room alone were three beds, and four mattresses on the floor. Something bad happened to the postal service. No letters reached us and the postboxes were suddenly sealed. Smuggling letters out became another of Private Snaith's duties.

New arrivals were put in tents. The rain seldom stopped. The place was a quagmire, the houses leaked and I shuddered to think what living in the tents must be like. Yet we led bearable lives. We held talks, debates, competitions. We pooled our books and soon had a small library. We had hairdressers, shoe repairers, even doctors and dentists. Newspapers were smuggled in: now we could keep up with how the war was going.

So we passed the time tolerably well until, after six weeks, we were told to pack our bags for a new destination: the Isle of Man.

6.3

It was Thursday in the first week of August when we said goodbye to Private Snaith. "We've a lot to thank you for," I said. "You kept us healthy and sane."

"Thank you, sir," he replied. He'd never called me "sir" before. "I'm sorry to see you go, I am truly."

"I bet you are," said Wolfgang. "Perhaps the next lot won't be as enterprising as we are."

"I shall pray for you, my boy," said Father Zeigler.

"Thanks," said Private Snaith in a vague sort of way.

That was the last we saw of him.

We were lined up, four hundred of us, shivering in the cold morning air on the scrubby patch of ground the guards called the Parade Square and we called something else. The officers faced us in a line and a sergeant called the roll for the last time. It was wrong again. But no officer moved or said a word so the sergeant had to sort it out by himself.

No coaches this time. We formed up in ranks, picked up our cases and walked to the station, still with its name-boards blacked out. The waiting train had four carriages.

One hundred men per carriage: thank heavens it wasn't far to Liverpool.

Our journey ended at a pierhead in the docks. A small steamer, once a ferry to the Isle of Man, was waiting. With its regular passengers and four hundred internees, this was an overcrowded boat.

We set sail at midday. As Liverpool disappeared behind us, dismal thoughts flooded my mind. I was starved of news from home. How was Ellen? I knew she'd cope without me: I'd never known such a resourceful woman. Paul and Anna, how were they? I had confidence in them too. But the promised German invasion could happen any day. How would the Nazis treat a defenceless woman and her children when they found out who she was married to?

Then there was Walter. A dreadful air battle raged over England. Pitifully few British aircraft against the greatest air armada the world had seen. The papers said Spitfires and Hurricanes were shooting down more Luftwaffe planes than they were losing, but the losses were still serious. Liverpool had been raided. We heard bombers overhead, the rumble of anti-aircraft guns, saw searchlights and bomb damage. And my son was in the eye of the storm. I feared for him, though I knew he would never fear for me.

As we sailed westwards the wind strengthened, rain swept in, and we docked in Douglas, seasick and drenched. Wolfgang came up to me. "You were having sad thoughts, I think," he said.

"Yes," I answered.

"I too. This is a war of partings and departures. Each place we leave makes the cord between us and our loved

167

ones weaker."

We disembarked at 5 p.m. A lorry waited for our luggage to be loaded, which seemed a good omen. The rain ceased, the wind dropped, the skies cleared and, as we walked in evening sunshine along the promenade, our spirits rose. The hotels and boarding houses looked inviting, but not for the likes of us, we thought. One hotel especially stood out as imposing. The Hotel Metropole.

"What a place," said Wolfgang. "Who could afford to stay there?"

The sergeant in charge shouted, "Halt!" and we came to a ragged stop. "Left turn," he shouted. Now we stood in front of the Hotel Metropole, looking straight through its open front doors.

"This is impossible," Wolfgang muttered.

But it wasn't. We filed through the doorway into the spacious foyer. "I always knew the Lord would provide," said Father Zeigler.

The Hotel Metropole really was ours. We had proper beds, hot and cold running water, competent guards and approachable officers. The CO, Major Frobisher, was a middle-aged man with decorations on his tunic, so he'd fought in the last war. I respected him at once, especially when he wished us a pleasant stay here.

"I think I'd be happy to see out the rest of the war here," said Wolfgang. "In fact I think I'll stay here for the rest of my life."

It seemed too good to be true. We could post letters and even send telegrams, though telephoning was frowned on. Letters and parcels reached us regularly. We could even swim in the sea. I wrote home to say that life, if not quite the lap of luxury, was certainly very tolerable. Of course, it didn't last. Nothing good ever does.

6.4

Word spread that unmarried men under thirty were to be sent away. "Where to?" they asked. They weren't told, but someone over thirty and married caused near hysteria by suggesting they were to be repatriated to Germany.

The answer came. Canada. The single over-thirties such as Father Zeigler were annoyed: a free voyage across the Atlantic meant safety and the start of a new life on release. The married under-thirties would have wanted it too, but only with their families. The rest of us were thankful that we wouldn't have to risk the U-boats. But the young bachelors were ecstatic. A passage to North America at the Government's expense – what could be better?

I listened to them with amused detachment. Then the list was put up with the names of those bound for Canada. My name was on it.

"You must appeal," said Wolfgang.

"See Major Frobisher," said Father Zeigler. "He's a good man."

That morning I asked Sergeant Trotter, in charge of the

170

guards, if I could. I was told to report to the CO's office at two o'clock. When I knocked, I was ushered in at once.

"Do sit down, Mr Vögler," said Major Frobisher. "I think I know why you have come."

"I'm on the list for Canada, yet I'm forty-one, married with a family, and have lived here for twenty years. There must be a mistake."

"If there's a mistake, the Home Office made it," he replied.

"Then I must see someone from the Home Office."

"That's not easy," he said. "Of course, you can appeal. I think it's odd myself and I'll certainly back you up. Leave it with me, Mr Vögler."

Three days later I received a note to report to his office again. Sergeant Trotter escorted me. Two men faced me, Major Frobisher and a thin man with a pinched face and glasses, a grey file open in front of him.

"Sit down please, Mr Vögler," said Major Frobisher. "This is Mr Newton from the Home Office. The final decision is his."

Mr Newton took his glasses off and peered at me. "Good morning, Herr Vögler," he said. "You want me to help you, I believe."

"Excuse me," I replied. "I live in England and I'm known as *Mr* Vögler."

He put his glasses back on and said, "So my information is wrong. I was under the impression that you are still a German citizen."

"That's true," I replied.

"Then you are *Herr* Vögler and that is how I shall address you."

That made me angry. "The orders are that single men under thirty are to go to Canada," I said. "I'm neither."

"I have your dossier here," he replied. "Your name is Matthias Vögler. Though you have lived here twenty years and seem a respectable member of your community, you maintain family ties in Germany and visit the country frequently. Your brother and his wife are known Nazis. Your nephew is a member of the Hitler Youth, so highly regarded that he was presented to Adolf Hitler himself at a Nazi rally. My information is that you were present at this rally with your family. I believe this was not accidental: attending it was the point of your visit."

"I can't deny we were at the rally, though it certainly wasn't the point of our visit. I found it an unpleasant and disturbing experience." I wondered how he knew.

"So you say now," he replied. "But your conduct is typical of a Nazi sympathizer. You are potentially a spy and a dangerous fifth columnist. You live in an area where there are several sensitive military establishments. We suspect you may have passed information about them to the Third Reich. There are many such as you in Britain and they are being arrested, imprisoned and will soon face trial."

"None of this is true," I said, trying to stay calm. "I have never, nor would I ever, dream of helping the Nazi cause."

Mr Newton looked down and smoothed the pages of my dossier. "You cannot deny the facts," he said.

"If you think I'm a spy, why don't you arrest me, instead of sending me across the Atlantic?" I said.

No reply. So I answered for him. "It's because this is an easy way to keep me out of the way without getting evidence, which you won't find. There are no hidden wireless sets in our house."

"That remains to be seen," said Mr Newton.

"Don't you dare ransack my home."

"I'm afraid you have no power to prevent anything we do."

This was too much. "I won't have you upsetting my wife and family," I shouted.

"Ah, your family," said Mr Newton. "Tell me about them."

"My son is in the RAF. He volunteered long before the war began. He was with Fighter Command in France and now he's at Biggin Hill."

"We make no comment about your son."

"My wife was an army nurse in the last war. She saved me from death. Have you the slightest idea what a bond that makes? It overrides everything else, parents, brothers, national loyalties. My wife had no need to put herself in danger in France. Like my son, she volunteered."

"We make no comment on your wife either."

"My son Paul. He's still at the grammar school. He's doing well. His teachers say he'll go to university, but my guess is that he'll volunteer for the armed services the moment he's old enough."

"Ah, your second son," said Mr Newton. "I understand that he speaks German almost like a native."

"I taught him when he was a young child."

"Commendable. Why did you not teach your eldest child? Could it be that you saw your second son as a better prospect to join you?"

I stood up, furious. "That's monstrous," I shouted.

"Please sit down, Mr Vögler," said Major Frobisher.

173

"You won't help yourself that way."

I sat angrily and said, "Do you accuse my daughter Anna as well?"

"Not for the moment," Mr Newton replied, yawning as if bored.

"What can I do to convince you of my hatred for Nazism and my loyalty to Britain?"

"Very little, Herr Vögler."

Then I thought of something, a last chance. "It was my dear Anna who led me to realize what I really felt about Hitler and the Nazis."

Mr Newton, plainly not listening, opened his briefcase.

"Do you know the story of the Lorelei rock?" I said.

Major Frobisher spoke. "No, Mr Vögler," he said. "Please tell us." Mr Newton looked annoyed and put the dossier back on the desk.

"How Lorelei sang for her lost lover and sailors on the Rhine were so entranced that they foundered on her rock and perished?"

"Ah," said Major Frobisher. "Like the Sirens luring Ulysses and his men in Homer's *Odyssey*. Why have you told us that story?"

"I hated the Nazi rally. It disturbed me to the roots of my being. Anna put what I felt into words. She said that Hitler reminded her of the Lorelei story. His speech was a beautiful song to everyone there but us. He was luring Germany onto the rocks and the people would founder and perish."

"Thank you, Mr Vögler," said Major Frobisher and smiled. "That was very interesting. You must be proud of your daughter."

174

Mr Newton put the dossier in his briefcase, stood up and said, "Your appeal is denied, Herr Vögler."

Major Frobisher also stood. "I'm sorry," he said. "But it's my duty now to see you are on the ship for Canada. You are dismissed."

Sergeant Trotter escorted me back. "For what it's worth, I think that Ministry man was wrong," he said. "I can tell you're no spy. Do you know why? Nearly all the blokes here, they're refugees, they've been in danger and a lot of their friends never made it. They've learned who to trust and who not to − and they've done it the hard way. If you're hiding something fishy I reckon they'd have rumbled you by now."

We reached my room. "I don't think the major believes it either," he said. "Pity what we say doesn't count for anything."

6.5

In despair, I told Wolfgang and Father Zeigler everything, including what Sergeant Trotter said about knowing who to trust.

"Of course the sergeant is right," said Father Zeigler. "Some of my supposed brothers in Christ betrayed me to the Nazis after telling me I had their support. I never doubted you, my friend, and never will."

"That goes for me too," said Wolfgang.

The news spread. Everyone's sympathy didn't soften the blow. Major Frobisher told me to write home telling my family. I was to put the letter on his desk and he would add it to his private mail so that no censor would see it.

That night I poured my heart out on paper, about Mr Newton's unfairness and Major Frobisher's dislike of what had been done. When I took the letter to his office, Major Frobisher received me courteously. "If I could reverse this decision, I certainly would," he said. "But I'll get in touch with your family and try to reassure them." He shook my hand firmly. "I wish you good fortune in Canada, Mr Vögler."

I felt reassured. We had a friend who might still have some influence. Or was that just another illusion?

Wednesday 28 August 1940. We packed our cases last night. Leaving good friends like Wolfgang and Father Zeigler
was hard. I joined the others in the hotel foyer, three hundred happy, young men. But as the day wore on and nothing happened, they grew restless, while I had a crazy hope that the voyage was cancelled and we were staying here after all.

9 p.m. Outside, a miserable drizzle was falling. Major Frobisher appeared. "Gentlemen," he said, "I'm sorry for the delay. Please pick up your luggage and form up in ranks outside. Goodbye and good luck."

So once again we walked the Douglas promenade, joined on the way by groups from other camps: there must have been nearly a thousand of us when we formed up on the quayside. A small, grey Royal Navy minesweeper was waiting. Surely we couldn't cross the Atlantic in that?

It was now 10.30 p.m. and we hadn't eaten since mid-day. We filed slowly up the gangplank. Some lined the blacked-out decks drenched by drizzle: others, including me, were pushed below, to crouch in darkness and stifling heat, with the stink of diesel fuel. I couldn't see my watch so had no idea of time. I couldn't stand it so I struggled back up the stairway to the deck, treading on sleeping men and pushing others out of the way. We were still in Douglas harbour and it still drizzled but at least I breathed fresh air. I felt wretched – sleepless, aching in every muscle, unwashed, unshaven and ravenously hungry. But

177

the ship didn't move and the drizzle still fell.

6 a.m. The minesweeper got under way at last. A new rumour spread. We were going back to Liverpool, to board a great transatlantic liner and sail in the lap of luxury. I didn't believe it. The drizzle turned to driving rain, the wind rose and the sea grew rough. I heaved up once, twice, three times, even though I hadn't eaten for nearly a day, and felt cavernously empty afterwards. We docked in Liverpool at 10 a.m.

The next two hours passed like an extraordinary dream. We were herded into a huge warehouse and waited, still with no food, huddled together in air as stale as below deck on the minesweeper. Large windows looked out over the quayside. After an hour, those nearest them began to whisper excitedly.

A huge white ship, an ocean-going liner, had tied up at the quay. We pressed towards the window to see this amazing sight. Cheers split the air and joy washed around me like a warm bath. I couldn't share in it. To me the ship was a monster, an evil thing, taking me away from all I held dear, and quite likely for the last time.

Without warning, the mood changed to anger. I pushed forward to see why. German soldiers, prisoners of war still in uniform, were filing up the gangplank, two hundred or more, under armed guard.

"Do we have to sail with them?" said someone disgustedly.

How strange that I should cross the Atlantic with men who, if life had turned out differently, would be my comrades. Seeing them still smart in uniform made me ashamed. We were unkempt, smelly, like tramps. I'd never felt so low as we shuffled up the gangplank into this great white ship, the *SS Ettrick*. Another ship, the *Arandora Star*, was moored behind us and more internees were boarding her.

The guards forced us deep into the bowels of the ship to a huge open space stretching almost its full length, lined with long tables and, as far as we could see, nowhere to sleep. We faced ten days in this place, in conditions nearly as bad as in the slave trade. We were the ship's guilty secret. I thought there would be a riot, until someone found a storecupboard full of hammocks. But where were we supposed to hang them? At eight o'clock, some army orderlies entered, put tin mugs and plates on the tables and doled out supper, precious little of it, with weak, sweet tea out of huge urns. Still, after over thirty hours with no food or drink, it was welcome.

At last we were told where to hang our hammocks. An orderly pointed out hooks in the ceiling, two for each hammock, and showed us how to sling them. So there we were, poised uncomfortably in the air directly over the tables we ate off. It took us half the night to sling the hammocks properly and by the time we'd finished we were sweating like pigs and too tired to sleep. So it was two sleepless nights in a row for me and, as I swayed unsteadily listening to the monstrous engines beating close by and enduring the smell of nine hundred men and several thousand gallons of diesel, I was in a pit of misery. There were no toilets. We were given buckets, one between two, and allowed upstairs each morning to slop out and wait our turn at one of the fifty washbasins.

At least we could see out through the portholes. On the first morning we watched the Irish coast slip by, the

Arandora Star and the two escorting destroyers ploughing through the waves beside us. The sight comforted us: we weren't alone.

On the fourth night we heard gunfire and explosions. The ship suddenly lurched sideways: we clung desperately to our wildly swinging hammocks. There was a muffled roar, then another and the ship lurched again. "Depth charges," said someone. "They've found U-boats."

We clambered out of our hammocks and huddled on the floor, waiting for the U-boats' torpedoes. I'd never experienced such blind fear, even in the trenches. Then, you could see the enemy. This was like kittens drowning in a sack. But the torpedoes never came and somehow the night passed.

Daylight came at last. We crowded to the portholes. Both destroyers were there. But where was the *Arandora Star*?

Now came rumours and panic. She must have been torpedoed with no survivors. We asked the orderlies. "She's joined another convoy," they told us. "That wasn't a U-boat you heard. Just a false alarm and a bit of practice."

"Why would she join another convoy?" someone asked.

"These Navy people do funny things," was the reply. Nobody believed it.

On the fifth day we ran into a storm. The floor was wet with vomit: the smell was appalling. For two days the storm raged but on the seventh evening it blew itself out. On the eighth day we were allowed up on deck in shifts, two hours at a time. Out we staggered, troglodytes blinking in the blinding light. The cold, stinging air was like strong drink and we took great gulps of it. We looked at each other, pale, wasted, hardly able to stand straight, as if we'd been walled up alive. We sat, wrapped in blankets, on lifebelts, coils of rope, anything we could find, and talked. Soldiers took pity on us and brought cigarettes and food from their canteen. The German soldiers were on a roped-off part of the deck, looking as wretched as we did. We weren't allowed to speak to them, though I felt deep down that I might like to. Perhaps an old friend, an old comrade, might be among them.

Our depleted convoy sailed on. Each night was a time of breathless terror waiting for U-boats to attack. On the tenth day, calm, cold and fine, we skirted Newfoundland. Far in the distance were snow-capped mountains. On the eleventh day we entered the Saint Lawrence River, though the banks were still fifty miles apart. On the twelfth day we could make out towns, houses, trees. We packed our luggage, and stowed our hammocks. And at last came the order to leave our prison.

We came up on deck to bright sunshine. A police boat hailed us as we entered a large port. "Quebec," someone said. Police, soldiers and doctors came on board. "This ship must be riddled with disease," said another man gloomily. "They'll vaccinate us and put us in quarantine for six weeks." But, to our surprise, they didn't.

We lined the sides as the ship slowly drew up to the wide quay and was made fast fore and aft. An hour later the gangplank was lowered and we staggered down it, hardly able to stay on our feet after the heaving swell of the Atlantic. As dusk fell we touched Canadian soil and I took a last look at the *Ettrick* with loathing in my heart.

We were made to load our luggage into a line of vans

before we started our march in darkness. Then came a surprise. Our march lasted barely a hundred yards and ended at a line of coaches and buses. We were driven through narrow streets of small houses, lined with people who shouted and shook their fists at us. "They think we're Nazi prisoners," said someone. Soon the streets were left behind and we passed through the city centre, thronged with people, bright with lights, shops, cinemas, restaurants. After blacked-out Britain I had forgotten such things. We left the city and struck deep into dark countryside. An hour later we saw more lights – searchlights from watchtowers set in a high fence. Round the fence were rolls of barbed wire.

The buses stopped at checkpoints: papers were looked at, handed back and we drove through. Before us were lines of huts and high forbidding barrack blocks. So this was my new home. I stepped off the coach, lined up yet again, then marched with fifty others to one of the wooden huts and was shown my narrow iron bedstead and thin mattress. My journey was over. Now I must start my long exile, far away from home across a wide, wide, dangerous ocean.

December 1940

HELMUT PERPLEXED

7.1

Christmas 1940. *Gelfolgschaftsführer* Helmut Vögler was now too important to work as a postman. However, every morning he performed the sort of good work that a Hitler Youth was proud to do because it showed that Germany was united and the strong must help the weak. Three houses away lived the Lindemann family. Their ten-year-old daughter, Lotte, was disabled and in a wheelchair. Since Helmut had been promoted he had wheeled her every morning to the *Grundschule* for young children. Frau Lindemann had too much to do now she was on her own while her sailor husband was torpedoing British ships in the Atlantic.

Helmut liked Lotte. She prattled away ten to the dozen, though he didn't understand a word and said, "Yes, Lotte" or "No, Lotte" when she seemed to need an answer. Frau Lindemann was only too pleased when he volunteered to take her. "But I will bring her back when school finishes," she insisted. "You have far more important things to do."

"Yes, I do," said Helmut. "My responsibilities are very heavy."

He started taking Lotte to school at the beginning of October. He waited outside Frau Lindemann's house every morning while she made sure Lotte was ready, tied a scarf round her neck if it was cold and kissed her on the cheek. It seemed strange to Helmut to be going to a school. School was a place of books, learning and culture, and had not Hitler said such things were decadent unless they asserted true Aryan purity? All other books were for burning: Goering once said that when he heard the word "culture" he reached for his gun, though they said he loved paintings. Hard, brave and brutal, that's what the Führer wanted German youth to be. Books, learning, education, unless they extolled the virtues of Nazism, had no place in Helmut's life.

However, he took Lotte every morning for six weeks and assumed he would do it until he left for the SS. But on 13 December Frau Lindemann was alone and he saw she had been crying.

"What's the matter, Frau Lindemann?" he asked. "Where's Lotte?"

"She's not here," she replied.

"Where is she?" he asked, though deep down he knew.

"They came for her last night," said Frau Lindemann. "They've taken her to a new hospital being set up at Hadamar."

"I've heard of it," said Helmut. "It's between here and Marburg."

"They'll look after her better. It's built for children like her."

Helmut shivered. *Built for children like her* was dead right.

"They tell me they have fine doctors and nurses. It's

188

very up-to-date. It's for the best, isn't it, Helmut? I only want the best for Lotte."

He knew well what this meant. As a *Gefolgschaftsführer* and future SS man he had been told many secrets of the Third Reich. Hitler had formulated a policy that all those classed as idiots, feeble-minded, degenerate, anti-social or with physical disabilities could have no part in society. Their veins flowed with bad blood. Not only did their care cost money, which the Reich could ill afford, but they might marry and have children who would pass this bad blood to the next generation. The Aryan race must be kept perfect. Such children should be taken away for "special care". Most people thought this was only for Jews, gipsies, *Untermenschen*. But it wasn't.

He knew about "special care". Euthanasia. Quiet, secret killing with death certificates giving pneumonia as the cause of death. Of course, he believed in the policy's rightness. It was a fact that had been deposited in his head, not to be questioned.

"When did they take her?" he asked.

"Last night," said Frau Lindemann. "The Führer has decreed it for children like Lotte, so it must be right. Isn't that so, Helmut?"

"Yes, Frau Lindemann," Helmut replied.

But something inside him thought otherwise. This fact, which seemed so sensible and necessary, was different now it meant little Lotte, who he'd known ever since she was born. *This policy applies to real people*, he thought, *bad blood or no bad blood*. How, even with her disabilities, could anyone think Lotte's blood was bad? But all that about such fine doctors and nurses – it was a lie. Little Lotte, who

189

chattered away happily every morning and thanked him when he handed her over to the teachers, would be dead before Easter.

"I'm sure everything will be all right," he said, nearly choking on the words.

His mind wasn't really on the parade that day. When they went to the anti-aircraft site for their regular training he kept giving wrong orders. The boys looked puzzled and the army *Unteroffizier* in charge bawled furiously at him.

Helmut winced. He must put this Lotte business out of his mind. It was correct that she should be taken away for the greater good of the Third Reich. He'd let his boys down and he must make up for it. He was so brutal and single-minded for the rest of the day that some went home crying, which is not what members of the Hitler Youth should do.

This was the second wartime Christmas and Germany was victorious everywhere. True, Britain had not been invaded after all. But Dr Goebbels said that Britain tried to claim it had won a great victory against the Luftwaffe, while really Hitler had just got bored and told Goering not to waste the pilots' time any more on that insignificant little island. Every mainland country in the west had been conquered. It was the east that mattered now, and they all knew what that meant, even if Stalin in the Kremlin didn't. Russia would be next.

The Vöglers liked their traditional Christmases − the carp for Christmas Eve dinner with the giving of the presents and the goose for Christmas Day: going to church to give thanks − this year not only for the birth of Christ but

190

for the safety and continued success of the army, navy and air force. If there were any unchristian prayers for the annihilation of Britain and Russia they weren't said aloud.

So the Christmas spirit was strong in the Vögler household, as it was over all Regelstein and the rest of Germany. Nobody mentioned Uncle Matthias in England. *And a good thing too*, thought Helmut. So when they saw the New Year in, all they could imagine ahead were even greater triumphs for the Fatherland.

But when Helmut finally went to bed two hours after 1941 had been rung in and fell into a deep sleep, he dreamt of Lotte. She was lying very still on a trolley in a brightly lit room with walls of gleaming white tiles and hard black shadows, surrounded by figures wearing coats as white as the tiles. He went cold at the sight. Then the shadows seemed to join up into a solid shape, menacing, terrible and silent, promising revenge. When Helmut woke up, the fear stayed with him for some time until he angrily shook his head to get rid of it. But a seed of doubt grew in his mind, long after the vision of Lotte had faded.

March–December 1940

1940

ELLEN ALONE

8.1

The first weeks after Matthias was taken away were like a bad dream. His first letter arrived and made me feel resentful. He was lazing on the racecourse in the sun with fine new friends. Then came his next – what a contrast! He was trapped in an awful place, half starved and hopeless.

That night I had a vivid dream in which I heard, over and over again, the vow I'd made back in 1914: *"in the years that this war lasts I'll be someone worth their weight ... next time I'll make sure things happen the way I want them."* And when I woke I said aloud: "What's the matter with you, Ellen Vögler? You've never been like this before, you've gone out and made your own luck. So get out of bed and start DOING."

I got up and went downstairs nearly my old self again. I breakfasted properly with Paul and Anna for the first time in weeks and then watched them walk to the bus stop. Before she left Anna said, "I'm glad you're cheerful again, Mum."

When they'd gone I made a cup of tea, took a sheet of paper and a pencil and sat at the table to think. I couldn't bring Matthias back, nor Walter. It must be something else. I sat with pencil poised, then wrote: *Go back to nursing*.

I hadn't set foot in a hospital since leaving Abbeville. Still, as Ma once told me, if you don't ask you won't get. There would be wounded soldiers and air raid casualties but not enough nurses. I still had my certificate. I knew nurses now were State Registered or Enrolled but surely the training at London Fields Hospital still stood for something. Where should I go? The cottage hospital in Wicester? The big general hospital in Northampton? Or would there be new military hospitals?

Then I found myself writing, as if the pen had taken over: *Get Matthias home*. No, that was beyond me. I must concentrate on what was possible. I'd met Mrs Ogilvie, matron at the cottage hospital, at a school parents' evening, so I rang her up and we arranged to meet next day. That evening I told Paul and Anna what I intended.

"Good for you, Mum," Anna said at once.

"What about us?" said Paul.

"Paul, you're fifteen," I replied. "If you can't look after yourself by now there's not much hope for you."

"It's not me I'm worried about, it's her," said Paul.

"Don't worry, Mum, I'll see he stays in order," said Anna.

So that was settled.

The cottage hospital wasn't much more than a large house, with twenty beds, three nurses, a sister, a matron and the town's four GPs, who regularly came in to see how their own patients were getting on. Anything serious was packed off to Northampton. But now there was a change. Two long wooden huts had been built in the grounds.

"I just want to start nursing again," I told Mrs Ogilvie.

She looked at my old London Fields certificate and said, "Mrs Vögler, I had no idea you were a nurse. What was your last job?"

I told her about Abbeville. "That's as different from what we're used to as I can imagine," she said. "You'll find it very boring here."

"What are those huts outside?" I asked.

"That's government orders. We're supposed to be an emergency hospital for air raid victims. Well, there aren't any."

"It won't last," I said.

"I know," she replied. "I think you might be needed here soon. When the war hots up we might get cases that you'll cope with while my dear ladies faint with shock."

We agreed that I would start the following week. Now for the hard part. Matthias. I asked the children what they thought.

"Go and see Mr Coppard," Paul suggested. "Policemen are supposed to know these things."

"It was George Coppard who took him away," I said.

"That doesn't mean he wanted to," said Paul. "Perhaps he wants to make up for it."

Perhaps. I called at his house when he came off duty. When I told him why he looked very doubtful.

"I don't know what I can do, Ellen," he said.

"I haven't asked you to do anything," I replied. "I've asked you to tell me what I can do myself."

He looked quite shifty. "I'm paid to uphold the law, whatever I may think about it," he said awkwardly. "If someone tells me something that the authorities ought to know then I have to pass it on, especially with a war on.

197

So if I say one thing, I can't go and do the opposite just for you."

I stared at him. "George, what on earth are you talking about?"

"Nothing, Ellen. I'm just telling you the way it is."

Was he hiding something? All that "duty" and "law" and "authorities" – this wasn't the George Coppard I knew. Had he passed on something about Matthias? The only thing I could think of was about the Nazi rally. But how could he possibly know that? We'd told nobody. This made me feel even worse than when they said we couldn't take evacuees.

"Did he help?" Anna asked that evening.

"No," I said flatly. "I don't know what else I can do."

"Ask the vicar," suggested Paul. "They're supposed to know everything."

"You said that about policemen," said Anna.

It was worth a try. Next day, I rang the vicarage doorbell and Reverend Strickland himself opened it. He ushered me into his study, which was full of books, on shelves, stacked on his desk and piled on the floor. The desk was by the window looking out at the church: on it was a typewriter. He took his glasses off and said, "I was writing my Sunday sermon. Sorry about the books, but I need to look up theological points."

I told him my problem, and knew at once it was a mistake.

"Well, Mrs Vögler," he said, "I'm sure everybody sympathizes with your plight, and I assure you that you and Mr Vögler are both in our prayers, but in the circumstances I don't think you can be surprised. Far be it from me to undermine the splendid work being done by the security services, even if it may bear hard on individual people."

"Thank you, Reverend," I said, getting up to leave. "I'm sorry to have wasted your time. I mustn't keep you from your sermon."

"Mrs Vögler, I don't mean to discourage you and I feel for you, I really do, but I fear I have no useful suggestions."

Not discourage me? That's exactly what he had done. Then he said, "Of course, you could always write to our member of parliament. Dealing with matters affecting his constituents is his job."

Suddenly I was glad that I'd come. "Thank you, Reverend," I said. "I'm really grateful to you." Walking home, I wondered why I hadn't thought of it myself.

8.2

Our MP was the Rt Hon. Arthur P. Colgrove. That night I sat down to write what might be the most important letter of my life.

I'd never written to a Rt Hon. before. Did I start *Dear Rt Hon. Mr Colgrove?* That didn't sound right. *Dear Member of Parliament?* That was no good either, there were six hundred of them. *Dear Sir?* That means you don't know who you're writing to. *Dear Mr Colgrove.* That made him sound ordinary, not an MP or Rt Hon., but it would have to do.

My husband has been interned as an enemy alien.

But he'd probably say, "Serve him right," and throw it in the waste bin. I must dress it up a bit and start with the family, not Matthias.

My family has lived in Peterspury for twelve years. We are all very sad because...

Even worse. He'd say, "So is every other family, some a lot sadder than you," and throw that in the waste bin too.

My family, and especially my husband, have been treated unjustly.

Better. I could build on this.

Dear Mr Colgrove,

I believe my family, and especially my husband, have been the victims of a great injustice. My husband and I have lived in Peterspury for twelve years. During that time my husband, Matthias Vögler, has become highly respected in the village, has worked hard to build up his business as the only garage in Peterspury and is also the main agent for Morris Cars in the area.

My husband was born in Germany. We were married in 1919 and he has lived in England ever since. He hates Adolf Hitler and the Nazi Party and all they stand for. Our eldest son is in the RAF, for which he volunteered before the war.

I hope you will agree that under these circumstances it is grossly unfair that my husband has been arrested and interned as an enemy alien. My children and I earnestly ask you to use your good offices to ensure his speedy release, for which you would receive the undying gratitude of us all.

Yours sincerely

Ellen Vögler (Mrs)

And if you can manage this I might even vote for you, I thought as I put it in an envelope. The Rt Hon. A. P. Colgrove MP, House of Commons, London should reach him. I stuck a stamp on the envelope, posted it and felt that I'd done all I could.

The day before I started at the cottage hospital, an envelope came though the letterbox. Paul ran to pick it up. "Hey," he shouted. "There's a House of Commons crest on the envelope. It's him already."

I tore it open. All it said was: *Your communication has been received and will be dealt with in due course.* I was angry. Then I thought, poor man, how many other cries for help must he get? I'd just have to get in the queue.

That morning I started at the cottage hospital. The three nurses and Sister Brazier didn't seem happy to see me. Mrs Ogilvie introduced me and told them about my nursing service. They listened respectfully enough but once she went seemed openly scornful. Lucy Carter, not much younger than me, said, "It's all very well dragging soldiers out of the jaws of death but what do you know of the poor old dears who come here in winter with 'flu and go out next spring in a box?"

"I know I've a lot to catch up with," I said.

"There's not enough work for the four of us, let alone a new one," said Sister Brazier. "I can't understand why she took you on."

"It won't always be like this," I said.

Gladys Carpenter laughed. "They've said that since the war started," she said. "Nothing's happened so far and I don't think it ever will, not here in little old Wicester."

"Not even if we're invaded?" I said.

"If Jerry comes here we'll be past caring," said Vera Phillips.

"We'll soon know if you're right," I replied.

Next week every news bulletin and newspaper was full of the story of the little ships crossing the Channel to bring the soldiers back from Dunkirk. Two days after the rescue, Mrs Ogilvie told us, "We're getting eight soldiers here. Nothing bad, just shock. We're to keep them quiet and give them tender loving care. Simple stuff but it's what's needed."

When the ambulances arrived I felt that I'd been here before. Our eight men were brought off. Three could walk with help. The rest were on stretchers. All were having a laugh with their bearers.

Mrs Ogilvie was right: all they needed was care and we were good at that. For three days things went well. Then, out of the blue, two army nurses and an army doctor turned up. The doctor, a major, told us to go back to our normal duties because they were taking over.

So for the next month I dealt with Ronny Fanshaw's painful tonsils and Mrs Arkwright's chesty cough while army ambulances took the men away one by one until by July the huts were empty, the major and his nurses had gone and we were once again a sleepy little hospital in a sleepy little town. I'd wanted so much more than this.

8.3

In August letters came from Matthias again. He was in the Isle of Man, staying in a big hotel and sounding quite happy. He was comfortable, had room to move, decent food and regular dips in the sea. At the beginning of September he sent another letter.

My dearest wife,

I have bad news. The list of those bound for Canada was posted last week. My name is on it. I was sure it was a mistake so I approached Major Frobisher, the commanding officer. He said he was as surprised as I was and that I should appeal. Three days later he called me to his office. A man from the Home Office was there. He accused me of all sorts of things. He knew we had been to a Nazi rally and heard Hitler speak and that Helmut is in the Hitler Youth and was presented to Hitler. Ellen, how does he know these things? I tried to tell him what I thought about it but he would not listen. He said my appeal was denied and I must go to Canada.

My darling, I am frightened of what the future may bring. Frightened for myself and frightened for you and the children if the war should go badly. Major Frobisher has let me write this letter and will post it himself so no censor sees it. He is a good man and does not believe this is fair. Neither does anyone else here and they have told me so. They share my sorrow and indignation, but the die is cast and there is no going back on it. Pray that the next letter you will receive will tell you I have arrived safely in Canada.

With all my love,
Your husband, Matthias

I read it three times before I could take it in: I may never see Matthias again. It was the blackest, bleakest day of my life. I went to the hospital to lose myself in work and it occupied me well enough. But I knew the other nurses would think that Matthias deserved it because he was German. Only old Mrs Arkwright noticed I was unhappy. "What's the matter, dear?" she asked as I gave out her medicine.

I told her. She laid her hand on my arm and said, "My boy Jim in the last war sailed across the Atlantic like your husband and them U-boats got him. They're wicked things, Nurse. I still don't sleep for thinking about it."

That should have made me more depressed than ever but for some reason it cheered me. After that I regarded Mrs Arkwright as my own particular patient.

Days passed and I began to feel hope. Then another letter came. Paul and Anna had just left for school. I saw the House of Commons crest on the envelope and tore it open: this might be the great release.

Dear Mrs Vögler,

    I have now made full enquiries into the matter of which you advised me concerning your husband.

    My information is that there is sufficient evidence against him to render his continued presence in this country inappropriate, not to say undesirable. I regret I have to agree with the Home Office's assessment that the removal of your husband to internment in Canada is in the best interests of this country.

    I am of course sympathetic to your personal position: however, I have to remind you that the security of Great Britain and the British Empire must be our prime consideration.

Yours sincerely
Arthur P. Colgrove

So much for our wonderful member of parliament. How dare he say such things?

I was late into hospital again. The others looked at me angrily when I turned up and asked me why. I told them what the MP had said. Lucy Carter sniffed and said, "I'm not surprised," and Vera Phillips said, "Better safe than sorry." I really turned on her then. "Safe? What do you know about *safe*? Matthias's ship could be torpedoed and I'd be a widow."

"There'll be a lot of widows in this war and your Matthias's friends will cause most of them," said Gladys Carpenter.

I went to Mrs Ogilvie's office and asked for three days off.

That night I phoned my brother. "Ellie," said Jack, "Enid and I will drop everything and be with you tomorrow. My garage can look after itself. Besides, Jimmy Warner might appreciate a bit of help for a few days."

Jack and Enid never had children. I was sad about that, not only for them, but I wished ours could have had cousins. Now I was almost glad, because it meant they could come at once.

They arrived next evening. Jack didn't like driving long distances because of his false leg, so they came by train and arrived here on the bus.

"If I'd known, Jimmy would have met you at the station," I said.

"Don't worry, Ellie," Jack replied. "You've got too much to think about and Jimmy's got a garage to run."

"How long are you staying?" I asked.

"Why, are you counting the days already?" said Jack.

"Take no notice," said Enid. "We're here for as long as you like."

"I'm looking forward to giving Jimmy a hand," said Jack. "It will be quite an honour to work in a real Morris dealer."

"Don't be so sarcastic," I replied.

He wasted no time in getting to the point. "What are you going to do about Matthias?"

"What can I do? I did all I could by writing to that blasted MP."

"They're all the same," said Jack. "I don't trust any of them."

Next morning yet another letter came. The writing was unfamiliar and the envelope was postmarked DOUGLAS

IoM. I opened it. Hotel Metropole notepaper, like Matthias's letters. I was puzzled.

Dear Mrs Vögler,

I feel I must write to you after your husband's departure for Canada. I can give you one piece of good news. The SS Ettrick docked safely in Quebec yesterday.

I believe that a wrong decision was made about your husband. He explained clearly and eloquently his feelings about Hitler and Nazism. His words rang true with me, though the Home Office representative chose to ignore them.

I have an ever-changing group of men in my care, mostly refugees from Nazi Germany who in my opinion should not be interned at all. Many have endured intense hardship and danger to reach Britain. They e learned the hard way who to trust and who not o.

I have not heard the slightest doubt about your husband expressed by the two men who knew him best or by anyone else. He has been liked, respected and trusted and that is my considered opinion as his commanding officer.

I would like to see Matthias Vögler returned to this country. If I can do anything to help bring this about, rest assured I will.

Believe me, Mrs Vögler, I remain

Your obedient servant
Charles Frobisher (Major)
Commanding Officer

I put the letter down. "It's only words," I said.

"Don't be so sure," said Enid. "I've got a good feeling."

For the next week it was just good to have them there. Every day Jack went to the garage while Enid lent a hand round the house. The news was full of the war in the air and I couldn't stop thinking of Walter. Hundreds of German planes were shot down and hardly any of ours: that's what they kept telling us, but still the enemy came and now they were bombing London. On 15 September came the greatest air battle of all and for the first time we heard the phrase, "Battle of Britain". Next day was quiet, and the next. Slowly it began to dawn on us that perhaps it was over.

"Hitler won't invade now," said Jack. "His chance has gone. You mark my words. We've seen him off."

"Ellen," said Enid. "I've been thinking. You should go to London."

"What for?"

"You must get inside the Home Office, find the top men and tell them they're wrong and Matthias *must* come home."

"Enid, sometimes you can be really daft," Jack told her.

"I really wish I could," I said.

"It's the only way," Enid insisted. "Letters are no good. If you want to get anywhere you must talk to them face to face."

"Enid, my love," said Jack. "She wouldn't get near the door. The police would have her in the cells before you could say Jack Robinson."

"Where there's a will there's a way," Enid replied.

"If only there was," I said. "It would be a dream come true."

8.4

Enid's idea grew in my mind. Jack might be right and I'd end up in a police cell. But if I showed them Major Frobisher's letter then surely they'd take me to the top man and he'd say, "Yes, Mrs Vögler. We must take the word of an army officer. Your husband will be home soon."

I thought about it for three days and three nights until at last I said, "Enid, I'm taking your advice. I'm going to London."

"I'll come with you," said Enid. "You'll need moral support."

"Thank you, but I must do this on my own."

"Ellie," said Jack. "I've always supported you in anything you do. Whatever other people thought, I stuck my neck out for you. But please don't do this. It will bring you heartache and perhaps a lot worse."

"I'm going," I said. "I'll ring Mrs Ogilvie tonight and tell her I won't be in. I'll get a bus to Northampton and catch the eight twenty-nine train."

"At least let me drive you to the station," said Jack.

"No thanks. You'd only try to talk me out of it and

when you couldn't, you'd turn round and drive back with me still in the car."

"I wouldn't dare," Jack replied, smiling.

Next morning I caught the bus to the station and bought a return ticket to London. Posters plastered everywhere asked: IS YOUR JOURNEY REALLY NECESSARY? *Yes it is*, I thought to myself.

The platform was crowded. Goods trains kept passing through, long, slow, headed by panting engines, trucks piled high with coal, wagons with tanks and guns covered in green camouflage netting, parts of aeroplanes. 8.29 passed, then 9 o'clock. A porter chalked "8.29 to Euston cancelled" on a board. Everyone groaned. More passengers arrived. Half an hour later the porter came again, rubbed 8.29 out and changed it to 9.29. From then on he reappeared every hour: 10.29 cancelled, 11.29, 12.29, 1.29. I wondered if there was any point in going. At last his message changed. "2.29 45 mins late." A derisive cheer went up. If this had been peacetime there would have been a riot.

At last the train arrived: a black, grimy engine, eight shabby coaches. We piled in: people sat on strangers' laps, others wedged themselves between the seats. I preferred to stand in the corridor to get some air and was jammed in between a fat woman and a soldier. But it didn't matter – we were on our way.

The train was painfully slow, continually stopped by signals to let yet another goods train through. An hour went by before we reached Bletchley. At Leighton Buzzard we stopped for a full hour. I tried and failed to push my way along the corridor to the lavatory. Another half hour at

Berkhamsted. The fat lady next to me was getting in a state. "I said I'd be with my daughter Ivy in Clapham this afternoon," she wailed. "She'll be worried out of her mind."

The train lumbered off again and so did my thoughts. What am I going to do when I get there? You fool, Ellen Vögler. You've come all this way and you don't even know what you're looking for. Then I cheered up. The Home Office will be somewhere near the Houses of Parliament and you can get there on the tube.

We stopped again just short of Watford. Darkness was falling. "Listen," somebody said. The mournful sound of the air raid siren. Everybody was quiet. My urge to go to the lavatory was almost uncontrollable.

The train limped into Watford Junction and stopped. Porters passed along the platform shouting, "All change! All change!" We clambered out and looked up to see the sky criss-crossed with searchlights. We heard thunder of anti-aircraft fire, drone of bombers, the higher whine of night fighters. Sudden glows in the sky were followed by ominous rumbles. "London's getting another pasting," someone said.

A voice came over the loudspeakers: "Owing to enemy activity over London, all trains terminate here." I was stranded. But the fat lady had stuck with me. "My cousin lives nearby," she said. "She'll put me up tonight and if you're in a fix she won't turn you away." She wasn't so much fat as pleasantly plump with a kind and motherly face.

"Elsie Kibble," she said. "If Brenda won't take you in I'll make her life a misery. Her house is big enough for ten." After thankfully using the Ladies on the station, we went out into the dark streets.

We walked to the scream of planes, crump of anti-aircraft guns and dull roar of far-off explosions. Searchlight beams swayed like snakes in a charmer's basket and the sky to the south glowed orange. Elsie took me into a road lined with big houses. "Alexandra Road," she said. "Our Brenda's gone up in the world since she married her insurance salesman."

She stopped at a house halfway along, marched up the garden path and hammered on the front door. Nobody came.

"They're not in," I said.

"Nonsense," Elsie replied. "They're tucked up inside their Anderson shelter." She hammered again until the door opened.

"Hello, Brenda," said Elsie.

"Elsie, it's you," said Brenda. "I thought it was the warden to tell us we had a light on. What are you doing here?"

Elsie told her and introduced me. "We're stranded, Brenda," she said. "If you can't help us I don't know what we'll do."

"Come in," said Brenda. "We'll put up the camp beds."

The all-clear sounded soon after, so I had a night's rest after all. Next morning, only the electric trains which went the long way round were allowed into London. Euston station was an empty, eerie place.

"I'll leave you now, dear," said Elsie. "I'm off to the Northern line for Clapham, if it's running. Which line do you want?"

"I think I'll walk," I replied. So we said goodbye, two people who briefly came together and then drifted away, like so many in time of war.

Outside the station I saw buildings in ruins, walls torn away, furniture still clinging to floors jutting out into air, piles of rubble between buildings like decayed teeth, firemen hosing dying fires, ambulances, people swarming, a sort of ordered chaos. I'd seen terrible things in the last war but I'd never imagined this.

Except for a few red trams and buses, there was no traffic. I walked down Charing Cross Road to Trafalgar Square, Admiralty Arch and the beginnings of Whitehall. The Home Office must be near here. Sandbags to absorb the bomb blast protected the buildings. Armed soldiers guarded them and policeman patrolled outside. One saw me and said, "What are you looking for, madam?"

"Can you tell me where the Home Office is?" I asked.

"Why do you want to know?"

"I want to see someone there."

"Is he expecting you? Let me see your pass."

"I haven't got a pass."

"Then you've as much chance of getting in there as you would into Hitler's bedroom," he said. "You go back where you came from, or I'll run you in for obstruction."

I walked away, not caring where, feeling humiliated. Something drew me through little roads and alleys down to the Thames. The last time I'd seen it was twenty years earlier and now the memories of those times were strong. I walked eastwards towards St Paul's, whose great dome stood untouched by any bomb, found a bench, sat down and at once knew this was the very bench where I sat before I left for France in the last war – and now here I sat again in another war. Everything I was was because of war. But this new war had defeated me. I thought of Walter. He might be wounded: we'd never know. We'd only hear if he was killed. Paul would join the services before the war is over. Neither might survive.

And there's Matthias, another child of war who has been dealt a very bad hand. War does extreme things to people, some terrible, some, against all the odds, wonderful. And I had experienced both.

I had no idea how long I sat there. The sun had passed its zenith when I stood up stiff and cold and started the long walk back to Euston station. I was going home with nothing accomplished. But I was calmer and more content. So perhaps the day had been worth it after all.

The six o'clock train steamed out an hour late and took three hours to Northampton. I couldn't face walking to the bus station so I found a callbox to ring home. Jack answered. "I'm at the station," I said.

"Stay there," he answered. "I'm on my way."

Forty minutes later he pulled up in a large black saloon car. "It's a Riley 12/4," he told me, almost lovingly. "A beautiful car. A chap brought it in today. He didn't want to lay it up for the duration, he'd rather have the money. So we took it but God knows who'll buy it off us. There was just enough petrol in the tank to get here and back."

He helped me into the front passenger seat, got in the other side and drove off. "Well, how did you get on?" he asked.

I told him. "I won't say I told you so," he said. "But I

told you so. I'm really sorry. You had a wasted journey."

"No," I replied. "I learned a lot, about the war and about myself."

"Enid and I can't stay much longer," he said.

"Of course you must go," I told him. "You've got your own lives to lead. Besides, there's Ma and Pa to think of. Oh, Jack, I'd be down in Lambsfield tomorrow if it wasn't for Paul and Anna and the thought that I might hear something about Matthias."

"I know," he replied. "But your place is here. They understand."

We were home at eleven. Enid was waiting for us. "Have you eaten today, Ellen?" she asked.

I'd had nothing since morning and suddenly I was weak with hunger. "I've made some onion soup," said Enid. "I thought you might like some."

The soup was wonderful, like nectar, and two great doorsteps of bread filled me up completely. Then Jack poured glasses of sherry for me and Enid and opened a bottle of beer for himself. I was dead tired and by midnight I just couldn't keep awake. "Thank you so much," I said. "I have to go to bed."

I lay listening to the silence, feeling almost guilty about being in a place where no bombs fell while fifty miles away people died every night. But Matthias was three thousand miles away and I might never see him again.

"Damn this war," I muttered to myself. And then I was asleep.

8.5

Jack and Enid left two days later. Before they went, Jack said, "We've decided what to do about that Riley. We'll lay it up until Matthias comes back. It will be his welcome home present. I've left a crate of beer as well."

Not long after they left, a letter came from Matthias. He was in a Canadian internment camp in Valcartier, near Quebec and very unhappy. He was oppressed by surly guards, didn't get enough food and feared for his health and sanity. I sat down and wept.

As October passed into November, I felt lonely again but strong as well. The London Blitz got worse and at last the hospital received some of its victims. I had no time to mope because it was all so hectic.

It was the first week in November. When I got off the bus after early shift at the hospital two men stood outside our house. Strangers. One was well built, with a mane of black hair. The other was small and bespectacled, his thin hair a mousy brown. He wore a clerical collar. As I walked through the gate the big man cleared his throat and said, in a thick German accent, "Mrs Vögler?"

I stopped. "Yes," I answered. "Can I help you?"

"Allow me to introduce us. I am Wolfgang Eberstark. My friend here is Father Zeigler. We are refugees from Germany and friends of your husband."

"Of course," I said. "He wrote about you in his letters."

"May we come in?" asked Father Zeigler.

I brought them into the kitchen and made some tea. Father Zeigler said, "We're here to find out if you have any news of Matthias. Please forgive us if you have and it is bad."

"I've had one letter since he's been in Canada," I told him. "He's in a bad place. He's half starved and his guards are awful."

"I feared as much," said Father Zeigler.

"Why aren't you in your internment camp?" I asked.

"The authorities have seen fit to release us," said Father Zeigler. "We are as harmless as your husband," said Mr Eberstark. "He should have been released with us."

"Mr Eberstark…" I began.

"Wolfgang, please," he interrupted.

"Wolfgang, what can I do? I've even been to the Home Office to try and get him released."

"Mrs Vögler…"

"Ellen," I said firmly.

"Ellen, then. And my friend here is Gerhardt. Your husband was the best friend anyone could have. We went through a lot together."

"Much of which was thoroughly illegal," said Father Zeigler.

"Take no notice of him," said Wolfgang.

218

"Major Frobisher told me he would do anything he could to help," I said. "But that was a long time ago."

"The mills of God grind slow," said Father Zeigler.

"My children will be home from school soon," I said.

"Ah," said Wolfgang. "Paul and Anna. Matthias told us."

"Will you stay and have a meal with us?" I asked.

The two looked at each other. Then Wolfgang said, "Thank you, Ellen, but no. We've seen you, we have the latest news about Matthias and now we must go."

"Though they say we are released, we have been put in a hostel in Northampton. There is a curfew," said Father Zeigler.

"This is where you'll find us," said Wolfgang. "If you hear more, please tell us." He handed me a sheet of paper with an address on it.

When Anna and Paul came home I was almost happy. "I've got news for you," I told them. "Your father's friends have been here and told me all about him. And look, I have their new address."

"Why aren't they in camp?" Paul asked.

"They've been released," I said.

"That's not fair!" exclaimed Anna. "Why should poor Daddy suffer when they're set free?"

"I know," I answered sadly. "But that's how things are and I don't think there's much we can do about it."

The nights had drawn in. The Blitz continued as the first fogs and frosts of winter came. Not even the prospect of the school Christmas concert with Anna playing a violin solo could cheer me up. Then another letter postmarked DOUGLAS IoM arrived and again I tore the envelope

219

open with trembling hands.

```
Dear Mrs Vögler,
    I have been in touch with a number of
contacts in the Civil Service, especially in
the Home Office and Ministry of Information. I
enclose a pass which may be of use to you.
    May I suggest that you take it to London and
show it at the Home Office? The person I have
contacted will be expecting you.
    I wish you every good fortune for the festive
season and a happy outcome to your endeavours.

Yours sincerely,
```

Charles Frobisher

```
(Major)
```

There was another enclosure in the envelope. A card with HOME OFFICE embossed on it. Underneath was written:

```
Mrs E. Vögler
Please admit the above-named person who has an
appointment with Mr E. J. Varney (Room 106) at
2.30 p.m., November 15th.
```

The signature underneath was illegible. The card was stamped with a very official-looking crest. I read it once, I read it twice and my heart sank at the prospect of trying to get into the Home Office again. I just couldn't do it.

Then common sense took over. *You've been given a pass.*

Major Frobisher wouldn't go to all this trouble if he didn't think it was worth it. So stop snivelling and GO.

Fifteenth November was five days away. I wrote at once to Mr E. J. Varney, then to Wolfgang and Father Zeigler, and rang Jack and Enid. I went to bed feeling happier than I had for some months. But as soon as I closed my eyes I was assailed by gloomy thoughts. Suppose this Mr Varney does say Matthias can come home, he must cross the Atlantic. What if the ship's torpedoed? Wouldn't I be torn apart for the rest of my life, knowing that if I'd kept out of it he'd still be alive and home when the war ended? I'd be as good as signing his death warrant. But what would Matthias want? His last letter worried me and I was sure he'd rather risk the U-boats. Yes, I must go to London and plead for him.

Next morning over breakfast I told Paul and Anna. "I've got some news for you," I said.

"What is it, Mum?" asked Paul.

"I'm going to London again," I said. "I've got a pass into the Home Office to see a man who might help to bring your father home."

Paul stood up. "Wonderful," he cried. Anna stood up too, threw her arms round my neck and said, "Oh, Mum, let's hope he can."

"There's just one thing," I went on. "If Matthias is released he's got to cross the Atlantic and the U-boats might get him."

"It's war, Mum," said Paul. "You might get caught in an air raid on London and be killed. I think Dad will want to take his chance."

"But if he stays where he is he'll be safe until the war's

over and then he can come home."

"Yes, Mum," Paul replied. "If we win."

"Dad's got to try," said Anna. "He'd never forgive you if you had a chance to get him out and didn't take it."

"Do you mean that?" I asked.

"Yes," they said together.

They hadn't let me down. I had wonderful children.

We were very busy at the hospital: the huts were full of casualties from the Blitz. We had helpers now: a few retired nurses coming back and some rather snooty ladies, some of whom had been VADs in the last war. Snooty or not, they were doing a good job. Even so, I felt guilty when I asked Mrs Ogilvie for more time off. But she replied, "Of course, Ellen, you must go. We'll all be thinking about you."

"Please don't tell the others," I said.

"Why ever not?"

"Some of them think Matthias is in the right place. I don't want them saying 'Good job too' if this doesn't come off."

"My lips are sealed," she promised.

The next days crawled past. The clock ticking on the mantelpiece seemed to get slower. And then the day was here. The fifteenth of November.

I got up at 5.30 a.m. This time Jimmy took me to Northampton station and I was in time for the 7.29 a.m. We left only ten minutes late and hardly had a single stop for signals. At 9.30 a.m. we reached Euston.

* * *

I had four hours before seeing Mr Varney. Once again I walked through London, down Gower Street, Great Russell Street, Charing Cross Road, down to Trafalgar Square, where the old admiral looked down unharmed, along the Strand, further east all the time, Moorgate, Old Street, Great Eastern Street, Gracechurch Street, further on. Spitalfields, into the real East End, turning where impulse took me. Hoxton, Canning Town.

All the way I saw ruin, great gaps where houses, shops, offices once were and with every step my sadness mounted. Then the clock on a miraculously unscathed church struck one. I was due at the Home Office in ninety minutes, so I had to move fast. Buses were still running so I hopped on one and was back in Trafalgar Square by ten past two. Fifteen minutes later I was outside the Home Office. I waved my pass at anybody who looked official. And it worked. No chance of being carted off to the cells this time.

I was ushered up staircases and along corridors to room 106. I knocked and a voice said, "Enter."

I was in a huge, high-ceilinged room with big windows. Seated behind a vast desk was a youngish man, brown-haired, broad-shouldered, more like a footballer than a civil servant. He stood, came round to the front of the desk and shook my hand. "Edward Varney," he said.

"Ellen Vögler," I replied.

"Please sit down." He indicated a large leather-uphol-stered chair facing him across the desk. He had a folder in front of him stuffed with papers, all, I presumed, about Matthias.

"Mrs Vögler, this must be short because I have much to

do," he said. "But I assure you it will be fair and as thorough as I can make it. First of all, I have to come clean. In case you wonder why I take an interest in this case, it is because Major Frobisher is my uncle. However, that doesn't mean that I have to agree with him. He's told me about your husband and how his fellow internees, who have no reason to like any non-Jewish German, see him. But, Mrs Vögler, there's a great responsibility on you to show me why I should agree with my uncle."

"I understand," I replied.

"So why is he right and my colleague Mr Newton wrong?"

Heavens, where should I start? "Perhaps springing such a question on you is unfair," he said. He leafed through the papers and brought out some sheets held together with a paper clip. "These are the questions Mr Newton asked and his comments on your husband's answers. I'm going to ask you the same questions."

I remembered Matthias's letter telling me that Mr Newton didn't ask questions but made statements.

"First, would your husband have stayed in this country if he hadn't met you? Could he have gone home and become a Nazi?"

"How can I answer that?" I asked. "We've often talked about how we might have acted if circumstances were different. None of us can know. We met, married, were happy, that's all I can tell you."

"I see. Yet he frequently visited Germany, often without you and your children. Why was that?"

"Why shouldn't he go back to see his own flesh and blood? At first his family weren't pleased he'd settled here and in the beginning they didn't like me. That grieved him. I said it would be best if I didn't go."

"So you weren't party to what they discussed there?"

"What do you mean?"

"Might they not have convinced him of Nazi ideals, love of the Führer, racial purity, all that sort of thing?"

"All I can say is this. He always came back a little more disturbed and worried. He hated what he saw happening in his own country."

"Of course, he *would* tell you that, wouldn't he?"

"I know by now if my husband is lying."

"This is what Mr Newton wrote.

"In my opinion there was ample scope for Herr Vögler to become well acquainted with how the Germans were thinking and to see the subsequent rise of Hitler, so much so that he would be a highly likely candidate for espionage, treason or fifth column activity."

"What do you say to that?"

"I have never," I replied, "*never* in all the years I've been alive heard such ridiculous nonsense from a man supposed to be so wise that he is allowed to decide people's fates."

"I see," said Mr Varney and the ghost of a smile crossed his lips. "The next point. Your parents-in-law, your brother-in-law and his wife are all active Nazi sympathizers."

"I don't know that," I replied. "They're ordinary people. I don't think they have strong opinions. They go with the tide like most of us."

225

"But what about Helmut, your nephew? They seem very proud that he is in the Hitler Youth."

"So would I be if my son was in the Boy Scouts."

He looked at me quizzically. "Is that quite the same thing?"

"It is if you live in Germany."

He didn't answer, but turned a page of the dossier over. "This Helmut. He is so well thought of that he was presented to Hitler personally? How did his parents regard that?"

"Just as I would if my Paul were presented to the king."

"Mrs Vögler, can you honestly sit there and say it's the same?"

"Not to me and not to you. But it is if you live in Germany."

"What would you say if I told you it's my belief that your nephew is on the way to being a fanatical Nazi, probably a future SS man or worse?"

"I'd agree. I expect he is by now."

"You don't seem very worried about it."

"What can I do? He's not my child. This is what people think in Germany whether we like it or not – I can do nothing about it except feel proud that one of my sons is in the RAF and the other will join up when he's old enough. Helmut is German; my boys are English."

"I see. And which is your husband, Mrs Vögler?"

"I honestly don't think he puts nationality first. My brother Jack was in the army. He once said, 'Home is where your kitbag is.' Most old soldiers feel that and Matthias is an old soldier. His best friends from the internment camp have visited me. You said yourself that they're

226

refugees from the Nazis yet they had no doubts about Matthias."

He smiled again. "Neither has my uncle, Mrs Vögler." He looked at the dossier and said, "Why did you go to the Nazi rally?"

"It was their great day out. We were their guests. Of course we went with them."

He closed the folder and looked at me. "Shall I tell you what I keep hearing? Your own words. 'It is if you live in Germany.' Or that you would feel the same 'if my son was in the Boy Scouts,' or 'if my Paul were presented to the king' or 'it was their great day out.' Mrs Vögler, these are serious matters, not days by the seaside. Do you make no distinction between right and wrong?"

I was so shocked I couldn't breathe. When I'd recovered I said indignantly, "Of course I know the difference between right and wrong. What I see in Hitler is evil. I know it, you know it, Matthias knows it. It's just that there's always a little voice at the back of my mind that says that nobody can be entirely right and everybody else entirely wrong and another that asks me if I was there would I have the courage to stand up against it? If Hitler conquers us, I wonder how many of us will join the Resistance? Many French people will, but I bet a lot will do what the Germans tell them."

Once again he smiled. "You make your point," he said.

"Why don't you ask me what I thought of the rally?" I said.

"Very well, Mrs Vögler, what did you think of it?"

"It was horrible."

"Is that what your husband thought?"

227

"Yes."

"I gather your daughter had something to say about it."

"You mean the Lorelei story? How did you know that?"

"Your husband mentioned it at his appeal. My colleague discounted it completely but it made a big impression on my uncle."

"It put into words for Matthias what he felt. We were angry, of course we were, but we were sad too because this is Matthias's family; they're people we like."

He looked down at the dossier again, then looked up and nearly spoke. Then, as if making up his mind, he closed it and stood up. "Mrs Vögler ... Ellen," he said. "Thank you for coming today. Believe me, I shall do what I can, but I promise nothing. You understand that, I hope."

I stood as well and said, "Of course." Suddenly feeling almost embarrassed, I said, "Mr Varney, I want to thank you. You listened and you've been fair to me,"

"Thank you, Mrs Vögler," he said. "Let's hope for a good outcome." We shook hands again and I left the room.

8.6

I stood on the steps of the Home Office slightly dizzy. People surged around me about their business. Words, phrases, things Mr Varney said, things I said, jostled through my mind. Did I give the right answers or had I just made things worse? I imagined Mr Varney saying to Mr Newton, "You did a good job on that Jerry. After talking to his wife, I say that wherever you've sent him you'd better lose the key."

I walked slowly back to Euston, to find it in chaos with no trains arriving or leaving, except the electric trains to Watford. A rumour spread that there was bomb damage on the main line. I tried to push my way to a Watford train, but there was such a crush that I couldn't get near. I looked at my watch. 7.30 p.m. Night had settled in, cold, damp and misty. Ravenously hungry, I wandered the streets and found a Lyon's Corner House opposite St Pancras station. Soon I was sitting with a cup of tea and a round of toast and butter and began to feel better.

I finished my tea and found a public telephone box. But there was a long queue moving very slowly. Why couldn't they just say they were stranded for the night, put the phone down and let someone else have a go? One large man in particular went on and on and when someone tapped on the window he made angry gestures and seemed to go on talking out of spite.

At last he came out and strode away. The others seemed to take just as long. I looked at my watch again. Nearly 10.30 p.m. Now I was in deep trouble: with all these people looking for beds, what chance did I have?

My turn at last. I had the right change, dialled the operator, gave her the number, put the money in and waited while the phone rang. And rang and rang. Of course, the children would be in bed by now. But at last I heard Paul's voice. "Hello," he said blearily.

"The trains aren't running," I replied. "I'll have to stay here."

"Mum, what if there's an air raid?"

"I'll just have to deal with it."

"Be careful, please."

"The trains will run tomorrow. I'll be home when you come back from school."

"What was Mr Varney like?"

"He was all right. I'll tell you tomorrow. I must go: there are people waiting outside."

"Night, Mum." He sounded almost asleep.

I stepped out of the phonebox as a clock struck eleven. The chimes had hardly died away when the air raid warning started and the droning sounded high in the sky. Somehow I always thought that at moments like this people would panic. But no: everybody made purposefully off in one direction and I followed them to the tube station.

The procession down the stationary escalators was crowded but orderly. The Northern Line platforms were lined with camp beds. *If I don't get one, I won't mind,* I thought. *I'll sleep on the stone floor as long as I can be out of London in the morning.* But I did find an empty bed and no sooner had I sat on it than a familiar voice said, "Fancy seeing you here." I looked round to see who spoke.

"It's me, Elsie Kibble. Don't you remember me and my sister in Watford? You've surely not been in London all this time?"

"No," I replied. "I only came down this morning."

She chuckled. "You won't be going back tonight, that's for sure."

"What are you doing here?" I asked.

"Me? I'm too nice for my own good, I am," Elsie replied. "I've been to my daughter in Clapham again. Honestly, she only has to crook her little finger and I'm down there. Still, mustn't grumble, it's nice to have someone who wants to see you. What brings you here again, dear?"

I told her and waited for her to say, "If you ask me, your husband's in the best place. We don't want his sort here."

But she didn't. "I do hope it all works out for you, dear," she said. At that moment a huge explosion sounded close overhead and the platforms and tunnels shook. "And I hope you get home to enjoy it when it does," she continued, quite imperturbably.

Before the explosion there had been ragged attempts to sing Cockney songs: "Any Old Iron", "Knees Up Mother Brown" and the like. They didn't catch on, though when

231

somebody started with Vera Lynn's songs "There'll Be Bluebirds Over The White Cliffs of Dover" and "We'll Meet Again", people joined in more enthusiastically. But after the explosion there was a profound silence. "If we're trapped, this will be our tomb," I heard someone say.

Voices yelled at him to shut up. The singing died away. We waited, silent and tense. Elsie whispered, "These people get this every night. Beats me how they put up with it."

There were more explosions during the night, more distant than the first. Then there was silence. The minutes ticked away. "It's got to be over," said a man a few beds down from me. "I'll go up and look."

When he came back, he said, "Don't worry, we can get out. But they've made a right mess of Euston station."

It was half past two. "Let's go," I heard someone say.

"I'm staying here, dear," said Elsie. "I can have a real good kip."

I was torn. I was a nurse, I might be able to help people, it was my duty to go... But it was pure accident that I was here and there was something more important to go home for... Yes, but what if this was a test? If you help, then you'll get Matthias back: if you don't, you'll never see him again. I had to go: there wasn't a choice.

I climbed the steps, dreading what I might find. The stationary escalators seemed like mountain slopes. I reached the top at last and followed the MAINLINE STATION signs. Euston had suffered a direct hit. I saw police, air raid wardens, firemen, smouldering fires. In the lurid arc lights I saw that the great glass roofs had been smashed, the platforms couldn't be reached for huge piles of rubble and wardens were pulling brick after brick away, looking for survivors. No trains would leave this station for a long time to come. But that didn't matter now. I saw broken bodies brought out of the rubble and knew that I had to get to work straight away. I looked around for someone in charge. An air raid warden, a big man in a black uniform and tin hat, was directing operations.

"I'm a nurse," I said. "Can I help?"

"Thanks, miss," he replied. "Dr Black over there, he's the man you want." He pointed to a tall, thin man bending over bodies on stretchers. "Looks like he needs you."

So I hurried over to him and said, "Dr Black?"

He didn't even look up. "Who wants him?" he grunted.

"I'm a nurse. I want to lend a hand."

"This isn't like your comfortable hospital," he said.

"I was a nurse in France in the last war."

At last he looked up. "Were you now?" he said. "Then you should know what you're doing." Not much of a compliment, but at least he seemed glad of my help. "Nurse," he went on, then stopped. "That's no good, we're not in hospital now, I need to know your name."

I told him and he said, "Well now, Ellen, have a look at the chaps over there, will you, please?"

There were about twenty, some on stretchers, others on improvised mattresses made out of cushions from the waiting rooms. It was the start of a night that I'll never forget, trying to comfort men and women in deep shock, who had limbs broken or crushed, who needed sedation to stay alive until ambulances struggled through to take them to overloaded hospitals for surgery and proper care.

There was one man in particular. He wore a railwayman's uniform, one leg was crushed and he had been brought out only semi-conscious. Now his eyes were open and he could talk, but I knew he needed morphine before shock set in. "'Ello, love," he whispered when he saw me. "I've gone and done it to myself this time."

"You'll be all right," I said, with more optimism than I felt.

"What's your name then? I'm Bert."

"Ellen," I answered.

"Well, Ellen, how come I've never seen you here before?"

"It's a long story," I said.

"Mine's not," he replied.

"You remind me of my father," I said, and meant it — and not just because of the uniform. "He was a signalman."

"What, on the London, Midland and Scottish?"

"No, the old London, Brighton and South Coast."

"Main line fifty miles long? That wasn't a proper railway. Ours is four hundred. Still, signalman — good job that."

"What do you do?"

"Wheel tapper, aren't I. I shouldn't be working tonight — if there's no trains, there's no bleedin' wheels to tap, that's what I tried to tell them. But they put me on other duties and now look what's happened to me. Still, if I did go home I'd probably find we'd been bombed out."

"I'm sure you wouldn't," I said.

He suddenly reached up and took my hand. His whisper became hoarse and urgent. "But I won't be going home, will I? Don't try and tell me different because I'm not daft; they should have let me go home when I asked. I did ask,

234

Ellen, honest I did."

I squeezed his hand. He looked more like Pa than ever. He shuddered suddenly and his hand dropped.

"Dr Black, he needs morphine!" I called and he came running.

He lifted Bert's arm and felt his wrist. "He needs nothing," he replied. "He's gone," and covered his face with the blanket he lay on.

Bert's death, so much like hundreds of deaths I saw at Abbeville, made me feel very low. For a moment, I was back in the tents, seeing never-ending lines of shattered soldiers brought in and unable to do anything but watch them die. But Bert wasn't a soldier, he was an ordinary man, and not a young one either, going about his ordinary job. I remembered the hosts of people scurrying up and down Whitehall and wondered how many would come to work tomorrow. I felt a cold chill: what if Mr Varney was killed in the raid and today had been for nothing?

I soon fell into the routine that was my life twenty years ago. At eight o'clock, when the worst was over, I went to Dr Black and said, "I'm sorry. I must go home. My children are waiting."

He stood there, tall, dishevelled, hollow-eyed. "Of course you must," he said and shook my hand. "Goodbye, Ellen, and thank you."

"I thought I'd find you here," a familiar voice said. I turned round and there was Elsie Kibble. "I've been looking for you to tell you there are trains to Watford up the Metropolitan line from Baker Street."

Two hours later we were sitting companionably together on the slow journey north out of Watford. When we came

235

to Bletchley and she got off I was sorry to say goodbye.

At two o'clock I let myself into the house and flopped exhausted on the sofa before having a bath and going to bed. The next thing I knew was the front door opening. They were back and I'd had two hours' sleep.

"Crikey, Mum, you look worn out," said Paul.

"Sit down," said Anna. "Let me get you something."

"A cup of tea would be nice," I said.

"When did you last eat?" she asked.

"I don't know. So much has happened that I can't remember."

"I'll scramble some eggs," said Anna. "Two for you."

"Anna, that's the whole of our week's ration."

But the tea and scrambled eggs worked wonders and soon I had recovered enough to tell them about my extraordinary time in London.

"So is Dad coming home or not?" asked Anna when I'd finished.

"I wish I knew," I replied. "I wish I knew."

8.7

Over the next few days, I went over my time with Mr Varney again and again. Could I have done better? Then I thought of Bert and how his hand went limp and Dr Black saying, "He needs nothing. He's gone." But most of all I kept wanting, praying for, news about Matthias.

A week afterwards, Paul said, "Can I have a word, Mum?"

"Of course," I replied.

"Well, I've been thinking. I'm going to join up when I leave school. I know you want me to go to university and I will – when the war's over."

I felt very sad. "Are you sure about this?"

"Yes, Mum," he replied. "I'm determined on it. If I volunteer, it will save me being called up whether I want to or not. And I won't join the RAF or the Navy. It will be the army."

"Oh no, Paul," I said. "Not the army." So many disturbing thoughts came to mind. Jack without a leg and suicidal, Matthias nearly bleeding to death, soldiers at Dunkirk wading out to sea while German planes strafed them with machine guns.

"Why not? Dad was a soldier even if he was on the other side and when his turn came he didn't hold back. And Uncle Jack – you said he volunteered in the first week of the war."

"Nobody knew what it would be like then. Anyway, you've got two years to change your mind in. The war might be over by then."

"Mum," said Paul, looking at me sadly. "If the war's over in two years, it's because we've lost it. Winning will take longer than that."

"I wish your father were here. He'd make you change your mind."

"I'd like to see him try."

He was right. Matthias wouldn't try to stop him, simply because he was German. He would accept that Paul was English through and through. I thought of Paul and Helmut climbing the tree, how long ago it seemed.

"Anyway, I don't have to be in the infantry like Dad and Uncle Jack," Paul continued.

"I can't see you driving a tank."

"I wouldn't know how to. But there's one thing I can do that they'll want. I speak German like a native. I could pass for a German."

"Paul," I cried. "Surely you don't want to be a spy?"

"Why not? I'd be a good one. I've even got a German name so I wouldn't have to remember a false one."

"But that's worse than the infantry. You'd be living a lie, always trying not to be caught out; you could be captured and tortured by the Gestapo and then they'd shoot you."

"People volunteer to go into enemy territory and come

back OK so why not me? But I don't have to. There are lots of ways to be useful."

"Such as?"

"I don't know yet. But I'll find out. Anyway, Mum, there's no point in trying to talk me out of it, I'm joining up and that's final."

I took him at his word and didn't mention it again.

The weeks passed. No word came from Mr Varney. Days at the hospital continued as normal. The Blitz went on. No news came in to cheer us up. Everyone felt resigned and hopeless. Mr Churchill made stirring speeches about fighting them on the beaches, airfields and everywhere else, and never surrendering. As he spoke we felt uplifted and brave, but then next day's news came and everything went flat.

Winter arrived. The days passed like leaden footsteps. Every morning was the same: up early, get the children off to school (but they're *not* children now: they're nearly grown up), catch the bus to Wicester and thank God that Mrs Ogilvie never asked me to work a weekend.

Christmas was nearly here. I couldn't look forward to it. People would die this Christmas. I wouldn't put it past the Luftwaffe to drop bombs on Christmas Day itself.

A week before Christmas, I caught the 6.20 p.m. bus home. The lower deck was full but the top deck looked empty so I climbed the stairs.

Yes, empty, except for a man sitting in the front seat. The conductor came upstairs. "Fares please," he called. I held out my sixpence. "Peterspury," I said and he handed

239

me my ticket.

The man at the front must have paid already. The conductor went straight downstairs. The bus came down the High Street and stopped outside the Greyhound, the old coaching inn. Nobody came upstairs.

The bus started. I kept looking at the man's head. At any other time I would have thought ... no, surely it couldn't be. Could it?

This was suddenly, weirdly, like that far-off day when Jack took me to the football match in Lambsfield. I stood up, walked tentatively forwards and sat two seats behind the man. Then I said, loud enough for him to hear if he wanted but soft enough for him to ignore, "Matthias?"

He turned. He too must have remembered that long-ago day because his face split into a broad smile as he said, "*Schwester Ellen!*"

I stepped off the bus still in a dream. This couldn't have happened, it was a hallucination. "It's true, my love. It's really me," he said. When he saw the house he leant on my shoulder and tears streamed down his face. "I never thought I'd see my home again," he said.

When we opened the front door, I called, "Look who's here," and Paul and Anna rushed to him.

When we had calmed down I made a meal and brought out the beer that Jack had left. Then we sat down together, looking at each other, still amazed. "I don't know what to say," began Matthias. "I've dreamed of this moment every night." He opened a bottle, poured himself a glass and said. "Pure happiness."

"Why didn't you tell us you were coming?" I asked.

"I didn't know," he replied. "One moment I was looking at years in that godforsaken place, the next I was called in to the CO and told to pack my things. He said I could send a telegram but I wouldn't."

"Why not?" I asked.

"When we sailed to Canada, two ships left Liverpool. One was torpedoed and sank with no survivors. I was on the other. With odds like that, I wouldn't put you through the agony of waiting."

We were all silent. Then Paul said, "Well, Dad, we're all safe and still alive. So if you don't mind I'll pinch a bottle of your beer."

"You drink what you like," said Matthias.

"By the way," said Paul. "There's a coming home present for you in the garage from Jimmy and Jack."

Among the Christmas cards was one from Mr Varney.

"I hope you are pleased with your early Christmas present,"

it said.

January 1941–
June 1943

HELMUT IN CRISIS

9.1

As 1941 dawned, Helmut was full of doubt. Since he joined the Hitler Youth he'd been consumed with ambition to join the *Waffen SS*: Hitler's elite, the sharp edge of Nazism, the world's most feared fighting men.

But he knew that the SS did other things besides fight. Mass shootings of *Untermenschen*, setting up concentration camps, ruthless carrying out of the Führer's will. Whatever the Führer wanted must be right, so he had always thought, and to bring it about had been his bounden duty. But when Frau Lindemann showed him Lotte's death certificate (the cause of death was "breathing difficulties") and said, "I know it's all for the best," he couldn't tell her what he was supposed to: "That's very true, Frau Lindemann. The Führer is always right, however hard it seems."

He hated to think that the Lindemanns might know the truth in their hearts. It was all right to believe that misfits, degenerates and cripples should be liquidated – as long as you didn't know them. But he'd known Lotte all her life. He remembered when she was born and sympathetic neighbours rallying round to help. A future SS man should say, "It is for the greater good of the Reich that she should die." He tried to say it himself, every night before he went to bed. But the moment he was asleep, a little voice said, "Admit it, Helmut. You don't believe it any more."

In April Lothar came home on leave, resplendent in his new SS uniform. "Haven't you joined us yet, Helmut?" he asked heartily.

"I'm not eighteen till next year," said Helmut. "I don't know if I'll be good enough."

"Of course you will," Lothar replied. "You're ideal."

"What's it like in the SS?"

"You've no idea how wonderful it is to carry out the Führer's will in the purest way possible," said Lothar.

"How do you do that?"

"I can't tell you: we have many secrets. But if I say that the world must be cleared quickly and cleanly of Jews and *Untermenschen*, you may understand what I'm talking about."

Helmut did, all too clearly.

"I'll let you into a secret," said Lothar. "The Führer is planning a great invasion, the most audacious campaign the world has ever seen. I think you'll guess where."

"Is it…?" Helmut began, but Lothar leant forward and touched his lips with his finger. "Sssh. Don't say it," he said. "Just think it."

So Helmut thought. *Russia.*

"There," said Lothar, smiling. "I knew you'd get it. I can read minds, you know. Something else the SS taught me."

"Are you in a Panzer brigade?" Helmut asked. "I think that's what I want to do, be in tanks."

"No," said Lothar. "I can't tell you my unit. But think of Jews and *Untermenschen* and you'll have a pretty good idea. It's noble work, Helmut. One day there'll be a final solution to this problem. You mark my words."

"Yes," said Helmut. If Lothar had any inkling of his doubts, he'd report him. He didn't dare think of what might happen then.

On 22 June, the invasion started. Operation Barbarossa. The German army swept east into Russia and nothing could stop them. The Führer was already master of Europe and soon he would rule Moscow as well. In spite of his doubts, Helmut was thrilled. All that counted was Germany's triumph.

Now he knew what he wanted. No death squads, no "final solutions". *I want to fight, cleanly and gloriously*, he told himself. *I want to command my tank and sweep across the Russian steppes. I shall volunteer for the Wehrmacht.*

He'd be eighteen in March. But he wouldn't wait for compulsory call up: he'd go when Christmas was over. It might be his last Christmas at home and he wanted something good to remember.

In October, Lothar was home again.

"You get a lot of leave," said Helmut.

"The SS has privileges," Lothar replied.

"How's the war going?"

"Everything you read is true," said Lothar. "We're breaking up the Soviets as if they are children's wooden bricks."

"Tell me about the battles you've been in," said Helmut eagerly.

"My work is more important than mere battles," said

Lothar. "It's my SS group that is clearing the land of lesser people to make it fit for Germans to live on. Russia is fertile and rich with oil. Much too good for the Russians."

"So you aren't actually fighting," said Helmut.

"Some people hack down the undergrowth, others are privileged to prepare the soil," Lothar replied enigmatically.

Helmut decided he didn't want Lothar as a friend any more.

Christmas passed, not quite as happy as the one before. Everyone knew that the Russian campaign wasn't going as well as Dr Goebbels made out. Helmut wasn't too worried. A new generation of troops was taking the field and he was one of them. All would be well.

He joined the Wehrmacht in January, two months short of his eighteenth birthday and volunteered for the Panzer corps. Because of his Hitler Youth record he was at once sent for officer training.

At last, in late 1942, as Germany digested the news that the great Desert Fox, Erwin Rommel, the general Helmut admired most, had been defeated by Montgomery at El Alamein, simply because the Afrika Korps didn't have enough tanks, Herr *Leutnant* Vögler, H, who now knew as much about tanks as anyone, took his place in the Grossdeutschland Panzer Division to play his part in the great Russian campaign.

9.2

June 1943. Here he was, only nineteen, commanding a Tiger tank and already a veteran. You grew up quickly on the eastern front. He'd endured a Russian winter, when men sleeping under their tanks froze to death in the night. He'd seen good men die in the inferno of a stricken tank. He knew every detail of the heroic struggle for Stalingrad, the noblest German sacrifice of the war. A whole army fighting to the last man. True Nazi philosophy. Nonetheless, he thought but didn't dare say, it wasn't very sensible. If Hitler had let the army withdraw they'd be here now, for this battle about to start would decide the war in the east. Winner takes all.

Lothar's remarks about breaking Russia up like children's bricks were true. Ruin on all sides: sullen people, skeletons of houses, unburied and decaying bodies, mass graves. Helmut knew the SS had summarily shot thousands: he had a recurrent nightmare of a bullet in the back of the neck and the victim tumbling into the grave he had dug himself. Sometimes Lothar gave the order: sometimes, when the dreams were at their worst, he did. If ever he had to, he'd do his duty, but he would hate it. This regimented death was wrong. Though if anyone guessed what he was thinking, he'd probably be shot himself.

He loved his Tiger tank and knew every inch of its mighty frame. He happily got his hands dirty with the mechanics when it needed repair. Often he spotted problems before the trained men did.

The tank squadron waited for the order to move. His heart beat fast: this would be the Reich's most vital battle of the war. Win it and the whole war was won. Lose, and … but they would not lose. They were stronger and their tanks were better. The battle of Kursk would start tomorrow and it would be swift and devastating.

Helmut was proud of being called tank commander. But he knew who was really in charge. *Unteroffizier* Rudi Durkheim, fifty if he was a day but still in the front line because he knew more about tanks than the rest of the brigade put together. Helmut depended on his wise counsel.

That night, strange news sped round the division. Hitler was sending two precious Panzer brigades to Sicily. It seemed that the British and Americans had invaded and threatened to run through Italy. Helmut couldn't believe his ears. Who cared about Sicily and Italy? *This* was the battle that mattered. He was beginning to doubt Hitler's judgment. But he drew back from the brink just in time. *Doubt the Führer*, he thought, *and there's nothing left.*

Next morning. Helmut waited in his tank, sweeping the wide steppe to its horizons with his binoculars. Rudi was by his side.

"What do you see, Herr *Leutnant?*" he asked.

"Barbed wire, tank traps," said Helmut. "T-34 tanks, hundreds of them. Why? We're supposed to be taking them by surprise."

"We don't take the Russians by surprise any more," said Rudi.

"Rudi, you're a pessimist. Our Tigers are better than their T-Thirty-fours."

"Are they now?" Rudi replied. Helmut noted his sarcasm.

The order came. The Tigers moved forward. Overhead, formations of Stuka dive bombers screamed down on the enemy. The titanic battle of Kursk, the greatest tank battle of all time, commenced.

June–December
1943

TAIL-END CHARLIE

10.1

Walter, or Sergeant Vögler as he now is, stands in a hangar at No. 26 Bomber Command Operational Training Unit, RAF Little Horwood in Buckinghamshire. Horwood is only fifteen miles from Peterspury but he has no intention of visiting. He has fulfilled the vow he made at Biggin Hill and remustered as aircrew. Now he is a fully trained rear gunner, a tail-end Charlie. Today they are crewing-up for flying training. By evening he will be part of a six-man bomber crew who will fly together and may die together.

It's a hit-and-miss affair, this crewing up. Pilots look for navigators, gunners for radio operators, everyone wants good bomb-aimers but most of all they crave a good skipper.

Walter loved his gunnery training. Sitting in a turret and firing at moving targets was seventh heaven. The targets were, of all things, his beloved clay pigeons. But here he had four Browning .303 machine guns and could blow them to dust. It beat Harry Brindley's shotguns any day.

Now the honeymoon is over. Rear turrets are only one

part of a bomber and he must find out about the rest. Most of what the RAF knows about bombing is copied from the Luftwaffe in the Blitz, while the Luftwaffe copied the flak and nightfighter tactics from the RAF. It's a funny old war, Walter sometimes thinks.

Apart from other gunners he knows nobody. He should have hung a notice round his neck:

REAR GUNNER NEEDS GOOD CREW.

Then he sees a completely unexpected figure. "*Mikey!*" he yells joyfully.

"Bloody hell, it's you, young Wally," says the familiar Liverpool voice and they pump each other's hands delightedly.

"What are you doing here?" cries Walter.

"I was going to ask you that," says Mikey.

"I got fed up with being bombed and shot at. I thought I'd do the bombing and shooting myself," Walter tells him. "What about you?"

"They made me i/c stores," Mikey answers. "Asking for trouble. I tried to sell two RAF lorries to Bedouin tribesmen in Egypt and thought I'd better get out before I was found out. So I volunteered for aircrew and now I'm a bomb-aimer."

"I don't believe you," says Wally.

"Of course I'm a bloody bomb-aimer," says Mikey.

"No, I don't believe you sold lorries to Bedouins."

Mikey smiles his familiar smile. "Think what you like, young Wally," he says. "But I'm here without a stain on my character, and that's a miracle. So I'm raring to drop a few bombs on the Jerries, to pay them back for what they did to the 'Pool.'"

"We'll stick together," says Walter. "I wish we'd got a notice to say we don't want to be split up."

"Funny you should say that," says Mikey. "I've been waiting for a use for this." He goes to the wall and Walter notices a large piece of wood painted black leaning against it. Mikey produces a stick of chalk from a trouser pocket and scrawls on it:

REAR GUNNER AND BOMB-AIMER, FULLY HOUSE TRAINED, SEEK GOOD SKIPPER ABLE TO KEEP THEM ALIVE.

"That should bring 'em running," he says.

For some time it doesn't. Then a tall man with a lean, tanned face and wearing the uniform of a flight lieutenant comes over and drawls, "My oh my, exactly what I'm looking for."

Walter and Mikey snap to attention and whip up smart salutes. "Sir!" they bark together.

"We're all in this together, so 'sir' isn't what I want to hear," says the flight lieutenant.

"Excuse me, sir," says Walter. "Are you Canadian?"

"What did I just ask you?"

"All right, excuse me but are you Canadian?"

The officer laughs. "Canadian? No insults, please. I'm from the good old US of A."

"Why aren't you flying B-Seventeens then?" asks Mikey quite truculently.

"Look, boys," he replies, "I joined the RAF long before

Uncle Sam entered the war. I guess it seemed a good idea at the time. When the USA came in I could have transferred but I kinda like you guys. By the way, Chauncey's the name, Chauncey Stevenson the Second. Before you ask, Chauncey Stevenson the First is my father."

The way he pronounces his name sounds to Walter like "Chancy". He isn't sure he likes the idea of a skipper called "Chancy". "That's a funny name," he says daringly.

"It was the name of a famous president of Harvard University," is the reply. "My grandfather was at Harvard so he gave it to my father and he handed it onto me. I suppose he hoped I'd go there."

"But you came here instead. You must be off your rocker," says Mikey. Walter nudges him, "Don't push your luck," he mutters.

Chauncey Stevenson the Second laughs. "You're probably right. My father's a doctor but I didn't want to follow him. I told him I wanted to be a flyer and he said we'd be in the war soon so I'd get my chance. No, I said, that was no dice, I'd do like a lot of other Americans and join the RAF. 'Son,' he said. 'The British are good people. I worked in one of their hospitals in the last war and saw them do wonderful things. So go, and take my blessing with you.' Mom didn't like it, but he soon calmed her down."

Walter nearly says something, but decides against it.

"I've done one tour of duty in Halifaxes," Chauncey continues. "Now I'm converting to the Lanc."

Walter is impressed, "A whole tour? Not many survive thirty missions."

"I know. But I did," says Chauncey.

258

"You must have the luck of the devil," Mikey tells him.

"Luck nothing. I survive because I'm a damn good flyer. Boys, put your trust in me and you won't go wrong. Don't say yes straight away. Talk about it among yourselves."

They withdraw a few yards away and mutter to each other. "He can't get through another tour, his luck has to run out," says Walter.

"He knows what he's doing," Mikey replies. "Some pilots in this room hadn't even *seen* a plane this time last year."

"True," says Walter. They go back over and Mikey says, "Suits us, sir."

"What did I tell you just now?" says Chauncey. But he's smiling as he says, "Shake on it. There, we're nearly half a crew already."

They need a navigator, top gunner, flight engineer and wireless operator. An hour later they have them and Chauncey makes out the full list.

Pilot and skipper – F/O Chauncey Stevenson II

Navigator – P/O Arthur Bryant

Flight engineer – W/O Bill Warren

Bomb-aimer – Sergt Mikey Kennedy

Wireless operator – Sergt George Willis

Mid-upper gunner – Sergt Alf Jones

Rear gunner – Sergt Wally Vögler

"This," says Chauncey, "will be the best goddam crew in all the Allied air forces. And it will need to be."

The twin-engined Wellington bomber is a remarkable aeroplane. Walter loves the way the fuselage is made as a honeycombed mesh of aluminium. Geodesic construction, it's called and makes the plane amazingly strong. Sometimes it's called "the cloth bomber" because it's covered with canvas. But it's known mainly as the Wimpy, after a character in the Popeye cartoons. It's not much used for front-line bombing now Lancasters and Halifaxes have taken over. This is why so many are on Operational Training Units, flown by people not quite sure yet about what they are doing.

For Walter and Mikey the Wellington is for tomorrow. First, they have much to tell each other over pints of beer in the sergeants' mess.

"Do you ever see Doreen?" Walter asks.

"You're well out of that, mate," Mikey replies. "She's got herself lumbered with a sprog by some Yank soldier. Serves the daft cow right. You don't still fancy her, do you?"

"Not a chance," says Walter. "I only thought of her when I saw you. I've got better fish to fry than Doreen."

"Tell me all, mate."

"Her name's Julie. She's a Waaf I met at Biggin Hill. She's a bit of all right is Julie. No, she's more than that, she's wonderful."

"Got it bad, have you, young Wally?"

"You could say that."

Walter speaks flippantly, but he knows he has got it bad, very bad indeed. Thoughts of Julie rule his life. She's now at Fighter Command headquarters at Bentley Priory, north of London. They write to each other every day. They make their leaves coincide and go to a cheap no-questions-asked hotel in Yarmouth, where Julie puts on the Woolworth's ring he bought and they sign in as Mr and Mrs Smith. Not that the hotel staff are fooled. But these are days of fleeting unions and sudden death.

"I hope she knows you're not in a job with what you might call a secure future," says Mikey.

"Julie knows the score," Walter replies. "But I might get away with it. Someone has to."

"I hope you're right," says Mikey. "If you go west, I go too."

"What about you?" asks Walter. "Any joy on the woman front?"

"Me?" Mikey replies. "I play the field. I thought we might go out on the pull now and again."

Just for a moment, Walter is tempted, then thinks of Julie looking at him reproachfully and says, "No, I'd better not."

"Well, if you're spoken for I'll have to go on my own, though if there's Yanks around I haven't got a chance in hell."

Walter swigs at his beer. He is very happy. He has his sergeant's stripes, he lives in the comfort of the sergeants' mess, tomorrow is his first flight as a tail-end Charlie with a skipper he trusts and, best of all, he's met up with his old mate. Whatever fate is his will be Mikey's also.

10.2

Walter, in flying suit, boots and helmet, strides out with the crew to the Wellington parked on a concrete apron. It may be old and clapped out, but it still looks sleek and sinister. The undersides of the wings and fuselage are black: this is a plane of the night.

Inside, it is very cramped. They take their positions. Mikey lies face down on a mattress in the nose, where he can see the whole panorama below him. He has three jobs: observer, front gunner when he needs to be, but most importantly he will spot the target and let the bombs go at what he hopes will be the right moment. Walter is slightly envious: Mikey is always busy while he must wait until he sees the enemy. Also, Mikey sees where they're going. Walter only sees where they've been.

Walter enters the Frazer-Nash hydraulically-operated rear gun turret. He has sat in such things many times before. But being actually attached to the rear of a real bomber is a different matter. His parachute is stowed on the other side of the turret doors. Now that he sees what it means in practice, his heart sinks. How can he get it if the plane is hit? He really is the tail-end Charlie, with the emphasis on the "Charlie". Yanks would call him "the fall-guy". He'll have as much chance of getting out as Harry Brindley would of becoming a fighter ace.

Still, the Frazer-Nash turret is a pretty smart affair. He can point his four guns up, down and sideways. He can make the turret rotate. He has an amazingly wide field of fire. "Not bad," he says to himself.

Before they board the aircraft, Chauncey briefs them. This is a real boost: unlike the other pilots, Chauncey knows what it's all about. The crew walks out jauntily while the rest slouch apprehensively.

The two Bristol Hercules engines burst into life. The mechanic in him listens and decides they've seen better days. The Wellington moves clumsily onto the runway, jangling over the asphalt like a tin bath full of cans. Then faster and faster, until Walter sees the runway as a blur, there are no tin cans any more, and the Wellington is free and in its proper element at last.

This will be the first of many flights by day and night: fighter affiliates, where they learn tactics against fighters and Walter shoots them down with photographs, not bullets; bombing practice so Mikey can drop bombs without explosives. Sometimes they fly over Peterspury: he looks down and sees the straight gash of the A5, the turning to Peterspury, the church, the Crooked Billet, even Vögler's Garage. He imagines Mum hearing the Wellington and looking up with no idea that he's looking down on her. "It's the nearest I'll be coming," he mutters to himself.

Gradually, guided by the experienced hand of Chauncey, they begin to work as a crew. Walter is thankful for him. Other Wellingtons are lost. One ploughs into a row of houses in a nearby town, killing the crew and ten sleeping civilians. Another hits a power line and crashes into a wood. With Chauncey they are spared such fates.

During the long hours Walter spends in the sky, he considers many things. He thinks of Julie and feels a warm glow. Then his thoughts turn to Peterspury. At least he has written to them saying what he is doing. He knows his father is home, that Paul volunteered for the army and hasn't taken up his place at university. "What good is he to the army?" he asks himself. "He's scared of his own shadow." As far as Anna is concerned, well, if she wants to be a musician then good luck to her, as long as she doesn't expect him to listen. But Mum… In spite of their great row the last time he was at home, she's the one he wants to see. If his father wasn't back he might have gone there and taken Julie. Now there's no chance.

His thoughts always end there because it's now that the fighters come to show them what it's like in battle: Spitfires are flown by pilots out for relaxation and harmless fun in between combat duties. They appear from nowhere, buzz round like angry bees, pass so close that he can almost smell the Brylcreem on the pilots' hair. He shoots at them and hopes there aren't too many pictures of empty sky.

Some new gunners are scared of fighter affiliation. Not Walter. He revels in it. The photos show he would have downed well over half.

Their time in Wellingtons is nearly over. Soon they will be posted to RAF Langar, near Nottingham, to the Heavy Conversion Unit and meet the Lancaster. But there is one last hurdle to cross. They must make a proper operational mission, so they know what it feels to risk being shot at with live ammunition.

Walter doesn't like the sound of it. He's always known the training has a sharp end: he just hoped it would be delayed a bit longer. They are to fly east, rendezvous with Wellingtons from other OTUs and set out over the North Sea with a big load to drop. Not bombs. Instead, thousands of metallic, silvery strips which would make wonderful paperchains for Christmas decorations. They are called, Walter has no idea why, "window". If you drop enough they jam the German radar so that they won't spot the bomber fleets on their way to Cologne, Berlin or wherever, though they may mistake the Wellingtons for the main force.

Walter doesn't like this. If the Germans think a bunch of half trained chumps who don't know what they're doing (except Chauncey of course) is the main force, won't they send up all their fighters? The nearer he gets to enemy territory the more uncomfortable he feels.

When the Wellingtons are over land, there are no crackly voices over the intercom: if they don't speak, Jerry won't know they're here. Then he hears Mikey's voice. "This is bloody dangerous."

"Shut up, Mikey," comes Chauncy's voice. "Drop that window and let's go home."

"OK, Skip."

Walter surveys the dark skies. There are no fighters and their return flight across the North Sea is safe. As the sun rises they land at Horwood, taxi up to their apron and stagger out. In the end nothing has happened, yet Walter feels more frightened and shaken than he ever did at Biggin Hill, even during the great raid. He tries not to show it and he's sure the others, except Chauncey, are trying not to show their fright either. God help them when they have a bomber packed with real bombs.

10.3

The Lancaster is wonderful. Though cramped inside, compared to the Wellington it is cavernous. Walter is well in the routine now, flying in a modern long-range strategic bomber, better than anything the Luftwaffe ever had and, he and everyone in the RAF believes, far superior to the B-17, the Flying Fortress, that the Americans fly.

Then everything changes. They are sent away for three weeks at Survival School. What to do if you're forced down in enemy territory. Walter learns how to kill wild animals, skin, gut and cook them. What follows is worse. How to kill people by throttling them from behind. How to strangle them face to face. He prays the situation won't arise. Then, when they've learnt how to slaughter their fellow human beings, they are taken to a remote place on the windiest, wettest night imaginable, left there and told to find their way back home. After quarrelling about how to do this, they realize their plight is so awful that they must co-operate. So, cold, soaked, fainting with hunger – they haven't even seen a wild animal, let alone eaten it – they return home.

At last it's over, though whether they are any better at surviving is doubtful. The day before they leave, a squadron leader gives them their final advice about what to do if they come down in Germany.

"First," he says, "there are three sorts of people who could pick you up. Number one — the ordinary police or the regular army. Say nothing except your name, rank and number. They'll try for more, but that's your answer to everything. The Geneva Convention says they can ask you anything they want as long as they ask it nicely. Soldiers and policemen will probably ask you nicely, and when all they hear is name, rank and number they'll get fed up and send you to a prisoner of war camp. Though some bastards might hand you over to the Gestapo.

"SS and Gestapo. Tough luck if you get picked up by them. They'll ask you a lot of things as well, but not nicely. You'll be beaten up, tortured, cigarettes burned on your skin, electric shocks in places that'll destroy your prospects, head held down in water, anything else they might dream up. When they get fed up with hearing your name, rank and number fifty times they might send you to a POW camp. More likely they'll shoot you. Don't try to save your skin by telling them anything, because they'll shoot you anyway. Am I making myself clear?"

There is a subdued murmur which suggests he is.

"Right. Now, let's assume you're a prisoner of war. Your first duty as a fighting man is to escape. No matter what risk, what danger, what odds against, that is your overriding duty. Never forget that."

They look at each other unhappily.

"However," the squadron leader continues, "there is

268

another way." He looks round almost furtively, as though someone may be hiding in a cupboard and taking notes. "For God's sake don't tell anyone I said this. My advice is to stay put until the war's over. Life in a Stalag needn't be much worse than square-bashing. It just goes on a lot longer. But the Geneva Convention says you can have Red Cross visits, send letters home and get letters back. You may get food parcels too. For God's sake don't eat them all yourselves. Share with your guards. The poor devils probably get fed worse than you do and it's the best way to have a quiet life. If I were you I'd use my time properly. Do a correspondence course. The Red Cross can organize it for you. My tip is accountancy. You could be qualified by the time we win the war and there'll be plenty of need for accountants afterwards. Any questions?"

Mikey stood up. "Yes, sir. You said there were three sorts of people who could capture us. Who's the third?"

"Thank you, Sergeant, I nearly forgot. Civilians. Ordinary people. If they find you after you've just destroyed their houses and killed their families, then you've had it, I'm afraid."

There's silence. Then the squadron leader says, "Cheer up, lads, you'll probably miss. Now, what's the answer you give to any question they ask?"

There's an indistinct mutter.

"Come on, I can't hear you."

A sullen growl. "Name, rank and number."

"Louder! Mean it!"

A raucous shout. "*Name, rank and number!*"

"Good. All right, men, dismiss. And keep away from civilians."

269

Walter hasn't enjoyed the survival course and, except for the bit about the correspondence course, which doesn't sound a bad idea, he hasn't enjoyed the talk either. Still, accountancy. Hmm. That would be one in the eye for Paul and his fancy degree at Bristol University.

10.4

They are back at Heavy Conversion Unit and will soon be posted to their new squadron, a trained crew ready for the thirty missions that make up a tour of duty. If they're scared at the prospect, they must keep it to themselves.

Ever since he first met Chauncey, something has nagged at Walter. Twice he has nearly spoken to him about it: each time his nerve failed. But now he decides it's now or never.

"Excuse me, Skip," he says. "Can I ask you something?"

"Go ahead, Wally," says Chauncey.

"Did you say your father was in a British hospital in the last war?"

"Sure did," Chauncey replies.

"You don't happen to know which one it was?"

"Sorry, I've no idea."

"Does the name Abbeville mean anything to you?"

"Abbeville," Chauncey repeats musingly. Then his face lights up. "Yes, that's it! I remember him talking about it. And something about a mad dukess or whatever you Limeys call them."

271

"Duchess," says Walter. "Did he mention any of the nurses?"

"Ah, that I don't remember."

"What about one called Ellen?"

"No, I can't recall that name. Who is she?"

"She's my mother."

Chauncey looks at him shrewdly. "I'll write and ask him. I'll show you what he says, even if it's 'never heard of her'. Is that OK?"

"Yes," says Walter. "Yes, it is. Thanks, Skip."

"My pleasure," says Chauncey Stevenson the Second.

Three weeks later they leave HCU for a week's leave before going to their new bases. Walter has plans. His railway warrant is made out to Yarmouth. He has booked a double room in their usual hotel and paid next to nothing for it, for who wants to stay in a windswept town in winter, facing east winds over a heaving, grey North Sea? He's made another, very important, arrangement as well, but he'll pick his time to tell Julie about that.

As he waits on Yarmouth station for her train to arrive, his heart is beating very fast and he can hardly breathe. The train from Liverpool Street is an only an hour late, though it seems more like three days. He watches Julie step down from the carriage and his heart, as always, leaps. They run to each other, kiss, then Walter picks up the cases. They walk, Julie clinging to his arm, to the rundown hotel behind the closed and forlorn Pleasure Beach. The week he has looked forward to so much is finally here.

And it is a wonderful week. Walter is raised to a pitch of ecstasy he has only ever imagined. But it goes too quickly.

On their last full day together, before he goes to RAF Coningsby in Lincolnshire and Julie returns to Bentley Priory, he says, "Are you quite sure about this?"

"I've never been more sure of anything," Julie replies.

"You realize I might not get through this tour of duty?"

"Of course; I'm not daft. But you will. That's the sort of person you are. You were locked out of the shelter at Biggin Hill and everyone in it was killed. You ran through the bombs to the ops block with that telephone engineer and you didn't get hit. You survived when the ops block was hit. You got away with murder that night. That's you all over, Wally."

"If I do get through, you know you're stuck with me for good."

"It's what I want."

"That settles it then," he shouts joyfully. "Let's do it."

That night tops anything in his most fevered fantasies. "If I die now," he whispers, "I'd die happy."

"Don't talk like that," says Julie. "It's unlucky."

Next day they part tearfully on Yarmouth station. Walter watches the Liverpool Street train steam out. Julie leans through the window waving, until he can see her no more. He turns emptily away and waits numbly for his own train. There is a look of desperate sadness on his face, as if he has seen a wonderful mirage through a prison window.

They have been at Coningsby for two weeks getting used to their brand new Lancaster. They've even been on a "gardening" run, laying mines outside French channel ports. Gardening runs count as missions and thirty would make a whole tour without a scratch. Some hope!

At the end of the fortnight, Chauncey calls Walter over. "I wrote to my father," he says. "I got a reply this morning."

"What does he say?"

"See for yourself." He hands the letter over, a flimsy airmail envelope and points to a section.

Walter begins to read.

You could have knocked me down with a feather when you asked me this. How strange to be faced with that name after all these years and to find that her boy is in your crew. But war brings people together who would never have met otherwise and it would be a funny thing if there weren't coincidences like this. We shouldn't be surprised when they happen. What would be amazing is if they never did.

I've often looked back on those times and wondered if things might have turned out differently. I've never told anyone before, least of all your mom. I'm telling you now, not only because you're a big boy and a fighting man and you might not come through, but also because I sometimes think your generation believes mine are old fogeys who've never lived. Well, we aren't.

Ellen wasn't much more than a girl when I watched her stop a young German soldier bleed to death and I thought to myself, here is one amazing woman. Anyway, I guess I couldn't get her out of my head and soon I was a bit too fond of her. The British wouldn't let doctors and nurses get to know each other then, certainly not when they were off duty. But I sure as hell wanted to get to know Ellen, and I really messed up. I got

274

everyone in the hospital against me so I told them Uncle Sam had ordered me back and ducked out before they could rumble me. As I drove away I felt a real heel.

Son, I often look back on those days and regret what I did. Don't think I regret anything that happened afterwards. I married your mom when I got back to the States and so everything was for the best, but I've often wondered what happened to Ellen. To think that you've met her son, he's part of your crew and you depend on each other to get through, gives me a strange sort of satisfaction. If he has half the guts of his mother you've got yourself one hell of a crew member.

Best of luck to you both, son. I'm praying for you.

Walter hands the letter back. "Thanks," he mutters.

"Well?" asks Chauncey. "What *did* happen to her?"

"She married the bloody German soldier," Walter replies bitterly.

"Holy cow," says Chauncey. "I'm so used to Yanks with German names from General Eisenhower downwards that I never noticed."

"Well, now you know, I suppose you'll sling me out of the crew."

"Oh, Wally," says Chauncey. "How can you think such a thing? You're the best damn rear gunner I've ever known and one of the best crew members too. Your name could be Hermann Goering for all I care."

Walter looks at Chauncey with a mixture of gratitude, admiration and envy. "Thanks, Skipper," he says.

275

"By the way, can I tell my father when I write?" Chauncey asks. "I'll only do it if you don't object."

"If you like," Walter replies. "To be honest I don't care either way. I'm still stuck with a Jerry father and a Jerry name."

The more he thinks about Chauncey's revelations, the more implications there seem to be. He needs time to get his head round them.

They're down for their first proper raid tomorrow night. Even that doesn't stop Walter thinking about Chauncey's father.

"What's up, young Wally?" Mikey asks. They are sitting in the sergeants' mess, nursing pints of beer. Walter isn't touching his. "Have you ever wondered how things might be if something different happened?" he asks Mikey.

"What are you on about?"

"Well, say that…" But this is private between him and Chauncey and must stay that way. He drains his tankard in one gulp. "Let's go to the pub," he says. "I want to get plastered out of my mind."

Six hours later, Mikey carries him back to camp and puts him to bed. Then he's sick and Mikey wipes it away so he doesn't choke. Mikey has never seen anyone so drunk. Next morning Walter has the worst headache of his life. He must sober up for their first proper mission.

The twelfth of December 1943. The night's target is Frankfurt. To Walter that's very fitting: near where his father's from and where the family have twice been without him. If he'd gone with them he might now have a

276

conscience about wiping it off the map.

Frankfurt hasn't been bombed all that often. It's not like Berlin and isn't in the Ruhr where the big manufacturing towns are. But it's a banking and transport centre and has a huge chemical works. It will be a cold, fine night with good visibility. Chauncey's crew is very quiet, the only ones in the briefing room for whom this is the first op. This is what all their training has been for. Walter is now alert, eager to get up in the sky and away. After his session with the gunnery leader he rejoins the crew and Chauncey gives them a last pep talk. When it's over, Walter nudges Mikey and whispers, "It's our first raid, but it's his thirty-first. His luck is our luck. When's it running out?"

"Don't be such a bloody misery," Mikey snaps. "If you think like that then you're not our tail-end Charlie, you're our Jonah."

"Sorry, I've got a lot on my mind."

"So have we all, old friend, so have we all," says Mikey.

10.5

Now tonight's target is known, Coningsby is cut off from the world with no telephone lines in or out. Walter draws his night's equipment: flying suit and helmet, boots and parachute. He also gets an escape pack, with compass, knife, cigarettes, matches, maps printed on silk, so no sharp ears hear paper rustling, and money. Walter isn't sure what a Reichsmark will buy, not that he would dare go to a shop and try to find out but it's reassuring.

Then they wait for the transport. The lorries arrive, fill up with crews and soon they are clambering into their waiting plane. Walter's heart beats nearly as fast as when he was waiting for Julie. They take their places on board: Walter, in the rear turret, hangs his parachute pack outside the door, checks the Brownings and the ammunition and tests the turret's hydraulics. Then he waits.

The four Merlins burst into life. The Lancaster lumbers forward heavily. Walter sees a long procession of Lancasters slowly following. The sight is both stirring and frightening. Airmen and Waafs, from group captains to admin orderlies, line the runway, watching. Walter imagines he hears cries of "God speed you."

He feels the Lancaster's surge of power. The runway is a blur, then the amazing moment of lightness and freedom as they leave the ground and they are climbing, climbing. He watches the following Lancasters. They move into a loose formation as they fly out to sea to the rendezvous point. Lancasters and Halifaxes from other squadrons join them: he never knew Bomber Command had so many planes.

They climb to 16,000 feet and head south-west across the North Sea. It will be some time before they cross the darkened enemy coast. Walter fires a few practice rounds into the air to warm the Brownings up and, now he has an interval of quiet, considers matters swirling somewhere beneath his consciousness.

He wants to think only of Julie but knows he can't. There'll be no more weeks in Yarmouth until thirty missions are up. But he'll get through, he will, he will, and come back, because she's his destiny.

Then Chauncey's father's letter drowns her out of his mind. "*I sure as hell wanted to get to know Ellen … I really messed up … I couldn't get her out of my head and soon I was a bit too fond of her … I often look back on those days and regret what I did.*" Did this mean what he thought it did? Chauncey Stevenson the First became very fond of his mother, wanted to take it further but then messed up. What if he hadn't? Walter knows about messing up. For three years he's lived in craven fear of messing things up with Julie. Women are strange creatures: you can mess things up for ever in a split second and never know what you're supposed to have done wrong.

But what if Chauncey Stevenson the First hadn't messed up?

The answer hits him like a stone in the middle of his forehead: his mother might have maried Chauncey Stevenson, the American doctor, instead of Matthias Vögler, the German soldier.

Then what? It would be *him* sitting at the Lancaster's controls, his name would be Chauncey and there would be a different rear gunner. Or he might be a doctor in America like his father. He would have a father to accept and love, and he wouldn't have broken with his family.

Then comes a vision from the past. He's sitting with Harry Brindley in Harry's father's old shed and they are getting drunk. Walter is wondering what if his father had gone back to Germany in 1919. "*I wouldn't be half and half ... I'd be all English,*" he says, and Harry answers, "*No you wouldn't. You wouldn't be here ... You wouldn't even* exist."

He can't remember any more because he was too drunk. But he didn't take it in then and he can't get his head round it now. If he'd had a different father, would it be him sitting here? If Chauncey'd had a different mother, would *he* be here? Well, no. There'd be another pilot and another tail-end Charlie. All this because Chauncey's father messed up.

But what if he hadn't? If that had turned out differently, might not everything else? Suddenly he's really angry with Chauncey's father for messing up because thanks to him he's strapped inside a death trap and still has a Jerry for a dad.

If I go on like this I'll be crazy before we're over Germany, he thinks. *I wish it hadn't happened the way it did, but I'm stuck with*

280

it. I can't do anything about it, but I don't have to like it.

A crackly voice comes over the intercom. "Enemy coast ahead." Walter's mind is suddenly clear and alert. It must stay that way if he's to get through the night.

10.6

The land below is dark and sinister. Flak and fighters might come any time now. The Germans will know about them well before they reach the target. He watches the long procession following like sinister mechanical vampire bats. Some are higher than they are, some are lower, but all fly on doggedly. Below, like the glistening trail of a snail, the Rhine winds its way south and the bombers follow. Then the phalanx banks to port and follows the River Main towards Frankfurt itself. There is no spark of light below: the city is a dark shape superimposed on a slightly less dark expanse.

Now the flak starts. Walter sees it arching upwards, bright flashes below, bursting shells lurid above, dangerously close. The Lancaster behind them is hit. Flames sprout from the starboard inner engine, the bomber tips over and spins out of control. Walter, horrified, watches the ruined aircraft plummet down, silhouetted for a second over the bright burning on the ground, then disappearing into it. There are no parachutes. He knows the crew, he's bought pints for them and they for him. Now they've all gone together. The other Lancasters fly stubbornly on through the flak.

Walter's fingers itch on the Bownings' firing buttons. "Come on, you bastard fighters," he mutters. "Where are you? Frit or something?"

Suddenly he gets his wish. Sleek shapes close on them, each fighter targeting a bomber. Walter's practised aircraft recognition eyes know them. "Bugger," he mutters. "Heinkel 219s. Twin engined, more firepower than Messerschmitts. Faster too. Turn on a sixpence."

Below him, little orange blobs burst like boils. They are over the target: earlier waves of Lancasters have already plastered it and now their own leaders are dropping their bombs. But it's not their turn yet. The wait is too long for Walter. He yells impotently at Mikey, "Drop the bloody bombs, can't you?" He longs for the sudden lightness as tons of explosive fall away. The Lancaster will be free, jump a hundred feet in the air, turn and head for home faster than it came. Debriefing, bacon and egg in the mess, a good day's kip, the pub in the evening, then back in the air in two nights' time. Perhaps minelaying again. After tonight they'll deserve another night's gardening.

But the bombs do not drop and the Heinkels are overhead. They travel at twice the speed of the Lancasters. One seems out to deal with Walter's Lancaster. He sees it for a split second, dangerous but vulnerable in the moment before tracer from its cannon pours into the bomber. Just an instant to show its defenceless belly.

Walter rotates the turret as he watches. He pulls back the Brownings, pushes on the firing buttons with an exultant scream: the .303 bullets shoot upwards, bright streams of angry wasps, deadly slivers of brightness. The turret fills with the cordite smell that he loves so much. He knows he's done the impossible. Flames spread on the Heinkel's underside: the plane is stricken. The flukiest shot of the year, million to one against. "Was it buggery a fluke!" Walter yells. "It was brilliant." He waits for its desperate, futile revenge, tracer ripping into the Lancaster. But there's nothing: the Heinkel is gone, it spins, twists downwards, a pilot bleeding over the controls, either dead or shrieking curses as his death rushes up to meet him. "Die, you bastard, die!" Walter shrieks and a demented surge of power courses through him.

He calms down and breathes hard. The Lancaster ponderously flies on. "Mikey, for Christ's sake drop the bombs," he screams. "I can't do everything on my own."

Then he feels the rip of tracer into the Lancaster's guts, and the shudder and lurch as control wires are cut. Instinctively he knows the plane is doomed and knows why too. Crews have reported a new, deadly ploy. German fighters are deliberately flying under bombers with a pair of guns pointing straight up to their unprotected undersides. This is what's happened to Chauncey's Lancaster. Walter is smothered by a wave of grief: he didn't see it coming and his mates will die, have already died. Heat and flame surge through the plane: the leather of his flying jacket scorches and the smell drowns out even the sharp cordite stink. He imagines Arthur, Bill, George, Alf, Chauncey and, most of all, his best friend Mikey, already killed by tracer or now burning alive.

The plane tips over to port. Flame licks its way through. The scorching, burning smell is overpowering. The engines' steady beat becomes a scream: the Lancaster is spinning, slower than the Heinkel but its speed increases exponentially as it nears the ground: the death throe is nearly complete. Surely there will be parachutes. But he sees none. Then he realizes he must do something to get out or he'll burn alive with the rest. The tail-end Charlie always draws the short straw: nobody can get out of the rear turret. *But I will,* he resolves. He unbuckles his straps enough to twist round, reaches through the door, somehow grabs the parachute pack and fumbles to attach it to his harness. Then he pushes the turret's visor open. He struggles out: his efforts are superhuman. Something rips at the side of his leg and blood flows into his flying boot. But he is free: cold air bites in his face: he has left the dead plane as it plummets to the ground.

He is falling: for a moment, the lightness, the rush of air is intoxicating. Another million to one chance. But a few more seconds of this and he will die because his parachute won't open in time. He feels for the ripcord. The parachute blossoms over his head, a gigantic, white flower. His fall is checked: he floats down like a tiny galleon and feels almost content.

The ground approaches. At first he fears he will land in the inferno below. But the parachute drifts in the wind, carries him clear of the target area and wafts him gently towards open country. Even so, the ground comes to meet him very fast. He closes his eyes, braces himself and lands in something soft. He lies still for a few moments, listening. The silence is eerie. He smells dung. Oh my God, what has he fallen in? He feels round tentatively. Thankfully it's straw.

The glow in the sky from the stricken city gives enough light to see that he is in a farmyard. The dark shapes of buildings are near: not even a chink of light shows in them. There's a blackout in Germany as complete as in Britain.

He reels in the parachute as if landing a huge white fish and scrumples it into a tight ball. He'll shelter in a barn and hide it under straw. Then he'll work out what to do next. He has no idea what the time is. He looks at the luminous dial of his heavy-duty aircrew watch. 2.30 a.m. GMT. That's 3.30 a.m. in German time. Should he get out of here, make his way somewhere safe, the Swiss border perhaps? But he doesn't know where the border is and it definitely won't be down the end of the next street. Wait though, there's a compass in his survival pack. Where is it? But he won't be able to read the compass while it's still dark. The sky is overcast now: he can't even see the pole star. Then a shaft of pain makes him remember his leg: his boot is full of blood.

Which side of Frankfurt is he on? He doesn't remember seeing the river as he floated down. He might have come down in that place Regelstein, where his father hails from. Perhaps he should have gone with the rest of the family when they visited, then he might recognize it. One thing is certain. He must get himself as far as he can from the hidden parachute, his helmet, flying suit, blood-soaked flying boots. Ah, but take them off and his RAF uniform is revealed.

So what? He has his ID card, with photo, name, rank and number. He remembers the squadron leader's talk at Survival School. Get picked up by the SS or the Gestapo and you're in trouble. If it's the ordinary army then the chances are you might be OK. Yes, he thinks, as he enters the barn, he fancies a cushy number sitting on his arse in a Stalag doing a correspondence course in accountancy. Then he'll be ready for when his Jerry father at last pops his clogs and the Morris dealership is his. Not a bad prospect.

Then the squadron leader's third option surfaces in his mind. Picked up by civilians: "*If they find you after you've just destroyed their houses and killed their families, then you've had it, I'm afraid.*"

Well, if it *is* civilians, he'll tell them it wasn't him who dropped the bombs: he only fired the guns. Then he remembers who would have dropped the bombs and he's filled with grief for his friend Mikey. He feels bleak and empty with a dreadful sense of loss.

He also realizes he's horribly hungry but, hungry or not, he must stay in the barn, hide till morning and decide what to do then. Meanwhile, get a bit of kip. Unexpectedly, he is laughing. He has remembered something from years ago: Harry saying how in the last war his father escaped conscription by hiding in a barn. If Harry's hopeless old dad could get away with hiding in a barn he's damn sure he can. So he snuggles up in the straw and tries to sleep. He's dog tired and nearly drops off.

All at once, he is sitting up, every nerve alert. Voices outside, German, angry, urgent, male. He's sure they're looking for him. It was only a matter of time. Even in the dark, a parachute descending like a pale ghost will not go unseen in a country at war.

He hears approaching footsteps. Hobnails rasp on stone. The steps aren't regular: they're not soldiers. The noise is suddenly softer on the straw-strewn ground of the yard.

He hears voices talking in German. He almost wishes he'd picked up the language from his father when he was young, like that little creep Paul. But he knows enough to understand that these are the third and worst of the squadron leader's options. Civilians. Farm workers perhaps.

He listens. Have they worked out which barn he's in? A voice shouts, "Come out, *Engländer! Schnell! Schnell!*" He has to obey: he doesn't want them to come in looking for him. Things might go badly if they find him snivelling under the straw. Surrender, walk out with hands up, that's all he can do. The rules of war will prevail. These will be good, country people, like him. He'll go to that POW camp and keep his nose clean for as long as it takes. He scrabbles in his uniform for a white handkerchief to wave. That should settle it.

The cry again. "*Schnell! Schnell!* Come out, *Engländer!*"

Yes, I am an Engländer. *I will be all right.*

Then a voice in his head says, "You've got a German name. They'll see your ID. 'Hullo,' they'll say. 'What have we here? Walter Vögler? An English airman with a German name? A traitor. Shoot him.'" He sits down again in the straw.

"*Raus! Raus!*"

There's another noise, metallic, not loud, but ragged as if it's the same action performed by different people. He knows it well but for the moment can't quite place it.

"Do you hear, English terror bomber? *Raus!* Out! Now!"

Of course he knows that noise. It's how a shotgun sounds when you break open the breech to load it, one cartridge in each barrel.

Damn you, Father. You never let me have a shotgun when I wanted one and now I'm going to be killed by a dozen Jerries with shotguns. Damn you and damn my mother for making me. Damn that Yank doctor for messing up and making everything happen the way it has.

He is feverish with fear and impotent hatred. For all he knows he's at the mercy of his own blood relatives, the relatives he never wanted to see. Perhaps if they *had* met him they'd understand him, pity him, protect him.

But they won't. Unpleasant thoughts race through his head. *What if that Helmut's with them, the one who met Hitler? If he's there I've no chance because we're opposites. Would he realize who I am? My German relatives don't know me and I refused even to admit they exist. Except Helmut. And he's going to be out there. I know he is.*

Walter makes up his mind. He will not surrender to people whose existence he refused to admit. He will not throw himself on their mercy. He'll go down fighting, Julie or no Julie, though it's cruel even beyond contemplating that all his dreams of Julie have gone for nothing, that he will never see her, hear her, touch her again. His life has come to this: in these few moments he comprehends its inevitable path, and everything springs from the fact that *his father is a sodding Jerry.*

He is filled with a surge of recklessness, an adrenalin more deadly than when he downed the Heinkel. He stands up and takes a deep breath. "That's it and all about it," he shouts. "I'm coming out now. Do what you bloody well like."

His leg is now throbbing with pain, so he hobbles out of

289

the barn and into the open. "*Bastards! Bastards! Bastards!*" he screams.

He sees the flash of the shotguns as they fire but does not hear the noise they make.

1943–1945

HELMUT AT BAY

11.1

Helmut had fought the long fight. At Kursk, he had seen his tank exploding round him, watched his crew fry, heard Rudi's death screams – and still heard them, night after night. He had been miraculously thrown clear without a scratch or a burn. His first thought was: *I should have gone with them.*

But he hadn't and so he had a choice. Did he want to die or live? He took some time to decide on the second option. In the interval, he joined another tank crew, stayed with it through the long retreat – and always the refrain beat through his mind: *the war is lost, the Third Reich is finished, what will become of us?*

After months of rearguard battle, he was repatriated. A week's blessed leave: Regelstein almost unscathed, though Frankfurt had been badly hit, and his parents ecstatic to see him. A year had passed since the disaster at Kursk. In Germany he saw what he had only heard about and not quite believed. Destruction and ruin of cities, ragged, frightened people fighting in the rubble for food scraps, despair wherever he looked. He felt molten rage. The merciless British terror bombers had done this. Another mistake by the Führer, invading Russia because he thought Britain would give up. But Hitler wasn't the Führer any more. He was the Emperor with no clothes, Adolf the house painter, the failed artist, Mr Schickelgruber as the Americans called him. Everything Helmut once craved so fiercely was dust and ashes in his mouth.

The news that the Americans and British had landed in Normandy broke while he was still at home. He was not surprised.

"What will happen now?" said his father.

"We'll fight on. We'll survive even though our enemies close in."

"Helmut," said his mother. "Do you sometimes think we've brought all this on ourselves?"

"I fear you may be right, Mother," said Helmut. "I've seen the hatred in people's eyes when they look at me."

Next day he reported for duty. A time of training in another Panzer brigade, then off to the front, but this time to the west, to France.

April 1945. Another long, steady retreat in which Helmut somehow stayed alive while friends and comrades died all round him. Now they were pushed back deep into Germany itself. More by accident than anything else, he found himself leading a platoon consisting entirely of Hitler Youth, none more than sixteen, wearing uniforms too big for them. They were hard to control: their zeal, their bravery, broke his heart. In them he saw himself, five years ago when he was a dreaming postman. They didn't have an old soldier's caution: they threw themselves at the advancing Americans and were mown down before his eyes.

Now and again they met refugees fleeing eastwards. They heard rumours that a resistance group was forming: the Werewolves. "They're fools," Helmut told the boys. "Take no notice."

One night he dragged the surviving five of his flock into a barn as the unstoppable American phalanx swept past. "Stay out of trouble," he hissed. "Yes, Herr *Leutnant*," the boys muttered sullenly, all except Willi, once a *Scharführer* like Helmut, who they saw as their leader. He opened his mouth to remonstrate but Helmut would not let him. "Keep quiet and don't argue," he warned.

Finding the barn had been sheer luck. The boys made themselves as comfortable as they could. In the gathering dusk, Helmut could make them out only as darker shadows against the straw. "I want you to listen to me very carefully," he said. "Our position is hopeless. This place is crawling with Americans. They're angry, their blood is up. If they find us we won't last ten seconds."

"Then we should face them," said Willi. "Our lives don't matter. We should die for the Fatherland. The Führer would want us to."

"Put your rifles down," said Helmut. Nobody moved. "I said put your rifles down."

"Never," said Willi.

"This will come hard," said Helmut. "But I have to say it. We must forget Hitler. The heart has been ripped from our beautiful country. We followed a dream and found it was a mirage. Hitler alone has done this to us: we are in this state because of him. Do you understand me?"

There was no answer. He felt rebellion in the air. "Boys of the Hitler Youth," he continued. "You don't have to show your bravery to *me*."

Willi muttered, "We haven't come this far to be cowards now."

Helmut pretended not to hear him. "You've done enough, no, far more than enough," he said. "It's time to stop. It's finished."

Willi stood up: in the gloom Helmut could only see his silhouette.

"That's a lie, Herr *Leutnant*," he said.

"Willi," Helmut replied. "Four years ago I was like you. The Führer was my life. But I've seen what he has brought us to. I've been on the eastern front as far as Kursk: I've been on the western front as far as Normandy. I've seen what terrible things we did there. God help me, I did them myself. The world will have its revenge on us for all that we've done to it and the world, I have to tell you now, will be right."

There was an angry silence.

"We leave here tomorrow," he said. "We'll work our way north. If we have to, I would rather surrender to the British. They have a right to be in this war. They have suffered at our hands. The Americans haven't."

He knew Willi wanted to speak so he waited. But no words came. "Sleep now," he said. "We have a long and difficult day tomorrow."

He burrowed down in the straw and slept almost at once. He was woken suddenly in the small hours by something jammed against the side of his head. He opened his eyes. Willi was holding a revolver against his temple. He felt for the holster at his waist. Empty. With a pickpocket's skill, Willi had gently removed it as he slept.

"You're a traitor, Herr *Leutnant*," Willi whispered. "I shall shoot you."

Helmut's heart hardly missed a beat. "I don't think so, Willi," he said calmly. "A German soldier doesn't mutiny against his officer."

"The Führer hangs traitors slowly with piano wire," hissed Willi. "You're only going to be shot. You're lucky."

Helmut sat up. He could make out Willi's shape, feel his quick, nervous breathing hot on his face. The moon was up in a clearing sky: faint light came through a hole in the roof and he could see the dull glint of the revolver's grey barrel.

Very slowly and deliberately he reached out and moved the barrel to one side. At that instant, Willi pulled the trigger. The report reverberated round the barn: birds nesting in the roof flew away with raucous screeches of alarm. Helmut grasped the revolver, took it gently out of Willi's hand and replaced it in the holster.

Willi crumpled into the straw, sobbing uncontrollably. Helmut put an arm round his shoulder. "Don't cry, Willi," he said. "Once I would have done what you did. I admire you."

Willi wrenched himself away. "Don't touch me, Herr *Leutnant!* I've failed."

"Willi, that's the very last thing you've done. You're strong, brave, intelligent, you can lead others. Germany will depend on people like you. All this senseless death and sacrifice – can't you see? Now Hitler's doomed he'll drag us down with him. Is that what you want?"

"No, Herr *Leutnant*," said a voice in the darkness. Manfred, two months younger than Willi. Helmut had a torch in his pack. He took it out and switched it on to see the boys' frightened faces.

"I'm going to give you an order," he said. He took the revolver out of its holster again. "I shall shoot anyone who doesn't obey it."

The intent faces looked at him expressionlessly.

"I know you all hide your Hitler Youth daggers under your uniforms, just as I still do after all these years. I want you to take them out, just as I have." He held his dagger up so they could all see.

There was a fumbling with belts and tunics until everyone except Willi held his dagger in his hand.

"Tell me what it says on it," said Helmut.

There was a ragged mutter. "Blood and honour."

"Louder."

"Blood and honour." The voices had more conviction.

"Right. All the blood we can spare for Germany has been given. Now we must think of our German honour and how to restore it. The days for daggers are gone. All of you, stand up and follow me."

They followed him without a word, even Willi. He led them outside, away from the barn until they were on meadow grass.

"Stop here," he said. They did so. In the moonlight he saw their puzzled boyish faces and wanted to weep for them.

But there was no time for that. "Good," he said. "Now, with your daggers, make a hole in the soil like this." He cut out a square of turf and put it to one side, dug a hole, gently placed the dagger in it, pushed the soil back, replaced the turf and stamped it down so that no trace of the dagger's last resting place remained. There was a horrified silence.

"Now, you dig too."

Four of them cut out turves and dug holes just as he had. Willi didn't move. Helmut ignored him. "Now put your daggers in the holes you've made and then heap the earth back over them."

"But Herr *Leutnant*, we can't bury our daggers," cried Manfred.

"I did. You have to," said Helmut. "The time for them is gone."

He could feel the unwillingness. Then Manfred did what he was told. He took one long, last look at the dagger and then put it in its little grave. He pushed the earth back in the hole, placed the turf neatly on top of it and trod it down. Though he tried to hide it, they could all hear him sobbing. After a few moments the others followed suit. Helmut noticed that, almost imperceptibly, Manfred had become their leader.

"Willi," he said. "I see you haven't buried your dagger yet."

"No," he answered stubbornly. "And I never will."

"I think you will. If you don't, I shall shoot you like a dog in front of your friends." He stood over Willi, pointing the revolver at his head. "Now, Willi, do it."

There was a long, unendurable pause. Then, slowly, Willi pushed his dagger into the earth.

For three days they moved northward along the Rhine

Valley, hiding in ditches when American soldiers in jeeps drove past, eating what they could find, potatoes, swedes and turnips rotting in long-deserted fields, berries off trees. They slept in ruined, empty houses. They heard rumours of the mysterious Werewolves, hiding in the hills and woods each side of the Rhine. One day they saw soldiers wearing steel helmets like pudding basins and army lorries like Helmut's father's prized Bedford truck roaring past and knew they had reached the British lines.

Helmut called his little band to a halt. "Now," he said. "This is the moment. We shall put our weapons down in a heap. We shall then walk in full view along the road. We shall surrender to the first British patrol that passes."

Willi spoke. "I will not do this." Even though his voice sounded forced and high as if there were no breath in his lungs, Helmut heard the contempt in it. He felt the boys' tension rise as he took out his revolver and pointed it at Willi. "Yes you will, or I'll do what I threatened before."

Just as last night, he felt their wills struggling with each other for mastery. Then it was over. Willi relapsed into sullen silence, Helmut put his gun away and they walked on westwards into the setting sun. Helmut heard whispering behind him. He ignored it because he knew he must. After an hour seeing nobody, Helmut said, "Halt. We'll rest now, then find something to eat."

He turned round, to see only four boys. "Where's Willi?"

"Willi's gone," answered Manfred.

"What do you mean, gone?"

"He said he was going to look for the Werewolves."

"He'll have a long search. The Werewolves are the very

302

last thing Germany needs. So much for poor Willi." Helmut studied the faces of the four remaining boys. "Do you want to follow him?" he asked.

There was an embarrassed shuffle. He waited ten seconds, then said, "Good. Even if your hearts aren't in what we're doing, your heads tell you that it's right. Five minutes rest, then we go on."

"Herr *Leutnant*, I hear a motor," said Manfred.

He was right. Round the corner came an armoured car, a Union Jack flying from it. They stood at the side of the road with their hands up and Klaus, the youngest, waved a rather dirty, white handkerchief. The armoured car stopped. The soldier on top trained his machine gun on them. "Don't shoot," said Helmut in English.

The soldier's eyes narrowed and his mouth set in a hard, thin line. Helmut saw white on his index finger as he started to pull the trigger. He was proud that the boys watched as unflinchingly as he did.

Then a major with a round, good-natured face jumped out of the passenger seat. "By jove!" he said. "A Jerry officer and four kids. Now then chaps, are you sure you've got no weapons?"

Helmut took his revolver from its holster and handed it to the major.

"Good man," said the major. "Well, hop aboard with your kids. We'll take you to camp and get you all something to eat. You look as though you need it. And then you can tell me all about yourselves."

They scrambled in. As they did so, the soldier spoke softly so that only Helmut could hear, his voice weary and bitter with the rage of years. "Major Hawkins is a soft sod.

I'd have shot the lot of you and laughed, you murdering bastards."

Helmut felt a profound sadness that human beings had allowed their world to descend to such despair.

"Prisoner, atten-*shun*!" yelled the sergeant. Helmut didn't move.

"Stand easy, Prisoner," murmured the officer, still writing. Helmut saw that they were about the same age and there were lieutenant's pips on his shoulders. So they had the same rank too.

"You may leave us, Sergeant Snaith," said the young lieutenant.

"But sir…" Sergeant Snaith began.

"Leave us," the lieutenant repeated, still without raising his head.

"But regulations say…"

"I know all about regulations. I'm using my discretion. I shall see the prisoner alone. I take full responsibility."

"Sir, I must…"

"That is an order, Sergeant Snaith. You may stand guard outside."

"Sir, I shall have to report this to…"

"Carry on, Sergeant."

Sergeant Snaith came to attention with an over-loud clatter of boots, did an about-turn that nearly broke through the floor, sniffed audibly and slammed the door behind him. The young lieutenant continued writing. Helmut stood fuming in front of the desk.

At last the lieutenant put his pen down. He looked up and said, in perfect German, "Why did you try to stand on my fingers when we climbed the tree?"

Helmut stared, then, for a second a boy of eleven again, said, "You tried to break the branch I was on. I could have been killed."

"I held onto you," said the lieutenant. "I saved you."

307

"Paul," said Helmut. When he'd got over the shock, he didn't know whether to feel hope or despair.

"Helmut," said Paul. There was a long, almost embarrassed silence. Then Paul said, as if it was an impossible request, "Please sit down."

Helmut remained standing.

"I noticed your name on the prison roll," said Paul. "I wondered if it was you so I made sure I did the interrogating. I knew you the moment you came in. That's why I sent Sergeant Snaith out, though it's against regulations to see a prisoner alone."

Helmut did not move: his mouth was shut in a straight, firm line.

"There are questions I must ask you," said Paul. "It would help us both if you would answer them."

At last Helmut spoke. "I did not try to stand on your fingers."

"And I did not try to break the branch," Paul replied.

Helmut was silent again.

"Believe me, I didn't," said Paul. "If you thought I did, then I'm very sorry."

"Then I apologize too," said Helmut.

"Please sit down," said Paul. Helmut stayed standing. "We have quite a large dossier on you," Paul continued. "I must go through it with you." He studied the page for a second. "Can you confirm that you are Helmut Vögler, born 1924 in Regelstein?"

"You know perfectly well that I am," said Helmut.

"Sorry," said Paul. "I have to go through all this rigmarole. Still, we'll skip the next bit. We'll come to 1938. You attended a Nazi rally in Nuremburg as a member of the

Hitler Youth and were presented to Hitler personally."

"You know that," said Helmut. "You were there."

"Yes, I was."

"What has it got to do with anything? Ah, I know. You think that because Hitler picked me out from the others it must mean I went on to a top job in the Nazi party."

"I think nothing," said Paul. "I want you to tell me."

"I suppose it was you who told your superiors all this."

"Good Lord, no," Paul replied. "But someone somehow got hold of it and passed it on. And as soon as my colleagues in the Intelligence Corps get wind of something like this they'll hammer it for all they're worth, for the very reason that you said. *Were* you a top Nazi?"

"No," said Helmut. "And by the end of the war, anything but."

"You got pretty high in the Hitler Youth. *Gefolgschaftsführer*, wasn't it? You had every intention of joining the SS."

"How do you know this?"

"You'd be amazed how many people there were in Germany passing information on to us. But you changed your mind. You didn't join the SS. Why was that?"

Helmut was silent. *Shall I tell him? Will he believe me? Won't he think I'm trying to save my skin? But I'm not. I'm laying my soul bare. Can I do such a thing for a man who four months ago was my enemy, even though he is my cousin?*

"Why, Herr *Leutnant*?" Paul repeated.

So Helmut sat down and told Paul about his early zeal, about Lotte and how it led to his gradual disillusion, how he endured the campaign in the east and began to realize its futility, how Hitler made men sacrifice themselves for nothing when they should have lived to fight another day, how he had lost the war against Russia when he took the Panzers out of Kursk and sent them to Sicily, which meant they were defeated on two fronts instead of just one.

"I was forced to face reality," he concluded. "The Third Reich was built on sand: we were deceived by a madman. I fought for my country. I would have died for it. But I wouldn't die for Hitler, not any more."

Paul wrote busily for a few minutes. Then he looked up again and said, "My father, your uncle, was interned as an enemy alien. He did not have a good experience. My mother fought hard to get him released and succeeded. My brother was in the RAF, in Bomber Command. He was killed over Germany. We've all paid big prices in the last five years."

"Yes," said Helmut.

"What do you want to do now? There's a huge task to get Germany on her feet again. The Allies won't repeat the foolishness of the Treaty of Versailles after the last war."

"I don't know," said Helmut. "I've thought a lot about it since I've been here. Later on I shall study. For now I think I want to work with my hands so I can see that I'm making a difference."

"Doing what?"

"Again, I don't know. I spent a lot of time before the war on the engine of my father's Mercedes. When we were given a British lorry after Dunkirk I helped to repair it when it broke down. I'm afraid it did, very often. I could repair the engine of a Tiger tank as well as any of the mechanics. I might go further with that sort of thing for a while."

Paul smiled. "The internal combustion engine seems to

run in the family." He stood up and Helmut stood too. Paul reached over the desk, his hand outstretched. Helmut took it and felt warmth in the firm handshake. "Leave it with me," said Paul. "I'll see you again soon."

But as time passed and Helmut heard nothing, he wondered whether he could trust Paul after all. Some prisoners were released: he watched them go enviously. Others were taken away under armed escort. Helmut had a pretty good idea of what was in store for them. Finally, as November came, Sergeant Snaith called him out again, escorted him to Paul's office and this time said nothing when Paul saw Helmut alone.

They sat down. Helmut saw papers on the desk.

"Have you heard of a place called Wolfsburg?" asked Paul.

"No," Helmut replied.

"That isn't officially its name yet, though it will be. The KdF factory is there, where Hitler was going to build the famous people's car."

"The Volkswagen," said Helmut. "Yes, I know."

"We're rebuilding the works. There's a fearful amount of work to be done. But the British army needs new cars and trucks, so we'll build Volkswagens. We've salvaged plenty of parts that survived the war undamaged. It's ironic that the first big customer for Hitler's people's car will be the British Army."

"What has this to do with me?" asked Helmut.

Paul picked up the papers on the desk. "Here are your travel warrants and personal ID. You're released. Go home to Regelstein, take two weeks' leave and then report to

Major Ivan Hirst at the KdF factory. He's in charge of the operation to re-establish Volkswagen. He expects you and will welcome you. You'll do well there."

Helmut took the documents. He could hardly speak. Then, with all the smartness from his Hitler Youth days when everything seemed so clear, he stood up ramrod straight, saluted and said, "Thank you, Lieutenant Vögler."

Paul also stood. "No," he said. "Thank *you*, Herr *Leutnant* Vögler."

They shook hands and Helmut said, "We'll meet again, Paul."

"We certainly will," said Paul.

1945–1946

ANNA

12.1

Some people tell me that they think in words. Others say they think in pictures. I do most of my thinking through music.

I've been like that ever since I can remember. After the lady on the train told us the story of the girl Lorelei I wondered about the song she sang. No, that's not quite right. I tried to *hear* it. But I never could. It seemed always just out of reach. Then, after I heard Hitler speak at the rally, even what I thought I knew before was drowned out.

It's been the same all through the war. Ever since it started, a sort of music has been running through my brain and getting louder, more insistent: music that says everything about the war, its horror, waste and sadness. And yet, as with the Lorelei song, I can't *hear* it. A sonorous, melancholy melody wells up of grief and despair, and yet it's just beyond me. I can't somehow hear it, play it, sing it, even hum it. At night, when I can't sleep, it nearly drives me mad.

The two nicest things to do with the end of the war,

because they were so unexpected, happened in June 1945. The first was just for me. The second was for all the family.

I'd got my place at the Royal College of Music, to start in September. I had grade eight qualification, for the violin, flute and piano and couldn't go any further with them. The violin was the instrument I loved best and I was determined to be a professional violinist. Wouldn't it be wonderful to be a soloist? Though being in a big orchestra like the London Philharmonic would be almost as good. One day, Mr Russell the music master said to me, "Anna, you really ought to learn another stringed instrument."

"I can play the flute and piano, sir," I replied.

"I know, but you're a string player first and foremost and you should know the other strings. Have you thought of learning the cello?"

No I hadn't. Cellos cost the earth. I was lucky to have Uncle Friedrich's violin. We couldn't have afforded such a good instrument.

"You know you've won the school music prize?"

I didn't, but to be honest I wasn't really surprised.

"Well, I've been thinking. There's a … no, I'd better show you myself." He led me to a shed in the school grounds just outside the music room. "This is the graveyard of dead instruments," he said and unlocked the door. It was full of old violins, violas and cellos without strings or bridges, all broken in some way, a pathetic sight. "I've been rooting around and found this," he said.

It was a cello body with a big crack in the wood and no bridge, strings or tuning pegs. The joint fixing the neck to the body was broken. "This was a really good cello once," he said. "It could be again if it was restored by someone who knows what he's doing."

"I see, sir," I said, though I didn't know what he was getting at.

"I've had a word with the headmaster. I know a good violin and cello maker and I'll get him to restore this to an instrument anyone would be happy to play. It can be your music prize."

I was so pleased that I didn't know what to say. At last I came out with, "I'd love it, sir. Thank you so much. And thank the headmaster for me, please." If Mr Russell hadn't been a teacher and I a pupil, I'd have kissed him.

That was the first nice thing. The second happened two weeks afterwards. The Higher School Certificate exams were over and, as I was leaving that term, I was allowed home quite a lot. That was why I was home on a Tuesday afternoon at the end of June.

It was a lovely sunny day. Mum had left her job at the hospital and we were weeding the front garden. As I knelt in a flowerbed I noticed a blonde woman coming up the road wheeling a pram with a baby in it. I watched her look at the notice saying "Vögler's Garage", then pause hesitantly at our front gate.

"Mum, she's stopping," I said. "Do you know her?"

Mum stood up. "Never seen her in my life," she replied and bent down again to the weeds.

The woman stood by the gate. "Mrs Vögler?" she asked timidly.

Mum stood up again. "Can I help you?" she said.

"It's about Walter," said the woman.

319

"Walter's dead," Mum replied. "He was killed in a raid over Germany. I'm afraid you won't find him here."

To my amazement I saw the woman was crying. She held out her left hand: on it was a wedding ring. "I know," she said. "I've come to see you…"

I could see Mum's mind working. She stared at the ring, stared at the baby and then said faintly, "You'd better come in." She opened the gate and the woman wheeled in the pram. Outside the front door she unstrapped the baby and picked him up. I heard her whisper, "Guess who you're going to meet, little Walter."

"Anna," said Mum. "Go and get your father! Tell him to be quick because this is important."

Dad was where he always was, with Jimmy Warner bending over a car and looking at the engine. "I can't, I'm busy," he replied when I asked him to come home. "It's important, Dad," I insisted. "Someone's here to see us."

"Who?"

"You'd better come and see for yourself."

So he followed me back to the house and in the kitchen we found Mum crying her eyes out and cradling the little child on her lap, while the blonde girl sat opposite wiping her eyes. Dad sized the situation up in a flash. He sat down heavily and said, "My God!"

"He's your grandson," the girl said softly.

"Does that mean…?"

"Yes, I'm your daughter-in-law. I married Walter by special licence in a registry office the day before he went back to his squadron and was killed in the raid on Frankfurt."

"But that's nearly two years ago. Why didn't you tell us?

Why haven't you been to see us?" Dad asked her.

"I was too frightened. I thought you'd throw me out."

"We'd never do that!"

"I had to pluck up my courage to come here at all," said the girl.

"I don't know your name," said Mum. "I can't keep calling you Mrs Vögler."

"I'm Julie. I met Walter at Biggin Hill when I was a Waaf. Did he never tell you?"

"I'm afraid we heard very little from Walter," confessed Dad sadly.

"I know he didn't get on well with you," said Julie. "He told me why. I said I thought that was terrible of him, he should swallow his pride and make it up with you, life's too short to have arguments like that. I'm afraid that for Walter it was."

"May I hold my nephew?" I asked.

"Of course," said Julie. Mum passed him over to me.

There was no doubt about it, I could see Walter in his face. Julie turned and looked at Mum. "Mrs Vögler, I loved your son," she said.

"I can see you did," said Mum. "I wish I'd known you before."

"Are you still in the Waafs?" Dad asked.

"No," Julie replied. "The RAF were very good to me. They gave me a compassionate discharge and I went home to live with my parents in Cheshire. I'd like to have a place of my own though."

"Will you marry again?" asked Dad.

"Matthias!" said Mum reprovingly. "What a question to ask."

321

"No, it's a fair one," said Julie. "I may do one day. Who can tell? But my memories are so close that for now I can't even imagine it."

"Yes, they're close to us as well," said Mum. "Walter has been a gaping wound in our lives since the war began. Seeing you with his son makes me hope it might heal one day."

"I hope so," said Julie.

There was an awkward silence. Someone had to say something or Julie would leave and we would lose a wonderful chance to lay the past to rest.

At last, Mum asked, "Will you stay and eat?"

Julie looked at her watch. "I must go soon," she said. "I've a train to catch."

"Nonsense," said Dad. "You stay here and have a proper meal. You must stay the night too. Ellen will make up a bed for you, won't you, my love?"

"Only if Julie wants me to," said Mum. Julie looked doubtful.

"We're your in-laws," said Dad. "You're part of our family now. You must stay the night. I'll take you to the station tomorrow morning."

Suddenly Julie was crying. "Oh, thank you," she gulped. "I thought you wouldn't want to know me, I thought you'd send me away."

Little Walter began to cry as well. I handed him back to Julie, who dried her eyes, smiled and said to him, "Say thank you to your auntie."

So Julie stayed the night in Walter's old room with little Walter asleep in his pram next to her and when we were eating breakfast next morning we seemed like a family who had been together for years. Before Dad took Julie to the station, Mum smiled and said, "We expect to see you here again, and often," and Julie answered, "Of course, and you must come to Cheshire."

So she left with little Walter and when they were gone Mum said, "Do you know, I feel as though the war really is over at last and all the questions are answered."

"Are they, Mum?" I replied.

She looked down at the floor and didn't answer at once. Then she looked up again and said, "No. Of course they aren't. That's what I thought at the end of the last war and I soon found out how wrong I was."

Prizegiving came and I was given my music prize. The guest of honour was Mr Colgrove, our MP. He was so used to presenting books as the prizes that he didn't seem to know what to do when it came to giving a cello. To save his blushes I picked it up myself and, as he shook my hand, he smiled and murmured, "Well done, Anna. I expect a ticket to your first concert."

That evening I took the cello out of its case, tuned it and started to play. It took a moment to get used to it, but soon I was getting the hang of it. Mr Russell was right: it was a good instrument with a lovely, mellow tone. Yet even as I played, I knew that my real instrument was the violin. The cello was wonderful, but I felt I was looking at it from afar, admiring it without being part of it. But listening to its rich, deep voice I suddenly realized something. The music that had followed me throughout the war was played on the cello.

12.2

In August, the Americans dropped atom bombs on Hiroshima and Nagasaki, and Japan surrendered. Now the war was really finished and we all cheered again. But when we saw pictures of what the atom bombs did and how terrible they were, we realized that if the Americans could drop them on Japan then equally someone else could drop them on us. Mum was right. The questions had hardly begun.

Paul came home for Christmas. He had been promoted. Captain Vögler of the Intelligence Corps.

"When are you going to be demobbed?" asked Mum.

"Not yet," said Paul. "There's too much to do in Germany – denazification, preparing for the war crimes trials. And then there's the rebuilding. You wouldn't believe the destruction: whole cities reduced to piles of bricks. When I think that most of it was done by us I feel very depressed. I suppose I should say, 'Wonderful. We did that. That's how we won the war.' But I can't and I'll never forget the sights I've seen. Don't worry, though. I'll be out soon and at university in September."

I watched Dad as Paul spoke. I wondered how he felt when Paul talked about war crimes trials, let alone the destruction. If it worried him he showed no sign. "I'm glad you could help Helmut," he said.

"Helmut has been through more than you and I can imagine," Paul replied. "He's got a lot to think about and a lot to come to terms with. But he'll come through. We'll be good friends one day."

Walter and Helmut. Both in their different ways victims of that horrible war. Now their stories seemed to be over, though deep down I knew that no story is ever over, it's just that there comes a stage when we think we can forget it.

Julie came down with little Walter while Paul was with us. I was glad Paul saw them both. He picked Walter up and said to him, "Don't go looking for shotguns in the shed because you won't find any."

This feeling that somehow things had come to a conclusion, even though I knew they hadn't, wouldn't leave me. Sometimes I lay awake at night thinking about those years.

I remembered Dad home for Christmas, 1940, and what a wonderful Christmas it was, even though there was no turkey or chicken for Christmas dinner but a rabbit Harry Brindley brought round. He could have got us a turkey on the black market but Dad refused to pay on principle. All our presents were secondhand or home-made. But it was a happy time even though the war still went badly.

Next year, 1941, Hitler invaded Russia. This was a sensation. Germany and Soviet Russia were supposed to have a friendship pact. When the news came through Dad couldn't speak for amazement. When he did, he said, "Hitler has lost the war. Has he learned nothing? No country can fight on two fronts, east and west, at the same time. It was too much in the last war and it will be the end of Germany in this."

"But, Dad," said Paul. "He isn't fighting in the west. He's conquered everybody and we can't fight him on our own."

"Wait till America joins in. They will, mark my words, just like last time. Hitler will fight on two fronts at once and it will finish him."

"It sounds too good to be true," said Paul.

Then Japan attacked Pearl Harbour and Dad's prophecy came true. The USA declared war.

In 1942 the Desert Rats under Montgomery beat Rommel's Afrika Korps at El Alamein. Dad said that to Hitler this was only a little sideshow, though it meant a lot to us. The big thing was the air war, with the Americans bombing by day, targeting factories, the RAF by night, huge raids, destroying cities, killing civilians. Many people weren't happy about this, but others said, "They did it to us, now we're doing it to them to give them a taste of their own medicine." But what the RAF did to Hamburg, Cologne and Berlin was twenty times worse than anything the Luftwaffe did to London. When I heard about it on the wireless I felt uneasy and wondered whether this was really the right way to fight a war, killing people like us in their thousands, no, their millions.

It was at this time that we received a rare letter from Walter, with the news that he was now one of the very people doing the bombing.

Of course Mum replied. She told him all the news – Dad coming home, Paul wanting to join the army, lots of little things that didn't really matter but which she hoped might interest him and even make him want to come home on leave. But we never heard from him again.

Just before Christmas in 1943 came the news that Walter was missing, believed killed, over Germany. We waited for more details but they never came. Nor did his personal possessions. We wondered why and Mum wrote to the Air Ministry. A month later a brusque letter arrived saying all his belongings had been sent to his wife.

Mum was furious. "How dare they tell such lies?" she shouted.

"Calm down," said Dad. "It's a mistake. They've made a mess of things, what they call a cock-up. These bureaucrats do it all the time. It's a way of life to them."

"I don't care," Mum stormed. "I'll write to them again."

So she did, but this time there was no answer.

Paul's Higher School Certificate was really good so we weren't surprised that he got into Bristol University. But they deferred his entry and he joined the army in 1944. The first time he came home, he said, "I've put in for a commission to be an officer."

"Does that mean you won't be a spy?" asked Mum. She hadn't forgotten what he said in 1940.

"Probably. I don't think I'd be a very good one. I want to use my languages, in the Intelligence Corps if they'll have me."

"Would that mean you won't be killed?" asked Mum. "I couldn't bear to lose two sons."

"Come on, Mum," said Paul. "You should know better than that. Anybody in a uniform can get killed."

"So can anybody without one these days," added Dad grimly.

Paul went back and the next we heard from him was a letter written from OCTU, the Officer Cadet Training Unit. And yes, they would use his perfect German in the Intelligence Corps. Mum was very relieved.

So the war continued. Titanic events. Stalingrad, D-Day, Germany caught in the vice from east and west that Dad had talked about. Dreadful things happening in the Far East against the Japanese. Setbacks, defeats – Arnhem, the Ardennes. But always now the relentless progress and the conviction that the war would be won. Then finally the Russians entered Berlin, Hitler killed himself in his bunker and the world began to find out about the awful truths of the concentration camps. It was all over.

VE Day in Peterspury wasn't like London with massed crowds outside Buckingham Palace. People danced in the High Street and the pubs stayed open all night. PC Coppard did nothing to stop it, in fact he got drunker than anyone. Boys let off crowscarers, the nearest we'd seen to fireworks since before the war, and we had to jump to get out of their way. It was a lovely, happy time, but some people didn't join in. They stayed indoors, looked at old photographs and cried quietly.

On Sunday there was a thanksgiving service in the

parish church. The choir sang Psalm 91. "*Surely He shall deliver thee from the snare of the fowler.*" *Yes,* we all thought. *That's exactly what happened.*

So it was over, victory over Japan would soon follow, and who knew what the future held?

12.3

I finally went to the Royal College of Music that September, the same time as Paul went to Bristol. There is no need to talk about it except to say that it was everything I expected. Christmas and two terms passed and in April 1946 I came home for Easter. When I got off the train I saw a poster on the station wall. A local amateur orchestra, the Northamptonshire Sinfonia, was giving a concert in the Town Hall next week. They'd got the great French cellist Paul Tortelier to come, and he was going to play Elgar's Cello Concerto.

I hadn't played my cello for some time. The violin was all I had time for at college. But I knew about Tortelier and been told that the concerto was a lovely work though I didn't know it, so I bought a ticket.

On the day of the concert I caught the bus to Northampton. It broke down three miles the other side of Wicester. As it was a fine evening we all sat on the grass verge while the conductor ran to the nearest village to phone the depot.

Half an hour later another bus arrived. But I didn't get

to the Town Hall until long after the concert started. The first thing I saw was a notice:

WE REGRET TO SAY THAT
M. TORTELIER IS INDISPOSED AND IS
UNABLE TO PLAY TONIGHT.

How annoying. He was the main reason I had come. Did this mean they wouldn't play the Elgar Concerto? I wasn't allowed in the hall until the overture, Berlioz's *Le Corsaire*, had finished and the audience were applauding. As I struggled to my seat whispering apologies to people I half heard an announcement about Paul Tortelier's absence and saying who would play instead. I didn't catch the whole name: it was Joseph something, nobody I'd heard of. There was disappointed muttering and someone booed, which I thought was going a bit far.

I found my seat and looked at the orchestra, men in black suits and white bow ties, women in white blouses and black skirts. The conductor, whose name was Arthur Swavesey, had left the stage but soon returned with the soloist, a young man, slim with black hair. He must be a fine musician to be playing such a work but he seemed shy and nervous. He tuned his cello and waited, bow poised, for the conductor to bring him in.

Usually a concerto starts with a long passage from the orchestra, but not this one. The soloist almost plunged into the cello, his bow really hitting the strings with four chords, urgent, angry and sad at the same time. His nervousness disappeared: it was as if he was asking his cello questions and the cello answered him. The orchestra made a quiet comment as if telling them both to calm down, but the questioning went on until the orchestra came in again with a restless, melancholy melody. The cello took up the theme and in its insistent swaying was a strange nervous energy. I knew that Elgar wrote the concerto just after the first war and that it expressed his despair at the misery it plunged the world into. This theme was a lament: I had a vision of a dark, bowed figure looking down on scenes of destruction and weeping for the folly of it all.

Suddenly I had one of those rare, strange moments when everything seems to come together. The music that I'd tried so hard to hear and failed, the music that said everything I felt about the war – *this was it.* Elgar was saying exactly what had eluded me, as if it had been just behind a curtain I could never twitch away until tonight.

It brought back all that we had been through: Dad taken away, Mum comforting a dying man in the air raid, Paul walking among the ruins and meeting Helmut, the dreadful events Helmut must have been through and, more than that, the far worse trials of millions of others, some, which we were only now hearing of, unspeakable, beyond human imagining. But most of all I remembered Walter dying, separated, estranged from us, and cursed the way events had turned out. I longed to see Julie and little Walter again: it wouldn't make things all right but it would ease the pain of the rift. But already the cello was gently moving me away from such private thoughts. The nameless soloist bent low across the instrument, seeming almost at one with it. And then I understood that the shrouded, brooding figure looking down on the ruins was the cellist himself.

The first movement was over: the second began. In the few seconds between, the audience breathed out a collective sigh of satisfaction. No booing now because the famous man had not arrived. A light, nimble theme: did it mean that life would be good again, settled, calm, without fear, without hurt? Once again I watched this incredible soloist. He was caressing the cello almost lovingly, as if it was a frail thing which could shiver into nothing in his hands. He made it sing of a happy time now lost, gone for ever, yet somehow gave it a nuance that whispered that such unalloyed happiness was never there in the first place.

The orchestra, like a quiet and tactful guide, led him almost shyly into a third movement of subtle, echoing, yearning phrases, which ended in a whisper and then nothingness and made me want to cry.

For the first time since he started playing, he seemed to come out of a trance. He sat back and looked round as if surprised that we were still there and he hadn't been talking to himself. The orchestra abruptly started a strong, energetic theme, which said, "Come on, you can do better than that," and in answer he again plunged into the cello, almost sawing it in half with the bow, as if desperate to keep up, to share in such exuberance – but somehow failing. The orchestra tried again: shining brass, ranks of violins, cohorts of cellos, seductive woodwinds, all urging him to join with them. But it didn't work: they gave up and he started another long conversation with his instrument, in which despair and a subdued anger unobtrusively combined. The orchestra came back, half-heartedly, as if they knew their attempt to raise the cello's spirits hadn't worked. The concerto ended with a profound sigh. The soloist lifted his bow gently from the strings: he had said what he and Elgar − and I − wanted to say. He sat expressionless, as if the music had haled the soul from his body.

Again, a silence. Then everybody stood: applause, cries of "Encore!" and "Bravo!" and waves of appreciation swept down on him like breakers on the shore. He stood and bowed, very slightly from the waist. The orchestra joined in the applause: the conductor stepped down from his rostrum and shook him heartily by the hand.

I must have been the only person in the hall who was not clapping. I couldn't: I just watched him. I was too full inside for applause; suddenly I was afraid of crying alone in the crowd. I had heard something that said perfectly everything that these last years, my childhood, all my life so far, meant to me.

I stayed for the last work, a Schumann symphony. I enjoyed it. But I couldn't shake off the feeling that this was only an amateur orchestra. I'd completely forgotten that in the Elgar.

I looked at my watch. The last bus left in half an hour. I mustn't hang around.

The bus station was almost deserted. I was the only passenger at the stop for Wicester, Peterspury and villages beyond. Six others joined me, the bus arrived and we filed on. As soon as I stepped on the rear platform the bus moved off. Before I climbed the stairs I looked back. A man was running towards us, desperately trying to catch up.

"There's someone coming," I called to the conductor.

"Tough. He should have come earlier. We've a timetable to keep to."

The man took a flying leap at the rear platform. I reached out a hand: he grasped it and got his other hand on the thin pillar at the corner of the platform. With me pulling and him straining, he finally scrambled on and collapsed panting on the floor.

"You're lucky, mate," said the conductor.

I guided the man to a seat and sat beside him. "Are you all right?" I asked. His face was somehow familiar.

"Yes," he replied. "Thank you." He had a foreign accent.

Then I realized. "You're the cellist," I cried. "I've just heard you playing the Elgar."

"Did you like it?"

"I thought it was marvellous."

"Yes," he said. "It is fine music."

"I know," I replied. "But I really meant your playing."

"Thank you," he said. "That makes me very happy."

"Where's your cello?" I asked.

"I have no cello," he replied.

"I don't understand…" I started. But he was looking out of the window.

I couldn't let this mystery go unsolved. I'd done him a service so he owed me an explanation. However, the question seemed to upset him. Perhaps my next question would upset him as well.

"What country do you come from?" I asked.

He stopped looking through the window and turned round again. "I am from Poland. I am in the Displaced Persons camp."

I knew where he meant. An old RAF station at Long Compton, four miles from Peterspury. It was closed down when the war ended and was now used as a temporary home for refugees, people whose lives had been broken by the war and were in this country with nowhere to go to.

Suddenly he answered my first question. "I sold my cello to a Nazi officer. There, you're shocked."

"I would love to know your story," I said softly.

He was silent for a moment, then said, "My name is Jozef Malik. I trained at the Warsaw Conservatoire and then joined the Warsaw Symphony Orchestra. I started on the second desk of the cellos, but soon moved up to the desk next to the leader. If it had not been for the war I would have led the cellos myself by now. I remember our last concert before the Nazis invaded Poland. We played the Elgar Concerto and Pablo Casals was the soloist."

I knew about Pablo Casals. He was Spanish and the finest cellist in the world.

"That performance gave me the most magical moments of my life. Every note, every tone and timbre stayed in my mind, locked in for the whole of the war. We all knew the war was coming, that the Nazis would invade us from the west in search of their cursed *Lebensraum* and then the Soviets would invade from the east. Poland would be like a nut crushed by nutcrackers and our beautiful country would be no more. That concerto told me all I needed to know: the folly, sadness, loss, the long regret the next years would bring us."

I was dizzied by his eloquence.

"I was an army reservist, as we all were. People think we were only half trained, pitchforked into defending our

336

country with horses, a few defective tanks and obsolete aircraft against the most formidable foe the world had ever seen. No, we were better than that. We gave them a good fight. But what chance did we have? *Blitzkrieg*, Hitler called it. Nobody had fought a war so ruthlessly before. I saw my country laid waste, its people killed without mercy. Yet we kept on fighting. We had this hope that France and Britain would suddenly appear and drive the Nazis out."

"But we didn't," I said. "I'm sorry."

He smiled. "It's not your fault. The blame lies with people in high places, as most of the world's ills do. I was foolish: I went to war taking my cello with me because I couldn't bear to leave it behind. Every night I played and my comrades gathered round to listen. And all I could play was the Elgar Concerto. Nobody minded. It was as if it spoke to them as well.

"Anyway, I was taken prisoner. *They'll shoot me for sure*, I thought. But no. I was brought before the commandant. 'Herr Malik,' he said. 'I'm pleased to meet you. I'm told you are a musician and played with the Warsaw Symphony. It is a fine orchestra.'

"'Thank you,' I replied.

"'And I'm told you have your instrument with you still,' he said.

"'I will always have it with me,' I answered.

"Then he said, 'Who do you hate more, us or the Russians?' What could I say? We were sandwiched between them: one was as bad as the other and both determined to destroy us. But my life might depend on the answer. So I said, though I didn't mean it, 'The Russians.' 'The correct answer,' he said, smiling. 'I'll make you an offer. We'll be fighting the Russians one day. Hitler is determined on it. Join the Wehrmacht and help to drive them out of your country.' I must have stared at him like an idiot. 'I mean it,' he said. 'The alternative is a labour camp and being shot when the work has worn you out. Of course, if the Soviets get you they'll see your soft musician's hands and put a bullet in the back of your neck at once. You're an intellectual with a mind of your own. They can't abide that.'

"'Do you ask everyone this?' I said. 'Only you,' he answered. 'You see, I'm a musician myself, though not professional like you. That's why I'm making this offer. You have a fine cello. I'll pay you good money for it if you join the Wehrmacht. If you don't I'll have you shot and take the cello anyway.' He still smiled as he said it."

I shivered as Jozef continued. "I said I'd join before I could change my mind. 'Good fellow,' he replied. He opened his wallet and counted out a remarkable number of zloty. 'This will keep you alive till your first German pay packet,' he said.

"I sat trembling, wondering what I had done. 'Of course, you can't go back to your comrades,' he said. 'They'd call you a traitor. I'll make out a travel warrant for you and orders to report for training. My orderly will fetch your cello. *My* cello, I should say now. You'll be put on a westward train tonight.'

"So there I was, with papers, a railway warrant to somewhere in Germany, handcuffed to an armed guard to make sure I got there. We got on the train in Warsaw, the guard sat down and I had to sit next to him. The train drew out and trundled slowly through Warsaw's ruined suburbs. We were the only people in our compartment. He yawned, undid the handcuffs and said, 'I've had a hard day, all this fighting wears you out. I need a few minutes' kip. Stay where you are.' Soon he was snoring. *If they find you sleeping on duty you'll be shot*, I thought, and felt almost sorry for him.

"The train rumbled on and the guard stayed sleeping soundly. I looked through the window at my devastated homeland and considered again what I had done. I had given up my beautiful cello for a pocketful of zloties and had entered into a pact with the devil. I didn't want the Soviets in my country, but I didn't want the Nazis either. Unless I did something about it, I would never sleep again for shame and guilt.

"It was dark now. The train was going slower and slower. We had to make way for freight trains loaded with guns and tanks. At last we stopped, miles from anywhere, in a pitch-dark landscape. We waited. My guard snored. Suddenly I made up my mind. I stood up, left the compartment, walked down the corridor, opened the door at the end and jumped down.

"Nobody saw me. I ran, expecting to be shot at. But the guard must have slept on. The engine whistled and slowly moved off, gathering speed until it was out of sight. I've often wondered what happened to the guard. I set off down a deserted road, stopped after a kilometre, got my breath back and looked round. I had no idea where I was."

We had come to Wicester. The bus would stop here for five minutes. Several passengers got off: more came on. While we waited he said nothing. When the bus drove off he started again.

"I was free," he said. "But I'd traded my cello for

339

money and my self-respect. I had to wipe out my shame. After days of searching I found Polish soldiers and airmen who had survived. I was welcomed, though if they'd known my history they'd probably have shot me out of hand. We stayed alive and somehow eluded the Germans. But what should we do? Some wanted to join up with the secret Home Army. Others wanted to get to France and Britain to fight alongside our allies. I thought long and hard and in the end I decided I'd go with those who wanted to leave Poland altogether."

The bus was out of Wicester and going down the A5 to home.

"I could write a book about what happened to us in the next months. Perhaps I will one day. But most of us did slip through Italy into southern France before the Germans got there and we found a ship to take us to England. Those who had been in the Air Force joined the RAF. The rest of us joined the new Polish Brigade. We fought through the war with the British. It was a long war for me and I don't know how I survived it. All the while I was haunted by my lost cello and the Elgar Concerto. I even carried two sticks around with me, one long, one short, and imagined they were cello and bow. I'd play the concerto night after night, hearing it in my head, getting the fingering right, every little twist of expression. By the end of the war I knew it better than Casals did at that last concert."

I looked out of the window. Three miles to go and I'd be home. Yet I wanted this journey to go on for ever.

"When the war ended I stayed in Britain. But the Allies had been treacherous to us. Winston Churchill and

President Roosevelt had told Stalin that after the war they would not interfere with the Soviets in Poland. So my country really was lost. The British put many Poles on ships home leaving them at the mercy of Stalin. But after VE day the policy changed. I and many of my friends were allowed to stay – stateless, displaced persons put into camps until they decide what to do with us. We're well fed and well treated, yet we still feel like prisoners. We are allowed out, but there's a strict curfew. One day I saw a notice about the orchestra, the Northamptonshire Sinfonia, needing new players. I got the permission of the camp commandant to join and the orchestra was pleased to have me, even when I told them they must lend me an instrument. They found one, though I couldn't take it back to the camp to practise. But I hardly seemed to need it: with years of pretending with two sticks I had somehow kept my technique.

"So I went to the first rehearsal. Yes, I thought, this orchestra is of a surprisingly good standard. Mr Swavesey the conductor told us the programme for our first concert. The Berlioz overture, the Schumann symphony and then, to my amazement, the Elgar Concerto.

"It seemed like a sign, a portent to say that some great thing would happen to me. I was so happy to be playing the very part that I'd played on my last ever concert in Warsaw. We rehearsed the orchestral sections until we knew them like the backs of our hands, not that I needed to learn much. And then it came to fitting all this to the solo part. We would have to wait until the last minute before Tortelier came for his one rehearsal. A piano was wheeled in and Mr Swavesey picked out the solo part on it.

"But it didn't seem to work very well. I don't quite know what possessed me to say, 'I know this work. I'll stand in for Tortelier.' Mr Swavesey said, 'Are you sure, Jozef? Well, we'll give it a try. Here's the score.' 'I don't need it,' I replied. 'I know every note.' Mr Swavesey looked at me disbelievingly and said, 'Well, if you're sure.'"

"I was right. We played the concerto right through from start to finish without a stop and when it was over everyone clapped and I had never been so happy in my life. I played for three more rehearsals but then the final run-through with Monsieur Tortelier was due and I had to go back to the cello section.

"Then he sent his telegram to say he was ill. 'We must cancel the concert,' said Mr Swavesey. But everyone shouted out, 'Let Jozef play it instead.' 'Could you do it?' Mr Swavesey asked and I answered with something I'd heard on American programmes on the BBC. 'You bet I could, buster.' I said and everybody laughed. So that's why I played tonight. And that's my story."

"But now you've nobody to play for and no cello," I said.

"That's true," he replied. "I had to leave the cello. I even had to borrow a black evening suit and white bow tie." He was wearing an old, threadbare jacket and grey, flannel trousers with no creases. "Now everybody is at the party after the concert, but I had to catch the bus to beat the curfew."

"It's like my father being interned as an enemy alien," I said.

"Why did that happen?" he replied.

I thought a moment before I answered. Then I said,

342

"My name is Anna Vögler. What does that tell you?"

He too thought for a moment. "I don't care," he said at last. "You listened, you helped me and you loved my music."

"I play the violin," I said, feeling quite shy. "I'm at the Royal College of Music in London."

"Just as I was at the Warsaw Conservatoire," he replied, laughing. "We have a lot in common, Anna Vögler."

We had reached Peterspury. "I get off here," I said. "Thank you so much for such wonderful playing. And for your story. I'll never forget either of them." Before I stepped off the platform I added, "And I hope everything goes well for you, Jozef."

"It will now," he answered. "This night has been full of signs."

12.4

I slept fitfully. Something nagged at my mind and I didn't know what it was until next morning. After breakfast, I went to my room and looked at the prize cello, stroked its varnished maplewood body, touched its taut strings, felt the fine horsehair on the bow. Then I sat down, took the bow and tried to play the first theme of the Elgar Concerto.

It sounded laboured and pedestrian. I could play the cello in the sense of getting the notes right, but I couldn't make it sing. That only happened when I played the violin.

I stood the cello against the wall and looked at it. It seemed to look back at me, saying something. I listened hard and then made it out. "*I don't belong to you, Anna. You know who I'm meant for.*"

I put cello and bow back in the case, called out to Mum, "I'm going out. I'll be back this afternoon," picked it up, went to the bus stop and caught the next bus to Long Compton.

The DP camp was a depressing place, looking exactly what it was, a rundown, deserted ex-RAF base. But there were still RAF policemen in the guardroom and, as I approached, one of them came out and shouted, "Where do you think you're going, miss?"

"I'd like to speak to someone here," I replied. "Mr Jozef Malik."

"Sorry, miss. Can't do that. You aren't allowed in."

"Couldn't he come out here?" I asked. "It won't take a minute."

"Not allowed."

"Please. It's important."

He smiled slightly. "All right, I'll try," he said. "I'll ask the sergeant. It all depends what mood he's in."

He went back into the guardroom and didn't come out for five whole minutes. When he did, he said, "It's your lucky day, miss. Sarge has won the football pools so he's being nice to everybody. We've sent someone for Mr Malik and he'll come out to see you. Mind you, you'll have to stand that side of the gate and he'll have to stay this side. What's that you've got there?"

"A cello," I said.

"Each to his own taste," he replied. "I prefer a good riff on a saxophone myself."

Jozef appeared from one of the low, wooden huts and walked quickly towards the guardroom. His face lit up when he saw me. "Anna Vögler," he cried. He came up to the main gate, a long barrier separating us like a level-crossing gate on the railway.

I impulsively picked up the cello before I could change my mind, thrust it through the gate and said, "I want you to have this."

He took it wonderingly and clasped it to him as if it

were an old friend or long lost lover, which I suppose it was. Then he let go, as if to hand it back to me. "I can't take it," he said. "It's yours."

"I want you to have it. I mean what I say."

He looked at me thoughtfully. Then he said, "Thank you. How long can I keep it for?"

"For ever," I replied. "Don't you understand? It's yours, really yours. It's my gift to you." He looked at me stupefied.

"Perhaps one day we might play duets together," I said.

He looked at the cello, then at me, a smile of complete happiness on his face. "Yes, Anna Vögler," he said. "We will play wonderful duets, you and I. One day."

"Where's your cello?" Mum demanded when I got home.

"I gave it away," I replied.

"You did what?"

"Gave it away."

"Who to?"

"A Polish DP."

"You gave your lovely cello to a stranger? I can't believe it."

"Jozef isn't a stranger," I replied and told her about the concert, the Elgar Concerto and Jozef's story. "So you see, he wasn't properly alive without a cello," I concluded.

Mum didn't speak for a moment. Then she said, "And what you did for Jozef will make him properly alive again." It wasn't a question but a statement.

I nodded.

She put her hands on my shoulders and surveyed me as if from a distance. I saw pleasure, contentment, even amusement in her face.

"Oh, Anna," she said. "You truly are my daughter."

———

"An engaging introduction to a pivotal moment in history."
Observer

England, 1914. When recruiting officers come to Ellen's sleepy Sussex village and her brother enlists, she knows that her life will never be the same again. This war will change everything and everyone – Ellen most of all. She hates working as a servant at the big house but her family needs the money. Then her brother returns from the front, injured and broken, and she realizes her true calling...

BY DENNIS HAMLEY

A powerful and emotional portrayal of the Apache's struggle for survival in a hostile world.

Siki is an orphan of the Black Mountain Apache. Her mother was killed by Mexicans three years ago and her father lost in an ambush the winter before that. When Siki witnesses the brutal murder of her little brother Tazhi, she vows to become an Apache warrior and avenge her brother's death.

BY TANYA LANDMAN